Dead as a Doornail

Grant Michaels

Dead as
a Doornail

St. Martin's Press
New York

✓ Title

This is a work of fiction. All names, characters, and events
portrayed in this book are fictitious. No identification with
actual persons, entities, or events is intended or should be
inferred.

ISBN 0-312-18077-2

First Edition: March 1998

10 9 8 7 6 5 4 3 2 1

for all hopefuls
whose dream house
is yet to come.

Once again my friends get the first round of thanks. The solitary work of writing begs to be countered by occasional bouts of dining, drinking, and what can politely be called dancing. No sooner do I begin sinking into a bog of isolation than someone calls with an idea for some fun and frolic. So, hearty thanks to my personal "cheer-meisters."

Thanks also to Doreen Treacy and Judy Bracken of the Boston Public Facilities Department for technical advice on acquiring real estate and on the foreclosure process. Any creative license regarding title searches and City Hall protocol is mine alone.

Thanks again to the Boston Center for the Arts and to the Mystic Studios Trust.

And finally, thanks to G.P., who verified that, in fact, under certain circumstances, auction property in Boston has been acquired before it actually went to auction.

1

It all started this morning, when I woke up alive.

"Freak storm!" buzzes a voice from my clock radio. "Welcome to April first, folks, and this is no joke. We are in the worst snowstorm in Boston's worst winter on record." The guy sounds jubilant, and it's only seven A.M.

I look out my bedroom window. Sure enough, the snow is blowing goddamn sideways out there. I must be dreaming. Didn't spring start over a week ago?

I pull the covers over my head and remind myself how lucky I am: I have my health; I have a few million haphazardly compounding in an aggressive stock fund (there's something to be said for choosing an investment adviser *not* based on looks); and in two weeks the IRS will be happy. What more could an ordinary mortal want?

My sleepy feet search under the covers for Sugar Baby, my longtime feline companion. Then sleepy logic reminds me that she's with my niece now, where I left her when I took a much needed vacation last fall. But when I went to pick Sugar up and bring her home, she refused to come. She clawed and growled and howled so horribly that I had to release her. Seconds later she hopped into my young niece's lap and purred contentedly. I suffered briefly from rejection, but Gemini resilience prevailed, and I soon reasoned that Sugar Baby was the fickle one, not I.

I doze for another half hour, then get up and have my breakfast with the TV. There's no newspaper today, so I guess the snow really is serious. I take a longer shower than usual, and by nine o'clock I'm ready to face the grueling day ahead—grueling for a former hairdresser anyway.

First stop: my vine-covered cottage. Yes, I own real estate now. What else do you do when you have too much money? Actually my place is more like virtual estate since it's uninhabitable. It was deemed "abandoned" by the city and I got it at auction. Well, kind of. Anyway, it's the last derelict townhouse in Boston's South End, the ultimate fixer-upper, basically a rotted-out shell of bricks—four floors of rubble or potential, depending on your outlook. At least it's on a choice corner lot. And with my future illusory and my past generally forgettable, I figure that refurbishing an old Boston townhouse is a worthy project for someone with too much time and money on his hands. I'm sure the owners of the meticulously gentrified property around my little eyesore are relieved too.

The weather seems to have brought the rest of the city to a standstill, so I call my contractor to confirm our nine-thirty meeting. He's a cute young guy named Tim Shaughnessy, and I'm his first client. Someone had to be. Where would I be now if no one took the chance to be *my* first client? And since Tim has been to Snips Salon a few times, I figured I'd give him a chance. His references are pretty good too, although I'm not sure if the enthusiasm is for his work or for his general appeal as a scrappy young guy from South Boston. The few times I've met him, Tim has an easy smile and an easy answer for everything. Maybe he can cut wood too. I'll soon find out.

As it turns out, Tim isn't home, but his answering machine talks directly to me: "Hey, Stan! I'm going to be hard to reach for a couple of days, but I'll be at the site nine-thirty sharp Monday morning. See you then, buddy, rain or shine. And I've got good news."

See what I mean by charming? He calls my moldering manse a site and he calls me buddy. I wonder what his other customers think when they hear that personal message. In fact, does Tim's fledgling business even have other customers?

Wet snow rattles against the kitchen window, reminding me of Boston's seasonal joke. What fool is going out in weather like this? Tim said rain or shine but he didn't mention the aberrant springtime blizzard. And if he went away for the weekend, he'd hardly be driving back in this storm. But New Englanders can't be weather wimps or they'd get nothing done. "April snow is the poor man's manure." That's the kind of cheery quip we're famous for.

I have nothing else booked for the morning—for the rest of my life actually—so I go to the coat closet and dig out my knee-high insulated boots. Then I bundle up in several layers of wool and set out like Little Nanook traversing the tundra in search of home sweet home. I certainly can't drive today, not in this weather. (My car is an Italian roadster that performs its sexy locomotion under blue skies only.) I won't wear a hat either, not on April first, even if it is snowing. I will not empower the weather. Besides, I haven't cut my hair since last fall, so there's plenty of insulation up there.

Driving snow, once you surrender to the incessant prickling on your face, is a very calming experience. Outside, even the hallowed dirt of Boston is blanketed by soft whiteness. I make my way from the Back Bay, where I live now, to the South End, where I will live soon. I see few other footprints along the way. As I cross Copley Square, I stop and turn to see the trail I'm blazing through the flat, open area. All is quiet. There are no cars around, no buses even. Only the wind moves the air. I recall some music my late lover once choreographed, "Footsteps in the Snow" by Claude Debussy.

I move forward again, and try to pick up my pace. I remind myself that's all past now. My lover is dead, I'm rich, I've regained my dumpling physique, and sometime next fall I'll be the proprietor of the hottest little guest house in Boston, if not all New England. The place will be *haute luxe*, complete with an intimate beauty salon and health spa. Life will be beautiful as glamorous jetsetters cross my not-so-humble threshold. This morning Tim is supposed to have the final plans for the massive renovations. I'm hoping the good news he mentioned is that all the subcontractors came in under their initial estimates.

The walk takes much longer than I figured, but finally I arrive at the property, *my* real estate, the apparent solution to life's insecurity. And sure enough, Tim's new truck is out front. It's one of those rugged four-wheel-drive things, and it's parked near a snowdrift where the curb ought to be. Fresh snow has already gathered on the cleared-off windshield. There's probably a fire hydrant under that snowdrift, but who's going to ticket him on a day like this? The point is, despite the weather, Tim Shaughnessy kept his promise, which makes him exactly the kind of little tiger I want working for me.

I turn toward the ruin that is my house and see that the snow on the wide outside stairway has been roughed up. Maybe Tim brought one of the subcontractors with him. Or perhaps it's his weekend companion, and they couldn't resist a buddy-boy tumble in the snow before my arrival.

I make my way up the front stairs and find the outer door unlocked. Tim's got keys, of course. I enter the building and, once again, the stench of rotted wood repels me. Tim has assured me the smell will be gone when the new work is complete. Here and there small clumps of snow dot the floor like vague anonymous footprints. I call out, but all is quiet. I call again, playfully, as though engaged in a round of hide-and-seek with two youngsters.

"Come on out, boys. It's your Uncle Stanley."

Still no answer.

I walk cautiously along the unsteady flooring. I see a small wet place near the staircase. It's dark, a possible stain. I bristle. This will not do. This is *my* house, *my* floor now, and I will not have stains. But, no matter. Soon enough the floor will be all new hardwood, nice solid tongue-in-groove oak, so what does a small stain matter now? Still, what is that wet spot? Something seems to be dripping from above, something melting. But there's no heat in the place. How can anything melt? Then I see that it's not water. It's dark and opaque, like paint. I look up to where it's coming from. My eyes follow a scarred wooden banister that once traversed a graceful arc up to the second-floor landing. I see a leg and an arm pressed against what's left of the balusters directly above me.

I go to the foot of the stairway and look up. It's Tim. He's sprawled on the stairs, inverted, as though he tumbled down headfirst. I call out to him, not so playfully this time.

"Tim?"

He doesn't move. Reluctantly, cautiously, I make my way to

the foot of the stairs. I creep up carefully, for everything shakes, all splintery and unsteady. I get to Tim and jostle his shoulder. His head rolls a bit and exposes a badly bruised neck. Blood oozes from his nose and one ear and trails silently in a sticky wet line along the stair tread where, at the edge, it gathers into a heavy droplet and plummets to the floor below.

I feel for a pulse on his neck. The skin there is smooth and firm, with hardly any beard, but it's too pale for a healthy young man, too gray. He feels warm—relative to the surrounding air, that is—but nothing moves under his skin. It appears that sweet little Tim Shaughnessy is dead.

Did he fall? Was he pushed? Whichever it is, it happened recently. Very recently. For some reason, I look at my watch. It's just after ten o'clock. I was late. If I'd been on time, would Tim be alive? For that matter, if I had simply bought a South End condo like everyone else, would Tim be alive? I look at him again. That's when I notice a single strand of black hair about five inches long lying on the collar of his jacket. I want to pick it up and examine it, but I know better. That's for the police.

Suddenly I realize if Tim was killed, the culprit might still be lurking within my precious realty. I get outside quickly and catch my breath. I try to make sense of the muddled footprints on the steps, but they're already covered by new snow. Around the corner on Tremont Street I find a public phone and dial 911. I quickly explain the situation, and the cops are on their way. But when I ask to speak to a particular officer I know, the 911 crew won't transfer me—I must call headquarters directly for personal matters—and they disconnect me. I have no change, and I have to use my calling card for the "personal" call back to the police. I ask for Lieutenant Detective Vito Branco, but he's not there. Then I phone my best friend, Nicole, but she's not home. I make one more call and find that she's not at work either.

So where is everybody? It's a bloody blizzard and nobody is where they belong.

2

I consider going to wait at Station D, a precinct station just a few blocks away. I'd be safe there, in case Tim's killer is still hanging around my place. But it would be a pretty stupid killer who did that, hang around after the deed. So, I return to the site, my real estate, which has now become a possible crime scene, and await the arrival of the police. I huddle in a small service entrance under the front stairs, partly to keep out of the storm, partly to conceal myself, just in case all my lovely logic is faulty and Tim's killer is still about after all—that is, if there is a killer. Trouble is, my fresh footprints give away my hiding place. Blow, wind, blow! Cover my tracks!

As if to answer my summons, a sudden roar shatters the quiet. The Metropolitan District Commission, staunch guardian of Boston's highways and byways, has sent one of those little toy plows to clear the very sidewalk that runs in front of my urban estate. The streets are impassable and the MDC is clearing sidewalks? I realize the snow may contain potential evidence—who knows what molecular secrets can be extracted from a snowflake these days?—and I scramble out from my hiding place and try frantically to stop the tractorette. But I'm too late. It churns by, burping and grinding, plowing its peculiar path to nowhere. So much for evidence.

I go stand on the newly cleared sidewalk and watch the miniplow turn the corner onto Tremont Street and disappear. Once again, all is quiet except for the wind and snow.

Then, like the forward guard of a cavalry battalion, a behemoth snowplow—a real one—rumbles down the street, clearing the way for the Boston police following close behind it. The squad cars stop in front of my place and the cops emerge. I instantly recognize the tall virile form of their leader, Lieutenant Branco.

"Stan?" he says, obviously recognizing me.

"Not the abominable snowman," I reply.

Branco's Mediterranean aura deflects the blowing storm as easily as Moses did the Red Sea waters. In fact, the snowy halo around the cop only intensifies his olive-toned skin, his black curly hair, and his steely gray-blue eyes.

He asks, "Did you call 911?"

"Like a good scout," I say. "You guys sure got here fast."

"Why didn't you leave your name?"

"I did."

"The dispatcher said the call was anonymous, made from that phone booth on the corner."

"Lieutenant, I know better than that."

"Never mind," he says brusquely. "What's going on here?"

"It's what *went* on," I say. "There's a body in there." I point to the old house, my old house.

Branco orders his crew to take up various positions around the place. Some of the cops file up the outside stairway, guns drawn, and enter my hopeless wreck of a real-estate venture. Others head down the side alley and go around to the back. Branco turns to me. "Wait in my car." He points to a snowy-white cruiser. I protest. I want to go inside with the big boys, but Branco says, "This is our work now."

"But I found him."

"There may be danger in there," he says.

"But I was just—"

"I said wait out here!" The cop's eyes glitter through the snow flying between us, and once again a simple formula defines our roles: The strong, angry man will do his important work and make the world safe for us lesser members of the human race.

As Branco turns to go in, I mention the black hair I saw on Tim Shaughnessy's collar.

He says, "We'll take care of it."

He goes inside, while I'm escorted to his cruiser and thrust into the back seat like a commoner awaiting His Grace's return. At least it's warm in there. There's a cop sitting up in front. His eyes study me in the rearview mirror, and I wonder how I landed up in this situation. As usual it's my own doing.

A sudden windfall of money gave me the luxury of choice, or appeared to anyway, and my first act of so-called choice was to embark on a quest to become a full-fledged man. That's a big decision for someone like me, a congenital sissy. At the time, it seemed no more absurd than those people who suddenly become fitness addicts after half a lifetime of idleness. But I did it my way: I decided to become a cop, which is about as manly as you can get short of the Marines. Thanks to Lieutenant Branco's discreet shepherding, my application bypassed some of the red tape, and I slipped into an anomalous vacancy on the academy's rolls.

Cop school kept me occupied for a while. There were basically two aspects to it: physical training and learning the law. As a rookie, you're expected to embrace the physical part like a religion: Don't think, just do. I painfully discovered that I have most of the same muscles everyone else does. Mine were simply dormant, awaiting revelation. As for learning the law, as long as I could maintain the mask of a hard-nosed cop or a fact-retentive lawyer, it was more like an acting class than serious education. It was almost fun.

The big surprise was finding that I possessed an unlikely talent: I am a natural marksman. That's right. I'm good with a gun. That is, once I get past my peculiar first response. See, whenever I hold a heavy hunk of deadly metal in my palm, my stupid dick gets hard. It lasts only a few seconds, but the first time it happened I was shocked, then embarrassed. Finally I got used to it. But back at the academy, with all those testosterone-laden cops and cop wanna-bes around me, concealing my temporary prong was a daily nuisance. And at that very first session on the firing range, I had problems aiming it too—the gun I mean—especially after the training officer saw me holding it in my left hand. He shook his head dismally and muttered, "Fuckin' southpaw!" Still, I tried to be very manly about it, gripping the gun with all my gay and glorious might. But every time I squeezed the trigger as instructed, the gun recoiled violently, flinging my arm into the air. Of course I kept it all graceful, like a Vegas showgirl in a feathered boa, but I never came close to the target. Finally, countless wasted rounds later, the training officer said, "Ya' too stiff, pal. Loosen up ya' wrist." Then he flapped his own hairy paw in front of me—very fay and limp—while he sniggered, "That oughta be easy f'*you!*"

Well, little did either of us realize the unique preparation all those years of styling, cutting, and curling motions had built into my clever hands and wrists. All I needed was a bit of inspiration—it was Barbara Stanwyck who saved the day—and suddenly I was the reigning sharpshooter of my class. *Ping! Ping! Ping!* I could put a bullet anywhere on the target.

The fag jokes stopped soon after that. Then some of my toughest colleagues asked me to teach them my "soft-hand" technique. So the tables turned, and real men were imitating me.

But inevitably I got bored with it all, which is the Gemini's bane, and I had to face the truth that a cop's authoritative nature isn't mine, except maybe for brief episodes, and only in high travesty. Without the DNA of a militia man—could I even write a parking ticket without pangs of conscience?—I knew I'd never make it as a cop on the street. So before they gave me the equivalent of a dishonorable discharge, I quit. Technically, it was a leave of absence, but I'm sure Lieutenant Branco still celebrated the event as yet another triumph for machismo, proof that we sensitive types can never soar to the ecstatic heights of genetic brutality. So, to compensate for my manly failing, I became a property owner in Boston's trendy South End.

And this is what I got.

I look out the frosty window of the police cruiser at my house. One of the assisting cops is scampering down the snowy stairs. He comes up to the cruiser and opens the front door, says to the other cop, "The lieutenant wants him inside."

As he escorts me into my own house, a female officer standing near the front door warns us to be careful, that the place is just about falling down.

Like I don't know, doll?

She points to where Branco is, on the stairway, bent over Tim Shaughnessy's body. Seeing the cop at work, all my whining about "men versus sissies" and "cops versus men" means nothing. Branco surpasses all nonsense.

My cop escort takes me over there. On the stairs just above

Tim's body, I see where someone's foot has gone through one of the treads. Probably some big-footed cop, certainly not Branco.

Branco sees me standing at the foot of the stairs. He comes down. His feet make no sound. He can probably walk on water too. He stops on the first stair, as if to emphasize his already towering height. Then he nods his head up toward Tim's body.

"Do you know him?"

I nod. "Tim Shaughnessy. He's my contractor."

Branco's eyes flash incredulously. "You own this place?"

"It has potential," I say with a shrug, maybe too flip.

The cop looks around. "Potential sinkhole," he mutters. "I figured you more for the condo type."

I shrug again and wish I was more butch. "I guess you figured wrong, Lieutenant."

"What were you guys doing here?"

I don't like his tone.

"Settling the final plans," I say like a potent property magnate. "The house needs a lot of work."

Branco eyes the crumbling walls and makes a little grunt. "Kind of a lousy place to meet," he says.

"Tim likes to be at the site as much as possible."

"Even on a day like this?"

"He's eager," I say. "He's just starting out." Then I add somberly, "I mean was."

Branco descends the last step, and a Roman legionnaire stands before me. "It's not clear yet whether this is an accident or if he had some help. How well did you know him?"

"Not well. Why?"

"Maybe he did this himself."

"Suicide?" I say. "No way. Tim wasn't the suicidal type."

"I thought you didn't know him well."

"I didn't," I say. "I hardly knew him at all."

"But you knew him well enough to know he wasn't suicidal."

"It doesn't take much to figure that out, Lieutenant."

Branco studies me in silence. "I forgot," he says. "You tried being a psychologist too."

"That was a long time ago."

He says, "But you still quit."

"There's quitting, Lieutenant, and there's knowing when you're not suited for something."

"There's also working harder when things get rough."

"The academy was your idea, not mine."

"Just drop it!" says Branco. "How did you meet this boy?"

"He came into the salon a while back."

"One of your customers?"

"I cut his hair a couple of times."

"Then what?"

"Then I got this place and hired him."

"And?" says the cop.

"It was strictly business, Lieutenant." I sound defensive. "You don't think I did this, do you?"

"I know you well enough by now," he says. "But this is your . . ." He has a hard time with the word. ". . . house," he says with a grimace. "And you claim this boy was your contractor."

"He's not a boy, Lieutenant."

"Maybe not," he says, "but there's something you're over-looking, Stan."

"What's that?"

"Take another look at him."

I look up the stairway. Tim's strong young body looks broken, the way it's sprawled there on the stairs.

"What's your point, Lieutenant?"

Branco's mouth is tense, his eyes impatient. "You're missing the obvious. He has red hair, just like yours."

I look back up at Tim, now as if for the first time. Branco's right. Despite the three hundred million differences between tough-buffed Timmy and Slavic-dumpling me, we share a nearly identical shade of red hair. Same style too: too long.

"So," says the cop, "since you're the owner of this . . . prop-erty . . . and since you bear a striking resemblance to the victim, it's possible that someone meant to get you this morning."

"I didn't think of that."

"Maybe you should," says Branco.

Me? Kinky perms aside, and a few off-key color jobs, what did I ever do that would drive someone to kill me?

I ask him what happens now.

He starts a litany. "The medical examiner is on the way, and the lab crew too. The driving's rough, so they'll be—"

"I meant what about me?"

Branco says, "I can arrange some protection."

"It's serious then?"

Branco shrugs. When he does it, it expresses some mystical, masculine, all-knowing authority. "It could be," he says with a cold look in his eyes.

I hope that hard gaze is nothing personal, just his way of maintaining the objectivity needed to be a good cop.

I ask him, "Did you see that black hair on Tim's collar?"

He says, "The lab will take care of it. And I think you and I better have a talk in my office. You can wait in my car."

"How long?"

"As long as it takes me!"

"Can I meet you at the station instead?"

Branco glares at me. He knows that I know—thanks to my aborted academy training—that without a charge, routine police questioning is voluntary on the subject's part, no matter how suspicious the circumstances. The use of force is a violation of rights.

He says, "Why can't you just wait for me, like anyone else?"

"I want to see a friend."

"Ms. Albright?" he says.

I nod.

Branco clenches his jaw. "All right," he says. "Just be careful out there."

"You really think someone wants to kill me?"

"I don't know!" he snaps. "But there's no sense in leaving yourself wide open. I'll get two of my crew to take you where you're going now, then pick you up later and bring you to the station."

"Thanks," I say, but my voice is shaking.

Branco says, "I don't mean to put the fear of God in you, Stan. Just keep your eyes and ears open."

I leave the place escorted by two officers. In the cruiser I ask them to take me to Snips Salon on Newbury Street. I see them exchange amused glances up in the front seat.

3

Boston suffers from climatic diverticula—a meteorological illness characterized by pockets of extreme weather. One neighborhood can be experiencing a full-blown nor'easter (or else torpor-inducing heat and humidity) while another sees only blue skies, calm seas, and a prosperous voyage.

On Newbury Street, which is Boston's version of Rodeo Drive or the Via Veneto, the freak snowstorm has magically expired. The sun is shining and the streets and sidewalks are almost clear of snow. Perhaps the guests at the Ritz-Carlton really do have privileged access to a beneficent deity. Either that or the fickle New England weather gods have been satisfied by Tim Shaughnessy's death and have called an early halt to their prodigal snowshow.

It's just after eleven o'clock, and Snips Salon is humming, despite the earlier weather. I spot Nicole's auburn hair and the classic chignon, just as she looks up from her manicure table. I go to her.

"Surprise, surprise," she says quietly, as she ministers to a dowager's gnarly fingers.

"Don't get up, doll."

We do a quick Eurokiss.

"I won't," she says, and she presents her other cheek for the second smooch. Then she turns back to her client and coos softly, "We're almost finished, Mrs. Haffenreefer. Just one more step—the magic step." She places the woman's arthritic claws inside a tiny forced-air oven. "Your nails will look like porcelain," she says as she gives the old wrists a reassuring pat.

Nicole loves portraying the wage-slave manicurist, which she claims is the best way to get her customers—whether Brahmin socialite or Hollywood celeb—to "tell all." The fact is, Nicole owns Snips Salon and the property it's on. In all the years I've known her, she has never divulged the awful truth of that little coup. I suspect it's connected to her modeling days in Paris, thirty-some years ago.

She turns the little nail dryer on and sets the timer. "I'll be back in five," she chirps to the old woman. Then she gets up from her chair, hooks her arm into mine, and drags me toward the back of the shop, where there's a small private office. Nicole's figure may be shot, but her runway strut is as reckless as ever. On the way to the office we pass one of my former rivals, Ramon, who grins vacantly at me. Nicole explains that he has his own station now, along with a growing client list, and isn't that nice? I bestow my own special grin of vacancy back to Ramon, for I recall when he was a mere shampoo boy. And it's an unequivocal truth that I taught the bitch everything she knows.

In the office Nicole sits down, then she places one hand over the other and nervously drums her fingers.

"Well?" she says.

"Well what?"

"Weren't you supposed to be going over the renovation plans on that . . . house . . . of yours?" Like Branco, Nicole has trouble with the word.

"Yes, doll."

"Then why are you here?"

"Aren't you going to light up first?"

"I've stopped," she says.

"Stopped, Nikki? Or want to?"

"It's been"—she ponders the vast passage of time since her last cigarette—"well, since last night, I think. That's not counting this morning, what with the weather and all. I did take a few puffs with my coffee, but I hardly inhaled, so that doesn't count. Now if you don't mind, I'd rather not talk about it. Tell me what brings you here this morning. A special client, maybe? Are you finally coming to your senses and returning to work?"

"No, Nikki."

14

I recount the morning's events in excruciating detail. When I finish I feel as though *I* need a cigarette, and I don't even smoke.

"Little Timmy?" says Nicole. "You mean that darling boy who came in here a few times?"

"He only acted like a boy. He was twenty-two."

"It's been quite a while since he's been here."

"His hair looked it too."

"Stanley! The poor boy is dead."

"His hair was still too long, doll."

"You mean like yours?" she says.

I ignore the dig. "Tim probably found someone else," I say. "You know how it is."

"Clients can be fickle," says Nicole. "But how did you end up hiring him?"

"The odd thing is," I say, "Tim found me. He called right after I got the house and told me he was starting his own construction business, just in case I needed any work done."

"Work?" barks Nicole. "That place needs razing. And now look what's happened."

"I know, doll. It's become a crime scene."

"You say the police think it was an accident?"

"They're not sure, but I know what I think."

Nicole says, "But why would anyone hurt little Timmy? He was like a"—she reaches for a word, not at all like her—"he was like a little *pet*, a darling puppy you just want to take care of."

"Well, doll, the police are wondering if someone may have mistaken darling little Timmy for me."

"Oh, Stanley, you two don't look anything alike."

"Thanks for your candor, doll, but look again." I bring one hand to the side of my head and lift a sheaf of coppery hair.

"Oh!" she says, obviously realizing the singular resemblance between the still-living me and the recently dead Timmy. "He had red hair too."

"You just discovered America, doll. And I doubt the killer asked Timmy for a photo ID."

"This is not good," says Nicole, "not if someone wants to hurt you."

I agree with her. "Not good at all."

"But who?" she says.

"As far as I know, Nikki, the last customer I fried left town years ago."

"What are you going to do?"

"For now," I say, "I'm supposed to lie low, whatever that means."

"Stanley, darling, I think you should come back to work here at the shop."

"You think a killer can't find me here?"

"What I mean, dear, is that you should get rid of that old house immediately. It was a big mistake, you have to admit that."

"Nikki, I thought you liked my idea for a guest house. You said running my own business would be good for me."

"It is, darling, and you can still do it, but you have to start out with a better piece of property. Where do you think I'd be now if I had opened this salon in Brockton?"

"You'd be in Brockton, doll."

"I always felt that old house was . . . well, *jinxed*, frankly. And now, after what's happened this morning, I say get rid of it."

"That's assuming someone will buy it."

"Well, *you* did." Nicole does not temper the mockery in her voice. For a moment her fingers twitch nervously, as though they are trying to conjure a lit cigarette from the ether. Then she continues more brightly. "And once you've dumped the old wreck you can start working here again. Face it, Stanley, you need to be with people more."

I purse my lips dubiously.

Nicole blathers on. "You've said it yourself, darling, ever since, well, ever since the other accident." I know she's referring to the runaway delivery truck that killed my lover. "You're alone far too much, Stanley, and you don't want to become doddery."

"Doddery?"

"You know what I mean."

"No, doll, I don't."

"It's when people don't have enough social contact with others, and they become . . . well, *strange*. They talk too much, or else

16

not at all. Things get out of balance. You know what I mean! We get them in here all the time, people whose only human contact is getting their hair done, or a manicure. Other than that they hardly participate in the world."

"Thanks, doll, for your impromptu confidence-building and character analysis. But for the sake of argument, if you don't mind arguing with a strange doddering creature, let's say you're right. Say I give up the idea of a guest house and sell the property. Then, as you advise, I come back to work here in the shop, and it's good-bye Gladys Gloom. I paint the picket fence and the magnolias bloom again. Then what?"

"Then you have a life," she says.

"And there's still someone out there who wants me dead."

"Stanley, you don't know that for sure. It really may have been an accident. And even if it wasn't, whoever did it may have meant to kill Timmy after all. And now they did, poor boy!" She shakes her head sadly, then sighs. "It must be connected to that awful house. Why else would it happen there?"

"I'm sure Branco has some ideas about that."

"Vito?" says Nicole, arching one eyebrow sharply. "Is he on the case?"

"Who else, doll?"

"And are you two back to your little games?"

"Nikki, you just took away my guest house. At least let me keep my cop."

"I thought it was finished between you two, after you quit police school."

"I didn't quit," I say. "I took a leave of absence."

"And after Vito pulled strings to get you in."

"Which in his rule book is grounds for excommunication."

"Which just proves how much faith he had in you, Stanley."

"Nikki, he had faith in his own idea, not me."

"But he's forgiven you now."

"I wouldn't go that far, doll. But things do seem to be back the way they were—just a little worse."

Nicole shakes her head. "You two," she says. "I don't know." She glances at her watch. "I'd better get back out front before those Brahmin claws go up in flames."

"Any message for Branco?" I say. "I'm going to see him now."

"Twice in one day?"

"Police orders," I say.

Nicole stands up and straightens her skirt. "You can give Vito my regards."

"And a big wet kiss?"

"If you like," she says. "You always do what you want anyway."

"What's the alternative, doll? To do what *you* want?"

She's almost out the door when she turns back.

"I'll tell you something I would like, darling. I wish you'd do something with your hair. You look like a hockey player."

Nicole leaves. I phone the Boston police and leave a message with Branco's staff that I'm on my way and I won't need a lift to the station. Then I shed most of my winter togs and leave them at the shop. I also change my snow boots for a spare pair of chukkas I keep there.

Outside, the sun is blazing, which seems to be a good omen. But as I'm crossing Newbury Street, I'm almost struck down by a big black Mercedes-Benz sedan. The car has customized gold-plated trim, and the rear window is lettered in gold leaf: GATEWAY TO PARADISE. I guess even the Grim Reaper has gone yuppy with a new 'Benz. All I can see of the driver is that she's got big hair, definitely high-maintenance stuff. She's gabbing on a car phone, oblivious to the near miss with yours truly. People with that much hair shouldn't be allowed to roam free-range on the public byways of Boston. I yell after her in impotent rage. Then I realize the near miss may not have been accidental. There is a possible killer on the loose, and I can't be too careful. I dash into a nearby boutique and pull together a quick disguise: mirrored shades and a suede-trimmed visor cap to cover my long red hair. No sense in attracting some wayward killer's attention and inciting him—or her—to action again. Funny thing is, with the visor cap and my big jaw and the long hair sticking out behind my ears, I really do look like a hockey player.

So I puff up my chest and swagger manfully toward police headquarters on Berkeley Street.

4

At police headquarters, Branco's office is a minefield of open packing boxes. He explains that he's preparing for the move to new headquarters in Roxbury. He sounds troubled about something, and I ask him about it.

"It's nothing," he says. "Just that I'd rather stay here. It's old, it's cramped, and it smells bad most of the time, but this is where I started. The new place . . . it's just too new."

"Then maybe you understand why I like my old house."

"That's different," says Branco. "That . . . *property*—if you can call it that—the whole place is falling down."

"The foundation is solid."

I hope.

Branco asks, "How did you end up with a place like that?"

I explain how I wanted some security for myself. But the words sound stupid. How much more secure can you be than with a few million in the bank? I tell Branco how I saw the building last fall, just after the first snowstorm, and how I wondered why it hadn't fallen down. And then how a friend of mine found out the property was going up for auction. So I visited the Citizen's Housing Office and made an offer. In my enthusiasm to become a South End property owner I overbid the taxes due by roughly a factor of eight, so the wreck was mine, and City Hall enjoyed a windfall. The only smart thing I did was not pay cash for the place. I got a special "rehab" mortgage. The interest on my few millions is better spent elsewhere. Like on charity.

Branco says, "Must be nice to have money like that."

"Somebody died first."

"And somebody died on that *property* of yours too."

"Which is probably where the answers to Tim Shaughnessy's death are—on my property."

Branco looks at me like I'm talking Sanskrit.

"What are you getting at?" he says.

"Isn't that house the obvious place to find an explanation for what happened?"

"*Obviously,*" says Branco, "it's the first place we look. Why do you think I have the place sealed off?"

"Well, since it is my house, I thought maybe you'd include me in the investigation."

Branco says, "You are included. You're here now, talking to me."

"But I mean as a helper."

"A helper?" says Branco. Another Sanskrit word.

"A cub reporter," I say. "Something like that."

Branco laughs. "You want to help me, Stan, you can start by telling me about your relationship to Tim Shaughnessy."

"What about it?"

"Just talk," says the cop.

"It was professional. I already told you that."

"And?" he says.

"That's all."

Branco fingers his chin. Even that part of him is meaty.

He says, "I still can't get over the resemblance between you and the deceased."

"You mean his cuddly cuteness?"

"I mean the superficial characteristics—things like his hair, his face, his general build."

His build? Tim was a tidy little bundle of young muscle. And me? The only thing tidy about me is—

Branco interrupts my mental meandering. "A good-looking boy like him, and here's you, you've been alone for a while. Maybe you and him—"

"He's not a boy, Lieutenant, and we were not involved! Why are you trying to put sex into it?"

Branco does his manly shrug. "People sometimes kill for sex."

"Well, it wasn't sex this time, not with me. Why don't we focus on Tim's killer instead of his dick?"

Branco freezes. "We?" he says.

"You alluded to it this morning, and you're doing it now. And I'm telling you again, Tim Shaughnessy and I weren't involved. I'm more worried that whoever killed him might have meant to kill me. Isn't that what you said?"

"If he was killed," says Branco. "It still could be an accident."

"Which is it?" I say. "I mean, should I worry or not?"

Branco says, "I don't know yet."

"If Timmy was killed, I want to know who did it."

"You think I don't?" says the cop.

"So, can't you use my help?"

"No," he says bluntly.

"But I'm good at psyching people out, good at questioning them without their realizing it. And I'm good at puzzles too, even if I don't use linear logic. Don't you think an alternate approach could help you?"

Branco is unmoved.

I go on. "At the academy they said I was well-suited for the intellectual kind of police work, and—"

"But you didn't finish the academy, did you?"

His office becomes quiet, except for a buzz from the fluorescent lights. Branco has stated an absolute truth, something that can't be argued or discussed.

Finally he says, "I'll tell you how you can help me, Stan. You can get out of town for a while."

"Leave town?"

"For your own safety," he says, "just in case that boy's death wasn't an accident."

"Like a killer can't follow me?"

"I can arrange some protection."

"With a sympatico guard that might not be so bad."

Branco shakes his head. "Always ready with a joke, aren't you?"

"It helps," I say, "and it's harmless. Look, I'm not going to run away, and I'm not going to cower in fear."

"It's up to you," says the cop. "Along with everything else I have to do, I don't want to have to worry about your safety too."

"I can look out for myself."

Branco's face suggests otherwise. "We've already got one body in this case, and that's one too many for me."

"But I haven't done anything to be killed for."

"That may be true," he says, "but we don't know what a possible killer might be thinking, do we?"

"What about Tim's papers?"

"Papers?" says Branco. I'm talking Sanskrit again.

"From his house," I say, "where he ran his business."

"What about them?"

"Did you get them yet?"

"Someone's out there now," he says dismissively.

"Since when?"

"Since now!" says Branco, and his eyes start to glitter, a sign of rising anger. "I'm awaiting a full report from my crew."

"And you'll question Tim's subcontractors, right?"

"Subcontractors?" says the cop.

I explain. "Tim had other people working for him. Maybe one of them has a lead on why this happened."

"Is that so?" says Branco. He jots a note on a pad of paper. Then he says, "As I recall you got excellent marks in firearms training."

I blush demurely, as appropriate.

He says, "Did you keep your gun?"

"I didn't see the need."

"You might want to reconsider." He opens a drawer in his desk, takes out a small leather holster with a gun inside. "If you won't stay off the streets, you'd better have this. It's from inventory. There's a permit too." He holds the gun and holster out to me.

I look at it dumbly.

"Go ahead," he says and offers it to me. "Take it."

I do. I feel its heft, bounce it in my hand like I'm weighing it. Neurological impulses jam my nether regions.

"What's wrong?" says Branco. "You're acting like you've never seen one before. Pull it out and get your fist around it."

I do as he says and slide the heavy piece from its sheath. My crotch starts doing a rhumba.

Branco continues. "You set a new record for marksmanship.

You can hit a target from any distance and angle." He sounds like he's reading *Ripley's Believe It or Not*. "You don't want to let a talent like that go to waste."

Meanwhile my dick is really pulsing.

I slide the gun back into its holster and hand it all back to him.

"What's wrong?" he says.

"Nothing," I reply. My mouth is dry. "I just don't think I need it. Nothing personal."

"Better to be safe," says the cop.

"Perry Mason never had a gun."

Branco's voice is suddenly harsh. "Perry Mason wasn't real, and you might need protection."

I show him my cap and mirrored sunglasses. "This is all the protection I need. If there's a killer looking for someone with red hair, all I have to do is cover my head."

"Maybe you ought to dye your hair."

Good point, cop. But I don't tell him that.

"Maybe I'll get myself a fright wig."

Branco shakes his head again. "Look, Stan, don't do anything to call attention to yourself, okay? No wigs, no blue hair. Just keep it simple. I know it's hard for someone like you, but just try to blend in, for your own good."

"Yes, sir!" I say with a playful salute.

"Jeez," he mutters, "no wonder you couldn't cut it."

I'm about to defend myself when his telephone rings. As he reaches for it, he waves me off. "I've got work to do."

Thus forsaken, I leave the station. Out on the front steps I once again don my disguise of cap and mirrored shades. Branco is probably right, that dying my hair would be better than wearing the cap. But as I stand outside police headquarters, I think of a good way to use my red hair to advantage. And along with that I decide I'm not going to lie low. I'll show Branco how a gay gumshoe earns merit badges, even without the blessing of his sacred cow police academy.

I head down Berkeley Street toward Columbus Avenue and the South End. The snow is melting fast under the sunny sky, creating a small rush of "spring waters." Young men are walking the sidewalks, carrying gym bags, on their way to and from their workouts in sneakers and flimsy shorts, despite the uncertain weather, or perhaps *in* spite of it. I spy one particularly fine rump, flexing copiously within the stretchy knit confines of a pair of black sweatpants. Since I have no direction, why not follow its lead?

5

As I follow the heroic butt to my destiny, I notice that its owner is limping slightly. An Ace bandage binds one ankle like an emblem of athletic valor. It flashes on alternate steps, like a beacon, in high contrast against the black sweatpants and black sneakers. His sweatshirt is black too, like his hair. From my rear-ward vantage, the only points of light on the guy are his hands, his neck and ears, and that Ace bandage. Then, without warning, the gimpy gait activates a kinky quirk of mine, and I feel an urge to nurse and heal the wounded warrior walking before me. This Flo Nightingale reflex is especially strong when the injured souls are athletes, since they appear more helpless than ordinary people when hurt.

He leads me many blocks to a café called Members Only. A friendly-looking dog is sitting on the sidewalk out front, patiently awaiting its owner inside. It looks like a cross between a standard poodle (uncoiffed) and an Airedale terrier, but with wavy black fur. Maybe it's some new breed—a Poodale or an Airepoo. The wounded warrior pets the dog, and the dog licks his hand. Then the hero goes into the café. It's one o'clock, just about time for a coffee break, so I follow him inside. Honest, all I want is a cup of coffee.

It's a smallish place, and it's jammed with guys who all look twenty-five years old with big square jaws, smooth skin, bright eyes, radiant smiles, and broad shoulders. They all seem related, if not by blood, then by looks and behavior. They chatter noisily through a rush of caffeine—or endorphins—depending, I guess, on whether they're heading to or coming from their respective workouts. I stand for a moment just inside the door to get the lay of the land, and in Members Only there are plenty of potential lays. So why do I feel like a stranger?

The general chatter seems to be about a new piece of workout gear just arrived from Southern California. One very bossy boy proclaims himself the sole New England distributor, and he pitches the product like he's competing for the Grand National Tupperware Championship. The product is a "men's upper body support system" called the Pec-Pouch. (The quotes are his.) It's basically a form-fitting Spandex athletic shirt, cut short to expose the midriff and "those *rrrrrr*ipped washboard abs." But the "genius" of the Pec-Pouch—that's what the man says—the "genius" lies in the strips of twill tape that form two scooping crescents from the center neckline to each of the underarms. The result is two pouches that "contain, support, and delineate the cultivated male breast."

Whew!

From one corner of the café someone calls out, "Oh, dollface, it's a Cross-Your-Heart Bra!"

Attention has been usurped from center stage, and we all face the challenger. He's sitting alone and sipping a tall coffee drink topped with a big puff of whipped cream. He wears a fawn-colored fedora, oversized sunglasses, and a pink cashmere jacket.

"They had those bras back in the fifties," he says with his firsthand knowledge of another generation, maybe even another planet.

The hostess of the Pec-Pouch party retorts, "Back when your tits started sagging, Myron."

"I was only a teenager then!" says the challenger.

But La Pec-Pouchette has reclaimed the spotlight. He encourages the café boys to try on the product. They eagerly peel off their shirts and release their plumped-up muscles from confinement. Suddenly the café is awash in naked torsos. The boys pull on the Pec-Pouches, fussing with the twill tape to set it properly into the deep contours of their heavy-laden chests. They flex their shoulders and chests repeatedly until, one by one, they discover the "magic clench" being demonstrated by the hype-meister. The café is filled with squeals of delight as various pectorali majori are levitated and thrust forward with explosive exuberance. And voilà! Jayne Mansfield everywhere!

I make my way to the café counter. I really do want some coffee. One of the boys there is too busy with his Pec-Pouch to wait on me. The other counter boy is—well, well! Looks like the owner of the bounteous butt also works the counter at Members Only. But he seems removed from the folly around him. His bright blue eyes envision something more important than frivolity; his dark features imagine something more profound than push-up bras. I immediately fall in love with his soul. It has nothing to do with his flawless Ken-doll physique.

He senses my adoring gaze and looks my way. I'm still hiding behind my mirrored shades. Maybe he's admiring himself in them.

"I'm not working," he says. "I'm just here to pick up my check." He smiles quickly, as if friendliness will compensate for no service, then looks away. A few moments pass. He looks at me again, smiles again, and says he'll take my order anyway. He asks me what I'd like, and I order a double espresso. He smiles again, and this time it's a very nice smile, as though he means it. I smile back. Then he launches into a sequence of silky smooth movements that even my dead lover would have called a dance. When he delivers the coffee to me he smiles one more time. I think I see something extra in that smile, a special engraved invitation. Maybe all charming smiles look like that.

"You move nicely," I say. Can I yearn for you and worship you? Please?

"Thanks," he says. "Some guys like to use their heads, I like to use my body, so that's what I do."

Now I know we are star-crossed. We are perfect complements, me with my mind and him with his . . . soul. My nursing instinct speaks for me.

"What happened to your foot?" Let me kiss it better.

"I hurt it at the gym," he says.

A voice behind me remarks disbelievingly, "Did you really? You? The master of your body?" The voice is carried on a cloud of very expensive cologne. "How tragic!"

I turn around and see the cashmere dandy named Myron making his way to the counter. Through his sunglasses he shifts his concealed gaze between me and the coffee boy, then settles it on him.

"Why is it that some people can get service from you even when you're not on duty?"

The coffee boy says, "Because some people don't demand it."

"Do I *demand* anything from you?" says Myron. "Have I ever? Aren't we friends? Aren't we? Chip?"

So the coffee boy has a name, and I almost wish he didn't. Some names are unspeakable in the throes of passion, no matter how hunky the host.

Chip says, "Lay off, Myron."

Myron says, "Or what?"

Chip says, "Or else."

"We'll see what else," says Myron. He sidles up to me and says, "Did you see his hands? Look at them. Did you ever see such strong, handsome hands?"

Myron is right. Chip's hands are truly handsome. I hadn't noticed until now, distracted as I was by his other attributes. His hands are big and square. Even the fingers look muscular, as worthy of worship as the less subtle aspects of his beauty. I look down at my own hands. They're big and meaty too, but compared to Chip's they look soft and feminine. Despite the many years of hairwork that have made my hands as powerful as a concert pianist's, they simply don't look as strong and angular as Chip's. And the illusion of strength is intoxicating.

Myron says, "Aren't they the most beautiful hands you've ever seen on a man? And they're always so perfectly manicured." He makes a move to take one of Chip's hands in his own, but Chip pulls away. Myron says, "There's never so much as a hangnail on you, is there, Chip?"

"I said quit it, Myron!"

"Ooh, I am scared." Myron turns to me. "What do you think of this folly around us?" He flutters his own chubby hand to indicate the Pec-Pouchers still chirping away in the café.

Just moments ago I thought the same word: *folly.* Do I share more with this character than I'd like to admit?

Myron says, "It's like a costume shop at Mardi Gras."

"They're having a good time," I say. "It's harmless."

"Then why aren't you playing?" he says.

"It's not for me," I say. "I don't work out."

"Oh, doll-face," says Myron, "isn't it too tedious? And the results are so transitory. It's like trying to have fun." He leans close to me, as though he knows me and wants to share a secret. "I say let them do the work and we can watch."

Maybe I'd better start being extra nice or I might turn into this guy. Or—horrors!—am I already a little like him?

Myron adjourns his private audience with me and Chip, and makes an annoucement to the café at large.

"Listen, you all! Listen!" he says. "Someone was killed just a few blocks from here!"

The Pec-Pouch crowd has only half-heard him, and they ask each other variously, "What? Who? What did he say?"

But Myron has got their attention. "If you boys would get your tits out of my face maybe I can tell you! I said, someone was killed a few blocks from here, just a few hours ago, right here in the South End."

"Who? Where?" say some of the young voices.

"Nobody has identified the victim yet," says Myron. "Not publicly. But I think we'd all better be extra careful. You boys may not know it, but this was once a very dangerous neighborhood. I was here then and I remember. Believe me, I remember. I'm one of the handful of people still living who made the South End what it is today."

Myron pauses, as though waiting for applause. But the boys are already bored with him. What good is the old geezer, beyond the gloomy voice of history? Myron is probably fifty, and if that isn't close to death, what is? These boys haven't been alive long enough to see the things he's seen. Maybe nobody has.

I ask Myron, "Where did you hear this news?"

"Eh?" he says, turning toward me and falling out of character for a particle of a moment.

"You said someone was killed, and I'm asking where you heard it."

"I didn't hear it, doll-face. I saw it."

"Where?"

"Over on Waltham Street. What a to-do! Police cruisers, ambulance, medical examiner . . . it was like a film shoot."

Did he see me at the crime scene too?

Myron says, "What's the matter, doll-face? Have I scared you? Do you need protection? Maybe Chip will take care of you."

Chip says, "Myron, if you don't shut up . . ."

Myron leans toward me again and murmurs, "The boy can't take a joke."

I lean away from him and ask, "Was it a man or a woman?"

Myron replies, "I'm sure it will be on the news." He says to Chip, "Why don't you turn the radio to a news station? Then we can all hear about it."

"Because I'm not working," says Chip.

"Maybe if doll-face asks you—" Myron turns to me. "Why don't you ask Chip to put on the news? I think he'll do it for you."

I look toward Chip. Will the young god do my bidding? But Chip's blue eyes are busy trying to scorch Myron's medulla oblongata. And Myron is quite pleased with himself.

He says to me, "I have a shop on Tremont Street, at the corner of Clarendon. Drop by sometime." He makes a minuscule adjustment to his hat, then he says to Chip, "Take care of those hands, Chippy." He leaves Members Only like royalty taking an exit. Deposed royalty. On his way out, Myron grabs a handful of cut-up brioche pieces lying out on the counter for sampling. Outside the café, the friendly dog on the sidewalk springs to life and wags his tail. Myron holds a piece of brioche in the air, and the pooch leaps up acrobatically to nab it from Myron's plump fingers. The two of them walk off together like that, continuing their little show.

Back in the café I ask Chip how much my coffee is. He says it's on the house. I offer him a generous tip. He pushes the money away. Then he leans forward and says quietly, "You can treat me sometime."

Maybe I'm right and maybe I'm wrong, but I think I remember what flirting is. I pull off my sunglasses and cap, just to let Chip see the goods in their undisguised glory. But once he sees me he averts his gaze, as though he suddenly finds me repulsive. But what's not to like? My big jaw, which is perhaps a bit too manly for my girly disposition? Do my green eyes bother him? Should they be blue like his? Is it my broad grin, which sometimes comes across as dopey? Is my red hair too long? Should it be dark like his, and styled in a "boy's" regular? The only glaring physical difference between me and the other guys in the café is that they have shoulders and I have hips. Whatever the reason, Chip can't look me straight in the face.

"Is something wrong?" I say.

"No, no," he says, forcing a smile. "Just for a second there, you kind of looked like someone else."

"Someone you'd rather forget?"

He hesitates. "I guess you could say that."

So much for our future as soul mates.

I put the sunglasses and cap back on.

Chip glances nervously at his wristwatch. Then he calls out to someone in back, above the fracas of the café. "Hey, André! I'll be back for my check later. I've got a client now." He fetches his gym bag from under the counter, and emerges with that slight limp. He leaves the café without looking back. Once outside, Chip manages the wet sidewalks with aplomb, and quickly vanishes.

I remain engulfed in the center-ring clamor of the café, but also wonder what critical molecule is lacking in my own DNA, the missing code that would enable me to exclaim along with the other members of my so-called tribe, "The gym! The gym!" like some oracle. Perhaps the real question is, *which* gym? The decision is as fateful as choosing one's god.

I leave the café to continue my self-appointed rounds as neighborhood woolgatherer. Weatherwise, what began as a freak snowstorm has transformed itself into lakelets of slush everywhere, thanks to the now-blazing afternoon sun.

6

A few blocks from Members Only I see a familiar Mercedes-Benz sedan double-parked in front of what looks like a hair salon. By the gold-leaf lettering on the car's rear window—GATE-WAY TO PARADISE—I know it's the same one that almost ran me down on Newbury Street. The engine is idling, polluting the air but keeping the interior perfectly climate-controlled, unlike the New England weather outside. The megamobile probably has a security system with a setting for "unattended idle," just like the brain of the bimbo who drives it.

It's obvious she plans to come out shortly, so I hide behind a nearby tree and pull my visor cap farther down to watch and wait. I almost feel like a real dick.

Inside the salon I see two women arguing. One is tall and slender, wearing a full-length fur coat and hat. She must be the car owner. The other is short and stocky and wears a sweatshirt and jeans. She's got to be the salon rat. The disparity in their height and body shape makes their argument appear cartoonlike. But their intense, aggressive jawbone action indicates otherwise.

Finally the tall woman comes out. She's in her late twenties, early thirties maybe. Her silhouette is extremely glamorous in a full-length chinchilla coat—worn open—and a matching hat. It's an ensemble Nicole would envy, along with the svelte figure underneath. Her face is partly concealed by massive sunglasses, like some sexy secret agent in an old spy film that was never made. She looks up and down the street as she cautiously makes her way across the sidewalk. Though it's been partly cleared, Miss Amazon Glamor-Girl is wearing spike-heeled kidskin pumps and she's trying to keep them dry. More fool she!

She unlocks the car door by remote control, then opens it. She removes her fur hat and tosses it inside, releasing her massive hair from confinement. She looks up and down the street once more, causing tresses of long black hair to fan out over the plush collar of the coat and into the sunlight. The blue highlights signal an expensive dye job, since those sapphire glints usually occur only in natural black hair. Hair like Branco's. Once she's settled herself into the leather club chair that doubles as a driver's seat, she drives away. I watch her depart and get a make on the license plate: GATEWAY. She jams on the brakes and skids to a stop farther down the street. She has spied me in her rearview mirror. I ease myself back behind the tree trunk, out of sight. Moments later she drives off, but I know she's seen me. With any luck my disguise has concealed my identity, just as her fabulous costume has hers.

"I'll get you, my pretty," I say softly. "And your killer-car too."

I turn my attention back to the salon and notice a hand-stenciled graphic sign on the door glass: XuXuX. Is that a word? Or are those X's supposed to be scissors and combs?

The other woman comes out now. In the sunlight I see that she's very young, maybe twenty, but tough-looking, with short black curly hair. The color of hers is real. She resumes clearing the sidewalk in front of the shop. Her face is rosy with good health, and the work of moving slush appears easy for her. Her eyes are dark and clever, like those of a *ragazza*. (That's Italian for a street-smart girl.)

I come out of my hiding place and smile at her.

She looks back warily.

I wave hello.

She stops shoveling. "You want something?" she says.

"I, uh, I'm new in the neighborhood, and I'm trying to get to know the local businesses."

"Sure," she says, like I'm some kind of nutcase who hides behind trees. "This is a hair salon," she says. "We do hair here." Then she continues shoveling.

I watch her. Her motions are efficient and strong, every action deliberate and focused, young muscles hard at work. She catches me studying her.

"Hey mister, I'm not interested in buying anything, if that's what you're up to. And no handouts either."

"No," I say quickly. "Like I said, I bought some property, and—"

She interrupts. "You want your hair cut, that's fine. Otherwise, this is a business establishment. And if you don't have any business here, then have a nice day."

I pull off my cap and shake my longish red hair loose in the sunlight.

Her mouth drops open.

"Remind you of anyone?" I say.

She stares for a moment, speechless. Then she says, "You mean a hockey star? Dream on."

She starts shoveling again, but her movements have lost their fluid efficiency.

I tell her I own the house at the other end of Waltham Street.

"Which one?" she says.

"The corner lot."

She stops shoveling again. "*You* bought that thing?"

I nod. "I'm going to have it renovated. Maybe you know the contractor, a young guy named Tim Shaughnessy."

She looks me up and down suspiciously. "Never heard of him."

"He's in construction, real cute guy, had red hair like mine."

"Lots of people have red hair," she says. Then she puts one hand up to her mouth. "Hey, what do you mean 'had'?"

I stare at her.

She says, "Did something happen to him?"

I nod.

"Are you shitting me, mister? Because if you are, I know people who can take care of you."

"Easy, doll."

"Don't call me doll! What happened to Timmy?"

I hesitate. "I suppose you'll hear it sooner or later in this neighborhood." I remove my sunglasses, for this deserves a direct eye-to-eye. Then I tell her, "Tim is dead."

She throws down her snow shovel, and it clangs against the

wet pavement. "Liar!" she yells and kicks the shovel. "I know who you are. Liar!" Her eyes get watery. She looks at me with utter hatred. "Did that bitch send you here?"

"Which bitch?"

"Salena."

"I don't know anyone named Salena."

"This is a real shitty joke."

"It's not a joke," I say. "Tim Shaughnessy is dead. It happened at my house this morning."

The young toughette kicks the shovel one more time and runs into the shop. I follow her.

Inside she's fighting to hold back tears. "Timmy's okay," she says. "I know he's okay. You're just trying to scare me. Salena put you up to this. She told me she hired someone to follow Timmy, and it's you."

"No one hired me. I told you, I found Tim dead in my house this morning. I had no idea you knew him. I'm just asking around the neighborhood. I'm sorry it happened like this."

Suddenly she screams, "Who was it!" But she doesn't wait for an answer. "I'll kill him! I'll kill whoever did it!" She cries and howls. She throws plastic shampoo bottles. She kicks one of the two styling chairs and sets it spinning. She kicks the other one, spinning it the other way. They're kind of pretty actually, the two chairs spinning like that, and they dissipate some of her screaming. Then finally she falls into my arms and breaks down into heavy sobs.

After a while she quiets down, and I realize she's in the best state of mind to answer questions. It's called defenseless.

I say, "Do you want to tell me about you and Tim?"

She blows her nose, fusses a while with the tissue, then, finally, she talks.

"Timmy and me were real close," she begins. She shakes her head, fingers a few of her dark curls, then goes on. "We met last year. He just got dumped by someone, but he didn't want to talk about it, not the details. I figured maybe it was something he was ashamed of, so I didn't ask him. I just told him it would turn out all right. After that we started going out together. He told me once about a priest who touched him when he was young. I told him it didn't matter, not now. But I know about those 'pure' feelings. Pure feelings can go berserk."

"Did someone touch you too?"

"No," she says. "I just know. Then one day Timmy tells me he never made it with a girl, not all the way. He said he was a virgin that way, and I told him it didn't matter to me."

"Tim said he was a virgin?"

"What's wrong with that?" she says.

"Nothing," I say. I'm not about to tell her Tim Shaughnessy was certainly no virgin the "other" way, not now, not after I've already dropped the bombshell of his death.

She says, "I think Timmy had all these doubts on his mind because he thought he was gay, but he really wasn't."

"What I knew of him, he seemed pretty sure of himself."

"Then you didn't know him at all," she says. "I told him I'd wait for him to figure it out, no matter how long it took."

"Maybe you were waiting for the wrong bus."

"What bus?" she says. "Timmy and me both drive." She looks at me warily, then continues. "So after we were going out a while Timmy tells me"—she bites her lower lip—"Timmy tells me he started seeing someone."

"Seeing? Like dating?"

"Yeah," she says. "Like dating."

"So he broke up with you?"

She looks down. "How can you break up if you're not really going together?" She looks up again. "I mean, him and me went out all the time, but it was like friends. And I guess I thought— well, when we went out neither one of us looked at anyone else. So I thought Timmy liked me the same way I liked him. That's what I thought. But then he got all tangled up with this other person."

"So it was serious?"

"Yeah," she says. "Serious."

"Do you know who it was?"

Her eyes flash at me, and I know the spell is breaking.

"Why do you care about that?" she says.

"It might help the police find Timmy's killer."

She ponders this, then says carefully, "I think I'm talking too much. How do I know you're even telling me the truth?"

"You have to trust me."

"Why?" she says. "Who are you anyway?"

The party's over. She won't tell me much more now.

She says, "You just come in here and upset me and get me talking, and maybe it's not even Timmy who's dead."

I tell her, "It's Tim all right. I found him. Look, what's your name anyway?"

"Angie," she says.

"Angie what?"

"Just Angie."

"Well, Angie, I think you ought to go to the police."

She caws loudly. I guess I made a joke.

"The police?" she says. Her street-smart eyes gaze hard into mine.

"You knew Timmy," I say. "You knew him well. You can help them find his killer. Go to headquarters and talk to a guy named Branco, Lieutenant Branco."

"*Who?*" she says, recoiling as though someone is going at her hair with rusty scissors. "Get outta here, you and your cops! Leave me alone!"

"It's all right," I say, trying to calm her again. "It's all right. I'm sorry."

"I don't need no cops, okay?"

"Okay, but you can help—"

"I help number one!" she says.

Angie has recovered her feisty self, or appears to anyway. Fact is, she's probably in shock, no thanks to my indelicate message about Tim, her supposed beloved.

I tell her I'm going to ask around the neighborhood, see what else I can find out. "Is there anyone I should talk to?" I say.

Angie thinks a moment, then says simply, "No."

"Didn't you just say Timmy was dating someone?"

"Never mind about that," she says.

"Angie, he's dead."

"You already told me!"

"Okay, then, what about Timmy's friends?"

Angie says, "He didn't have any."

"Come on!" I say. "A cute, friendly guy like him? He must have had a whole fan club."

"I'm telling you, he was a loner."

"Then what about his family?"

"They're all gone," she says.

"Gone? You mean dead?"

"That's right," says Angie. "That's how Timmy got the money to start his business. All he wanted to do was work, and all you guys ever saw was a piece of meat."

I protest, "I didn't."

"Sure," says Angie.

"Look, I hired him, didn't I? It was his first big job."

"Maybe you were hoping for something more later on."

"And maybe you're too suspicious for your own good."

"I know how you gay guys are," she says.

"We're not all the same."

"Sure," she says again.

"What about that woman who was just here? Did she know Tim?"

"Which woman?"

"The one you were arguing with."

"Who was arguing?" she says.

"It looked like it to me."

Angie says, "I don't think that's anybody's business." She looks at her watch. "Right now I got a date with the weights."

"You work out?"

She says, "Everybody's got to work out."

"Even when they get bad news?"

"Especially then."

I tell her I'll probably be back sometime soon.

Angie says, "You come back here and maybe I'll take care of you."

I can't tell if it's a threat or a promise.

She says, "Whoever's doing your hair now is a real doodah."

"I do it myself."

"Yeah," she says, "I can tell."

I leave XuXuX and head down Waltham Street toward Tremont. At the far end of Waltham I see that same big Mercedes-Benz sedan double-parked in front of my old house, the recent crime scene. As I approach the place, the black 'Benz pulls away. The house has been sealed and festooned with bright yellow tape: POLICE LINE—DO NOT CROSS. Not a good start for a future guest house.

As I enter the main commercial area of the South End, I wonder again about the bodybuilding industry and its legion disciples. Even this girl Angie works out. Is anyone doing epidemiological research? Or are all the researchers too busy working out? Will muscle awareness ever recede to allow some other social trend its moment, something not quite so . . . quantifiable? Or are we doomed from now on to compare and contrast each other with tape measures?

７

It's around two o'clock when I get to Tremont Street. There's a storefront diagonally across from me, right at the corner of Clarendon Street. The building has a white marble façade, and it looks as though it might have been a grand hotel once, back in the late 1800s. A giant sign blazons above two big display windows and identifies the place in large loopy lettering, lots of scrollwork, very feminine: MYRON'S DOMESTIC ART. Below that, slightly plainer letters read: FOR THE TRADITIONAL HOUSE BEAUTIFUL. Myron told me he had a store here. He forgot to tell me you can't miss it. I figure I might as well observe one of my soon-to-be neighbors in his natural habitat, so I cross the wide street and go inside.

Opening the door sets a small bell tinkling over my head. A quick look around tells me that Myron sells nostalgia—specifically, tableware and appliances from the fifties. It's all here, everything that once defined a standard prescription for gracious middle-class entertaining in America. Your mother or grandmother threw it all out, and now you can own it for ten times its original price. But what is money when you can have and hold the very artifacts that gave June Cleaver orgasms?

The scent of Myron's expensive cologne permeates the place. Now if he was a genuine obsessive-compulsive, he'd be dousing himself with Old Spice or Aqua Velva, not some two-hundred-dollar-an-ounce Eau de Butt Dew from Maison Malatête.

I just about get the door closed when a voice calls out, "Wipe your feet!" Reflexively I scrub my booties on the brown fibrous mat. I also remove my mirrored shades and cap—their constant squeezing is beginning to bother my head.

Myron pops up from behind the counter, flushed with exertion. Without his fawn-colored fedora he looks like Humpty Dumpty's love child. When he sees me he lets out a loud henlike squawk, so apparently Mother Goose is in the gene pool too.

"Oh, sorry," says Myron. "That was quite a shriek, wasn't it?" He sounds more impressed than sorry. "But I just had authentic-period linoleum installed, and it's just been waxed, and I don't need people dripping water all over it."

I say, "Linoleum is to walk on."

"Just wipe your feet!" he says, not sharing my outlook on things material. Then, as though he recognizes me, "Oh, it's you, doll-face, from the café. You took your disguise off. What brings you here?"

"You invited me."

"Most people don't take my invitations to heart."

"I can leave if that's what you want."

"No, no," he clucks. "You're here now, and you've already tracked water in with you, so you might as well look around. You've got the place to yourself, thanks to this insane weather. Just make sure you wipe your feet."

Once again I make the requisite motions.

Myron says, "Straight ahead is the aluminum. The displays are arranged by hammered, anodized, and brushed media. Within each category are platters, tumblers, trays, and other accessories. Beyond that is the stainless steel. To your right are the electrical appliances—coffeemakers, waffle irons, toasters, and some rare items you don't see anymore. To your left is dinnerware—Fiesta, Holiday, Homer Laughlin, et cetera. Glassware is against the back wall, and—"

"Thanks," I say. "I'll just look around."

I take a few steps, but somehow Myron manages to be standing beside me, spaghetti mop in hand, sopping up the odd drops of water around my chukkettes.

He says, "Everything here is American-made in the good old U.S. of A."

"Some of it looks brand-new," I say, trying to sound interested.

"And some of it is," says Myron. "Those are the gold mines, when you find a factory-sealed full-chrome 1958 Sunbeam Mixmaster with stainless bowls and all the accessories. That's a slice of heaven. They don't make things like that anymore. But even my pre-owned goods are unconditionally guaranteed. I don't sell anything I wouldn't have in my own home."

Satisfied that his linoleum is bone-dry, he returns behind his counter while I look at a few of the objects.

"What's on these tags?" I ask. "Stock numbers?"

"Doll-face, it's called the price."

Myron settles himself near the cash register, which is itself an antique. "Was there something in particular you were looking for? I have anything anyone could ever want."

That was debatable.

"Actually," I say, "I'm looking for information."

"Information," says Myron, nodding his head uncertainly, as if he's not sure he's going to see any money from me. "Are you a collector?" he says. "Do you have something to sell? I'm always looking for new inventory. I prefer full sets, of course, but there is a decent market for open-stock items. I do pride myself on offering top dollar for top-quality goods."

I say it bluntly, to shut the guy up: "It's about the person who was killed this morning, the one you mentioned at the café. I'm doing a little investigating."

"Investigating?" he says. "Does that mean you're a dick? Eh? Are you a dick? I've always liked the word."

"I'm not a dick," I say.

"Well, don't get huffy," says Myron. "I'm not Betty Crocker either."

Trouble is, it's the second time I thought of a word and next thing I know, this guy says it to me. First it was *folly*, now it's *dick*. I don't like the relationship we're building.

"Oh," says Myron, and he clucks his tongue. "Now isn't that sad?" Suddenly he's gazing past me out the front window of his store. "Isn't it just too bad about that?"

"About what?" I say, turning to look.

"That place, that display. It's a blight on the neighborhood."

I try to see what he's looking at.

"You mean the store across the street?"

There's a new storefront over there that looks like some futuristic designer's hallucination. The sign reads: THORIN'S DOMESTIC TECH, and directly underneath that, FOR TODAY'S URBAN DIGS.

I mention the similarity to Myron's sign.

"Yes," he says bitterly. "The poor deluded creature thinks he's competing with me. But my customers would never set foot in a place like that. Why would they? Just look at that window! I swear he does it just to provoke me, displaying all that snotty imported merchandise with all those naked men using it."

From what I can see, Myron's competition has created freestanding two-dimensional mannequins from photos of bodybuilders, blown up to life-size, then mounted on foam board and cut out.

"They're only photographs," I say, "and they're not really naked. They're more like giant paper dolls waiting for their clothes."

Myron mutters, "I never saw paper dolls with bulges like that."

"I think they're kind of cute."

"Some people have no taste."

"Some people have eclectic taste," I say.

"Which means they don't know how to design a unified living space! Thorin should stick to closets, since that's his real expertise."

"So you know the guy personally?"

Myron says, "I believe in knowing as much as I can about everybody. Where are you from anyway?"

"Boston," I say.

"Which part?"

"Back Bay."

"Well, no wonder."

"No wonder what?"

Myron says, "It's another world once you cross Columbus Avenue."

"Works both ways," I say. Then I get myself back on track. "Speaking about knowing people, did you know the person who was killed this morning?"

"Why should I?" says Myron.

"You mentioned it at the café."

"Yes? And?"

"So maybe you know who it was, you being the neighborhood archivist and all."

Myron looks at me with little brown-button eyes.

I ask him directly, "*Do* you know who it was?"

He smiles vaguely, almost charitably, but still with those lifeless little eyes. "I guess you really aren't a dick," he says. "Not if you ask questions like that. Look, doll-face, if you want to play Nancy Drew, why don't you just tell me who it was who got killed—since *you* obviously know—and then we can see if I know him too. Does that make your game a little easier?"

Why am I always compared to Ms. Drew and never to the Hardy Boys?

I say to Myron, "You seem to know the victim was a him."

"It's a fifty-fifty guess, doll-fa—"

"Don't!" I say, putting up my hand. "Don't say it!"

Myron puckers his mouth, then mutters quietly, "—face."

That's it! Cool-shmool, dick-shmick! I say, "His name was Tim Shaughnessy!"

"Is that so?" says Myron, obviously pleased to fluster me.

"And he was a building contractor."

"Really?"

"So, did you know him?"

Myron places his chubby hands palms-down on the countertop, then takes a deep breath and leans forward, sticking out his overfed jaw for emphasis. "Tim Shaughnessy, or Tamantha as some of us knew him, was a little pixie from Southie—that's South Boston, in case you Back Bay types don't know your local geography. Tamantha was—how can I put this kindly?—Tamantha insinuated himself around the neighborhood."

"Insinuated?"

Myron scowls, as though I've spoiled the flow of a well-rehearsed monologue. He says, "Tamantha was a construction worker. But you already know that."

"What's your point?"

"Oh, doll-face, what's yours? You already know everything I'm telling you. Who do you think you're kidding?"

"It's *whom*," I say. "And would you do me a favor?"

"What's that?" says Myron.

"Don't call me doll-face."

"Oh, he's a touchy dick, isn't he? Oh, that's right," says Myron, "you're not a dick. Well, whatever you are and *whom*ever you are, let me tell you something. The South End may appear to thrive on restaurants and retail stores, but there's another whole industry that thrives on the South End itself, and that industry is construction. And bless his provincial little Southie heart, Tamantha never subcontracted any of the local people, the boys who live right here in the neighborhood. He never ordered goods or materials from our local businesses, and he never contributed a thing back to us. Our little Tammy was an expert at take, take, take. That's all the cute ones ever do, isn't it? Gimmee, gimmee, gimmee! But we have a community to support here!"

I say, "Tim's business was just getting started. He needed to get on his feet before—"

"Don't you defend him!"

"You have some pretty strong feelings about this."

Myron brings himself up short. "I feel nothing," he says.

"Neither does Timmy," I say. "Not now."

"Don't get sentimental, doll-face. It doesn't suit you. And why are you so concerned? You say you're investigating, and you try to sound like some grave impartial force for justice. But I suspect your connection with Tamantha goes beyond that. I think you knew little Tammy on a personal basis."

"What do you mean?"

"Don't get touchy. Did I say sex?"

"It was strictly business," I say.

"Then you know as much as I do what happened to him this morning, and why someone would kill him."

"But I don't, Myron. That's the point. That's why I'm asking people about him."

"Being a dick," he says.

I glower at him, to no effect.

"By what authority?" he says.

"Freedom of speech."

"And by what motivation?"

"The police think I may have been the intended victim. It's the red hair, I guess."

"Yes," says Myron, "there is a similarity. Actually, it's rather striking at first, which probably explains my surprise when you first came in here without your hat. You probably reminded me of Timmy, poor thing, and it brought up some emotional things."

Myron the chameleon.

"It's understandable," I say with a voice oozing psychotherapeutic balm. I can play chameleon too. "After all, we are discussing the death of someone we both knew."

"Yes," says Myron. "And if the police think the killer meant to get you, well, maybe you ought to be careful."

Then Myron's eyes get a faraway look in them again. I turn around to see what he's looking at, but there's nothing new outside the window. His voice sounds distracted as he speaks.

"Well, even if Tamantha was a self-centered little cocktease, he certainly didn't deserve to die." The sudden superficial melancholy gives him the look of a beardless Santa who just heard the toymaker's union is on strike. At least it's a discernible emotion. Myron's voice quavers as he says, "No one deserves to die like that."

"Like what?" I say.

Myron's little eyes study my face. "Murdered," he says. "Whoever the victim was supposed to be, Tammy is the one who's dead and gone now."

"You said you saw the police this morning."

"Oh, doll-face! They were crawling all over that place."

"What else did you see?"

Myron gives me a reptilian leer. "Do you mean *what*, doll-face? Or *who*?"

"It's *whom*," I say. "And don't call me that!"

He dismisses me with a flutter of his plump fingers.

"What do you care what I saw this morning, or *whom*? You're safe enough, aren't you, working for the police?"

"I'm not working for them."

"No?" he says. "I could have sworn I saw . . ."

Myron seems to be recalling what he saw from outside my house this morning. Does that include me being driven off in a police cruiser?

"Are you sure you're not with the boys in blue?" he says.

"I ought to know."

"Then maybe you're working on your own," he says. "Or aren't you working at all? Oh, that's right. I keep forgetting. You're not a dick."

My patience with this clown is just about up. Besides, I keep seeing little particles of myself in him—words and perceptions that we almost share—and I don't want to believe that old maxim that says we become whatever we fear the most.

I say, "Maybe I'll be back sometime."

"No hurry, doll-face."

"By the way," I say, "how's your dog?"

"My dog?" he says, with a curious scowl.

"I saw you leave that café this morning with a dog."

"Oh, you mean my *dog!*" says Myron.

"Didn't I say dog?"

Myron says, "Betty is a star."

"Is that her name?"

"His," says Myron. "Betty is a he, and he's in back. Some people don't appreciate him in the store."

"Is he named after Betty Crocker?"

"No," says Myron.

"Bette Davis?"

"No," he says again. "And that great woman's name is pronounced 'bet,' not 'betty.' "

"Is that so?" I ask dubiously.

Myron eyes me impatiently. "Look, doll-face, it's obvious you'll never guess, so I'll just tell you. My dear Betty's namesake is Betty Furness. You probably don't remember her."

"Afraid not, Myron. What kind of dog is he, anyway? A poodle?"

"A *poodle!*" says Myron. "Do you think I'd own a *poodle?*"

"Actually I figured you more for a collie or a beagle."

"A *what?*" says Myron.

"Since you're such a purist for the fifties."

"I can make exceptions," says Myron. "Betty is a Portuguese water dog."

"And I'm sure there's a good reason you chose him."

"There certainly is," he says. But before he tells me, we hear the muffled sound of a woman's voice raised in anger. Her words are indiscernible, but the emotion is clear. I glance toward Myron. He wrinkles his forehead impishly.

"These walls are like paper," he says, and rolls his eyes toward the common wall he shares with his neighbor. "Not like the old days. You hear everything now."

I head for the door, ready to leave.

Myron says, "By the way, do you know who's handling the estate?"

"The estate?"

"Yes," he says. "I'm wondering about Tamantha's household items"

I shrug, then put on my visor cap and sunglasses and leave the place.

8

The storefront that abuts Myron's shop is a realtor's office. The sign on the door says GATEWAY TO PARADISE, and the place proclaims itself "Your First-Class Passage to the South End." I've seen that name twice before, and when I look in the window I see a familiar woman seated behind a desk. The dyed black hair, too big for the city, marks her as the same person who was arguing at XuXuX a short while ago, the same person who almost ran me down on Newbury Street this morning, and the same person who was lingering in front of my property.

Now, finally, in the light of day, unfettered by chinchilla or automobile, she is clearly visible and I see that she possesses what is popularly called beauty. She's got pretty eyes, a pretty nose, a pretty smile, and pretty lips. There's even pretty shoulders, pretty breasts, pretty arms, and pretty hands. Everything about the woman is pretty and picture-perfect, except for that hair. That's the singular flaw. There's just too much dyed black hair, even for a Barbie doll.

She's got her pretty arms wrapped around a lizard-skin tote bag that's bulging with papers and manila folders. She's fairly hugging it to her pretty chest. I wonder what's so valuable about the contents of that bag. Or maybe it's the bag itself. Myron would know if it's an authentic Barbie accessory.

Of course I go in. I've got to. This pretty woman almost killed me this morning, and she's going to hear about it. Just as I'm opening the door, a tall, handsome black man, as stylized as an Erté Nubian, is coming out of the place. His face is like carved ebony, with planes and angles that glow satiny smooth in the sunlight. He knows he looks good, and he's utterly poised. Until he sees me. Then his eyes light up and they look directly into mine— or at his own fabulous reflection in my mirrored shades. We both smile and nod, and in doing so create one of those rare moments when two people express an honest attraction to each other before their defenses can kick in and spoil it. It's harmless enough, like a mutual vote: I like you, you like me. Matter closed.

I enter the realty office, where the faux raven-haired woman is now on the telephone. She motions me to come in and close the door as she chirps away into the receiver. Even her voice is pretty. I turn and look back out the window to see the dark-skinned dreamboat cross the street. When he gets to the other side he turns to look back at me. I remove my sunglasses. He smiles. Then he goes into the store called Domestic Tech. I'll be sure to drop in there after my chat with Miss Black-Haired-Barbie-from-a-Bottle. Hell, I'm single, rich, and lonely, and when a guy looks at me with interest, I might as well find out what kind of interest it is. Maybe voting isn't so harmless.

Meanwhile, Beauty's conversation consists of phrases like, "I'm doing it as we speak" and "Don't worry, that's my job" and "Yes, yes, yes, no problem." I'm ready to hire her based on enthusiasm alone. Although that might be all you get with her.

A polished hunk of solid brass sits on top of her desk, engraved with her name: Salena Hightower.

She finally hangs up the phone, and when she looks at me, I see a flash of recognition in her pretty eyes, which she quickly tries to cover with her exuberant pretty voice.

"Great day for house-hunting! Are you buying or selling?"

I'm about to berate her for almost killing me earlier, but it occurs to me that she might know something about Tim Shaughnessy, especially since she knows Angie the hairdresser, who claims to have been Tim's friend. If I confront this pretty woman with her deadly driving, she'll become defensive, and that will get me nowhere on the Tim Shaughnessy front. So as the microseconds tick by I figure, she sells property and I own property. In her game I'm holding a strong hand, so I'll play it for all it's worth.

"Actually," I say, "I'm shopping for a realtor."

"Then you came to the right place," says Salena Hightower. "I'm at your service. Now, are you buying or selling?"

"Probably selling, at least for starters."

Salena looks at me uncertainly, but she does it in a pretty way.

I say, "I want to make sure I find the right person before I commit to anything."

Salena says, "We always try to match the property with the best possible person."

"And I want the best possible realtor."

"I understand," says Salena. "And I assure you that I adhere to the highest ethical and performance standards."

"I'm sure you do," I say. Except for your driving, doll. "But with all the competition, I'm concerned about being pestered by people who will want to represent me."

"Is your property so desirable?"

"It could be."

"Where is it?" she says.

"Here, in the South End."

"Single or multiple unit?"

"That's not certain yet," I say.

Her pretty eyes look at me oddly. "Is it a condo or a single-family?"

"It's a building," I say. "A whole building."

"Really?" she says. If eyes could drool, her pretty eyes would.

"But it's still under development," I say.

"Then why do you want to sell it?"

"I'm not sure I want to be a developer. Up till now I always rented, and this is my first house, and I think I might want to unload it before I'm in too deep."

Salena smiles the way a cat does before it pounces on a mouse. "How deep are you now?"

"About hip level, so there's still time to bail out."

Salena laughs, but her pretty eyes don't think it's funny. They're seeing a smorgasbord of profitable possibilities. So why is she laughing? Is this how she establishes rapport with a potential client? By acting fizzy and friendly and funny no matter what the other person is saying to her? So whose angry voice did I hear coming through the wall a few minutes ago?

I glance out the window and across the street for signs of the Nubian who left here as I was entering.

Salena's laugh quiets down. I turn back to her, and again I see that flash of recognition in her eyes.

"Have we met before?" she says.

I tell her I saw her about an hour ago. "You were coming out of Xu—er, XuX—that hair salon down on Shawmut Avenue. Maybe you saw me too."

"Maybe," says Salena. She's trying desperately to stay light and breezy in spite of the slush piles outside and the humongous nest growing out of her head.

I ask her, "Are you a customer there?"

"No, no," she says with a laugh. "I just went in to buy some shampoo. Is that a crime?" She smiles expectantly, as though she's set me up for a punch line.

"Depends," I say, "on your hair and the product Angie sold you."

"Who?" says Salena.

"The girl who runs the salon. What did she sell you?"

"My usual," says Salena.

"How can you have a usual if you're not a regular customer?"

"I don't get my hair done there, but I buy shampoo all the time. So tell me more about your property."

"Actually, I'd like to talk about Angie."

"Angie?" she says, as though the question mark proves she doesn't know her.

"It looked as though you were arguing with her."

"Arguing?"

"That's right," I say. "Apparently you hired someone to follow a friend of hers. Poor kid was really upset about it."

"I did no such thing!" says Salena. For a moment she loses the pretty patina of a South End realtor. Her eyes flicker nervously. "Look," she says, "I don't understand. Are you here to sell property? Or are you one of those lonely people who roams around and bothers the ones who are trying to work?"

"I guess I'm waiting for an apology."

"For what?" says Salena.

"For almost killing me this morning."

"Killing you?" she says with a pretty little laugh. Her marketplace lustre is back. "What are you talking about?"

"You almost hit me this morning on Newbury Street."

"When?"

"You were turning off Arlington Street, at the Ritz, and you almost ran me down. You were gabbing on the car phone."

"I'm sure you're mistaken," she says.

"It was a big black Mercedes-Benz with a 'Gateway to Paradise' sign in the rear window."

"Oh," she says. "I *was* down there this morning. I guess I didn't see you. Did you get wet?"

No doll, almost dead.

"Is that why you're here now?" she says. "To accuse me of something I don't even remember?"

"I'm not accusing you, just informing."

"Well, I am informed, and thank you. As for your property, that was obviously a smoke screen to get you in here."

"Not really," I say. "I do own property."

"Well, good for you!" she says. "Sorry I can't help you with it, but I'm busy enough without taking on temperamental clients. Now, if you don't mind, I've got work to do."

Then an odd thing happens. Salena Hightower twists around and unlatches something from the back of her chair. From out of nowhere, two long rods of flexible high-tensile steel spring up behind her chair. The rods twang slightly in the air with their many foot-pounds of potential energy. Attached to each steel rod is a stirrup. Salena stands up and grasps one in each hand. Then she sits down again and begins pulling at the stirrups in various directions, flexing the steel rods like archery bows. She breathes, pauses, counts, and releases, repeating the exercises with military precision. The springy metal sings softly under the tension of being pulled. Its quiet twanging belies the impending catastrophe if the stirrups should slip out of Salena's pretty hands and release the deadly force of those springs in my direction. I've already seen how this woman operates machinery, and I move away from the contraption.

"Sorry to cut you off," she says, "but I've got to get a workout in every day. And since I don't have time to run to the gym like most people, I have to do it wherever I can."

Has she got one of these things built into that big black 'Benz too?

She sits there counting and breathing, yanking at those powerful steel springs and flashing her pretty eyes at me.

I say, "Do you know Tim Shaughnessy?"

"Who?" she says with a pretty, if forced, smile.

"A young guy, a local, runs a small construction business."

"What?" she says, huffing and holding and counting. Then her face freezes in that smile, like her pretty lips are stuck to her pretty teeth. The portrait stays that way a few seconds. Then her pretty face goes red, the heat goes up, the ice melts a little, and she can talk again. "Sorry," she says. "Never heard of him."

"Really? I mean, here you are in the South End, the keeper of the keys—that is, if your sign is true—and you don't know a local contractor?"

Salena's smile is even brighter now, and the springs on her workout contraption are warmed up too, just about ready for a big refrain. She says, "I can't be expected to know everybody."

Once again I glance out the window for a sign of the man who went into that store across the street.

Salena says, "Is something happening out there?"

"Not yet," I say.

I decide it's time to go. She's too distracted, and so am I for that matter.

"Thanks for your time," I say.

"Wait a minute," says Salena. "Do you mean Timmy?"

I turn back.

She says, "I feel so stupid." She's laughing brightly now, showing all her pretty teeth. "I've always called him Timmy, never Tim."

"Tim, Timmy," I say, and laugh along with her, although my teeth aren't quite so pretty. "So you do know him," I say.

"Of course I do! I manage the property where Tim lives."

"You mean Timmy?"

"Right," says Salena with a pretty giggle. "Timmy."

"So you're his landlord?"

She scowls—not so pretty. "Property manager," she says.

"You collect his rent, right?"

Salena nods.

I say, "I think that's called a landlord, doll."

"Not in the South End," she says. "And pardon me for asking, but who are you anyway? You never told me your name, or why you're really here. It obviously has nothing to do with property."

"Actually, it may have everything to do with property."

"But you come barging in here off the street and ask me a lot of personal questions, and now you want to know about Timmy, and frankly, I'm not sure exactly what game you're playing."

I use her tactics—a big smile and an offhand manner. "I'm exercising the good neighbor policy. You know, when someone is killed in your neighborhood, you kind of hope the neighbors will help you find out who and why."

"Killed?" says Salena. "Who was killed?"

"Tim was. Timmy to you. Someone killed him earlier today."

For that news Salena offers no smiles, frozen or otherwise.

"Now," I say, "do you want to tell me why you were arguing with Angie this morning?"

"What does that have to do with it?"

"Tim and Angie were friends."

Salena Schwarzenegger takes a hydration break and guzzles water from a plastic bottle, like a baby feeding—again, not too pretty.

Once she's slaked her massive thirst—her kind of hair needs a lot of water—she says, "I don't know anything about that. I already told you, I was just buying shampoo."

"Sounds reasonable, but that can be verified."

"Verified?" she says.

"As Tim Shaughnessy's landlord—excuse me, his property manager—you have a regular connection to him, and so the police will want to talk to you."

"Why?"

"You might know someone with a motive to kill Tim."

I absentmindedly glance across the street again, then realize that I'm doing exactly what Myron did earlier—allowing myself to be distracted by South End street life. How can I possibly have anything in common with that little troll? Nicole is right. I have been alone too long.

Salena's voice brings me back. "I'm sure he'll be there waiting for you."

"What?" I say.

"The man you met coming out of my office just now. Isn't that who you're looking for across the street?"

"No, not at all," I say, too chagrined to fix her grammar.

Salena has caught me cruising, and she knows it. And she's not at all pretty now, inside or out.

"How do you know it was Timmy?" she says.

"People are talking," I say. Why tell her I found him?

"I didn't hear anything."

"Maybe you're too cloistered in that car of yours."

She says, "Exactly what is your connection to Timmy?"

I tell her, "I'm one of his customers."

"He's your contractor?" she says.

"Yes," I say.

"So you really do own property?"

"Yes."

Salena's cotton-candy brain churns a bit. Then she says, "Do *you* own that house?"

"Which house?"

"The corner lot at 101 Waltham Street. Is that yours?" she says.

"How do you know about that?"

Salena says, "It's my business to know about every piece of property in this neighborhood."

"You probably know a lot more."

She says, "I do know that property was sold recently, but I couldn't find out who got it. That's what alerted me that something was wrong. There was something irregular about the title transfer. And for the life of me I couldn't find out who got hold of it."

"What do you mean, irregular?"

"Last I heard," she says, "there was an old lien on that place.

Next thing I know, someone new owns it. Now I find out that someone is you. So you're Stan Kraychik."

"You know my name too?"

"Of course," she says. "Tell me, exactly how did you get the place?"

"There was an auction."

"An auction?" she says.

I spell the word for her.

She says, "I wasn't notified of any auction."

"I'm telling you, you spend too much time in that car."

"Look, you!" she says. "I handle almost every piece of real estate in the South End, at least anything worth bothering with. And I never heard about any auction for that place."

"And I never heard about anything irregular, doll, so I guess we're even."

Salena's other side, the demon Barbie, says, "I'm going to look into this little one-man auction of yours. And you, for all your smart talk, could be in very serious trouble."

"I'm not in any trouble. You're the one with the suspicious behavior."

Salena says, "Was it that old clerk down at the housing office who helped you? I've always thought he was a bit nancy."

"Nancy?" I say. "What era are you talking from?" But Salena has struck a chord in me, for an old guy down at the Citizen's Housing Office did seem awfully friendly, maybe a bit too generous with his time and attention. I hope he didn't bend the rules to help me get the property. Everyone warned me it would be a big problem, but it all went through without a hitch. Until now.

Salena says, "You boys stick together, don't you? Loyal to the end."

"Except on P'town weekends," I say. "Those wreak havoc on the bridal registries."

"I'm looking into this," says Salena. "And I mean seriously. I don't appreciate it when people acquire property through favors. That's not why I'm in business. It's bad enough when people buy and sell property without an agent, but this deal of yours sounds downright illegal. You may find yourself minus a house very shortly, and your old boyfriend downtown may be looking for a job. Now, if you don't mind, I've spent too much time with you, and frankly, since you're not buying or selling anything, you have no business in here."

Then she grabs the stirrups on her exercise machine and starts yanking at them rhythmically. Better to burn up that anger here in her office than behind the wheel of her car.

I take one of her business cards and wink at her.

"Just in case I ever do want to sell the place."

As I head for the door I hear a dog barking happily through the wall.

"Must be Betty," I say.

"You've met her?" says Salena.

"Him," I say. "Betty is a him."

"And what does that make Myron?" says Salena. Then she resumes the precise rhythm of contracting, holding, and releasing her pretty upper limbs with religious fervor, right there in full view on Tremont Street. Does she get a kickback from the company for using the machine in public? More importantly, would you buy a house from this woman?

I leave her office and cross the street to discover if the Nubian vote was real or straw.

9

On the other side of Tremont Street I gaze into the display window for Domestic Tech. Signs and logos abound among the merchandise. Apparently it's all imported stuff since many of the names have odd-looking letters in them—things like å, ÿ, and ø—and remind me of those tiny colored flags that identify the

countries on wall-sized maps of the world. The giant cut-out photos of the bodybuilders, mounted on foam board, also lend a festive air to the place, which anyone buying the goods will need,
since the prices are astronomical. And they're not in Danish kro-
ner either.

I look up to see the handsome black man looking out the window at me. I remove my shades. He smiles. I remove the cap. He
smiles again, invitingly—another vote—so I go into the store.
The air in there must be circulating through some kind of space-
age filtering and sanitizing device because even mountain air isn't
that clean.

"Anything I can help you with?" says the man. His voice is
smooth, rich, and dark, like a full-roast Kenya double-A.

"Depends," I say, looking around the place, trying to appear
half interested, as if that might help bring us together. It's a dumb
tactic that seems to work in movies.

He extends his hand—the fingers are long and slender, the
palm broad and warm—and it easily engulfs my own chubby mitt.

"I'm Thorin," he says.

"Thorin?" I burble. "You mean, you own the place?"

"Why are you surprised?"

"Someone told me your personal specialty was closets."

Thorin grins, then looks out the window toward Myron's store
across the street. "I wonder who said that?"

I look out the window too, and I can see into Domestic Art,
where Myron is fussing with some sacred object, moving it here
and there on the counter for best effect.

Thorin says, "Myron and I share a special—what should I
call it?—a special fondness for each other. He says things about
me that aren't very nice, and I arrange my windows to, er, stimulate him."

"Stimulate?"

Thorin smiles. "I like to fool with him a bit."

Would he like to fool with me?

He says, "Myron is the kind of person who thinks things are
one way, and one way only. But I think people need variety. Otherwise they get too comfortable. I mean, look at him over there,
all cozied up in his all-American breadbox. If I don't keep riding

him, he'll get too soft, and then I won't have any competition."

"And you like competition?"

Thorin says, "Competition keeps you keen."

From the window I can also see Salena Hightower in her realty office. Her workout has made its way up to her jaw now, and she's talking on the telephone again. Who knows what kind of self-serving deal she's wheeling?

Thorin says suggestively, "Did she pull your chain too?"

I reply, "Which 'she' do you mean?"

Thorin smiles. "The real girl, the land baroness."

"Not that I was aware."

"It's okay," says Thorin. "I know her well enough to talk about her. And once you get past the frosting, the cake goes down pretty hard."

"We didn't get as far as the cake," I say.

"Well I have," he says. "We're married."

Thorin savors my surprise.

"That's right," he says. "Salena is my wife."

So this guy enjoys it too, pulling chains, just as he accused his wife of doing. Should I be surprised that two neighboring, young and attractive South End entrepreneurs also join loins and dance—and pull each other's chains while they're at it? Or is Myron right about Thorin? Is he really a closet case, and his marriage to Salena one of convenience? How else do you find the answer to a question except by asking it?

"Is Myron right about you and the closet?"

Thorin grins as though he's holding a big surprise for me in one of his big lanky hands. "That's like asking someone if he still beats his wife."

"I'm more interested in the closet."

"You?" he says. "You're not in the closet."

"That's right," I say. "And you're married yet you're coming on to me."

"Am I coming on to you?"

"Your smile and your eyes sure say so."

"I thought I was being friendly," he says.

"I guess I misunderstood."

"No need to apologize," he says.

"I'm not."

But he's clearly pleased to have pulled my chain again. And I am fascinated by the arrangement with his wife, Salena, whose office is directly across the street: I see you. Peek-a-boo!

I amble farther back into the store and Thorin follows me. The foam-backed mannequins in the window are arranged throughout the store as well. They're all wearing the same black bikini-style bathing suit too, and their faces are all the same, or appear to be anyway. I mention it to Thorin.

He says, "It's the same guy all right, but I plan on changing him every month."

"Your own boy-of-the-month club."

"It's harmless," he says.

"Doesn't hurt business either."

"Not in this neighborhood," says Thorin. "Most people think they're by Herb Ritts."

"They're not?"

"Every shot is my own work."

"You took these pictures?"

Thorin nods, pleased with himself, as he should be.

I tell him the stuff looks as good as Herb Ritts's.

He says, "I hope my work goes beyond that."

"Beyond what?" I say.

"Just look at it," says Thorin.

I guess I'm supposed to say, "Oh, Thorin, you're right. It's art. It's really *art!* You are an artist with the male body." But the truth is, the photos all carry the same clear message: Buy these products and you'll be sexy like me.

I ask him, "Do you know a young guy named Tim Shaughnessy?"

"Sure I know Timmy," he says with no hint of surprise.

"When did you see him last?"

Thorin's eyes shift down briefly. When he looks up they've lost their chain-pulling twinkle.

He says, "Do you mind telling me who you are?"

I give him my name.

He says it sounds familiar. Then he asks, "Why were you talking to my wife?"

Do I tell him because she almost ran me down? Or because she was arguing with Angie the hairdresser? Or because she was double-parked near my property?

"Because she's a realtor," I say. "I thought she'd know Tim. And since she does, I thought you might too."

"Oh, hey," says Thorin, laughing, suddenly relieved. "Now I understand. You're the guy who bought that house, right? The one Timmy's fixing up? So you're Stan Kraychik!"

"That's right," I say. "You know about my house too?"

"Know about it? Man, do you know how much merchandise from this store is going into your place? Haven't you talked to Timmy yet? We've got a truckload of fixtures and storage systems on order for you. Timmy has been waiting for you to sign off on the contract. Is that what you're here for now? To give the go-ahead? Well, hot damn! This is going to be a good day!"

"Not quite," I say. "There's a problem."

"Why? What's wrong?"

"Tim is dead."

Thorin looks at me as though my words have oddly slashed letters in them.

"What do you mean?" he says.

"I mean he's dead, Thorin."

The man loses his regal poise and slumps a bit, as though the plug has been pulled on his vatful of charm, and it's draining away fast.

He says, "But I just saw Timmy this morning."

"When?" I say.

"Wait a minute! Wait a minute!" Thorin says quickly. "You mean, Timmy is *dead?*"

"Yes," I say.

"But how?" he says. His smooth ebony voice sounds a little scratched now. "When? How do you know this? What's going on here?"

I tell him I found Tim's body.

And that's when Thorin falls apart in front of me. The guy just falls to his knees and breaks down into long howling sobs. He grabs onto my legs and pulls himself toward me, crying into my thighs, getting kind of close to my crotch. I'm not prepared for this, and I'm afraid someone might come and see us like that, closets and storage systems notwithstanding.

"I love that boy!" he wails. "I love him!"

I'm also worried that Salena and Myron can see us from across the street. But since I can't see them from this vantage point in the store, I guess they can't see us either.

Thorin's crying continues a while, then it stops, as though it's been turned off—blam!—just like that. He gets back on his feet, then wipes his face with a pristine white hankie from his pocket. He looks at me, eyes still red, but no more tears.

"I love that boy," he says quietly.

"Said the married man."

"What does that matter?" he says. "You're just using labels now. Married, straight, gay. What does any of that mean? A man can love another man without it being dirty. Timmy and I never touched each other, not once. That wasn't how we were. People like Timmy and me live for illusions, for things we cannot touch, but we know they are there. And that was how we loved each other. It was a pure love."

He walks back to the display window and looks out. Salena is off the phone now, and Myron is out of sight.

Thorin says, "How did Timmy die?"

"The police aren't sure yet."

"Do they know who did it?"

"Not yet."

"Are you working for them?"

"No," I say.

"Then what are you doing asking all these questions?"

"I'm working for myself." I feel my face flush. I realize I'm acting like I'm officially on the case, as though Branco has hired me, when no such thing has happened. I say to Thorin, "It's possible that someone meant to kill me, not Tim."

"You?"

I run my hand through my mop of long red hair, the same kind of hair that Tim Shaughnessy had.

Thorin looks at me. "You know," he says, "you do look a little like Timmy. But is that enough reason to think someone meant to kill you?"

"It also happened at my house."

Thorin pauses, as though he's trying to figure a complicated sum in his head. "You mean the old place you're fixing up?"

"That's right."

"Are you sure?"

I nod. "I found his body."

Thorin steps away from the display window and goes toward the back of the store. I follow him to an alcove where there's a small leather sofa. He sits down. Then he shakes his head slowly. "Who would want to kill him? Why?" Then he looks up at me. His eyes are sharp again. Something has occurred to him. "How do I know you're telling me the truth? Did Salena put you up to this? I saw you talking to her. Is this her idea of a little game?"

"I don't know anything about that," I say. "I never even met your wife, not until today." When she almost ran me down.

"Then why were you talking to her just now? I mean the real reason."

I tell him, "I saw her coming out of XuX—er, Xu—" Damn! "A salon here in the South End. A young woman named Angie runs it."

"I know about Angie," says Thorin. "Timmy told me she had a thing for him."

"A thing?"

He says, "Angie came on kind of strong. She's very young. Sounded like it was getting out of hand."

"What did Tim do about it?"

"He didn't know what to do," says Thorin. "So he did nothing."

A sexy guy on one side, an adoring girl on the other. Maybe sweet-tempered Tim liked to play the ends against the middle, which is where he was sitting pretty, and maybe also where he also got caught.

I tell Thorin, "I saw your wife arguing with Angie earlier."

"Really?" he says.

"And since Angie and Tim were so close, I thought maybe there was a connection between Salena and Tim too, through Angie that is."

Thorin says, "Salena is Timmy's landlord."

At least he knows the right word for the job.

"That's as far as their connection goes," he says.

"They had no other business together?"

"No," says Thorin.

"But they both deal in property."

Thorin says, "I'm telling you, there was no business between them."

"It still seems awfully coincidental that your wife shows up at Angie's salon a few hours after—"

"Okay, mister!" says Thorin. "I heard you, okay? Look, Stan, whoever you are, my wife and I had completely different relations regarding Timmy. Don't ask, don't tell. That's how we stay married. Maybe she doesn't understand how I feel about him, but one thing I do know is that she didn't do this. I am sure of that. She's his landlord. Period. If you really want some juice, why don't you go back across the street to that little shop of horrors and ask Myron about the Home Show last fall? Ask him about the scene he created with Timmy there. You can tell him I sent you."

"What happened?"

Thorin says, "I wasn't there, but Timmy told me all about it. And after that Home Show, you did not say Timmy's name in front of Myron unless you wanted to mop up the mess when the little gnome exploded."

Well, well. Chivalrous Thorin has come to his wife's defense by shifting suspicion onto Myron.

I ask him, "When did you see Tim this morning?"

"What?" he says.

"You said you saw Tim this morning."

"I did?" says Thorin.

"Earlier. You said you saw him."

"I don't think so," he says. "I didn't see Tim, not today."

Fine. Go hide behind your sexy cut-out men.

I know Thorin isn't going to say much more, so I thank him for his time and head for the door. On my way out I turn back and say, "You really ought to be more considerate about flirting with people."

"Why?" says Thorin. "It's harmless."

"I'm not so sure."

Then Thorin lowers his head into his hands and begins muttering, "This isn't really happening. This isn't real."

Maybe it's not. Maybe it's all an act for my benefit.

I open the door.

Thorin's voice calls out.

"Hey, wait," he says. "Just one thing. With Timmy gone now, who's going to finish the work on your place?"

I'm momentarily stuck for words. Finally I say, "I haven't really thought about it. It doesn't seem that important."

I leave the store, then cross the street to sing one more refrain with Myron.

10

I enter Myron's store and we do a reprise of our earlier duet. From somewhere within the store he calls out, "Wipe your feet!" and then I dutifully make the requisite motions. We're quite the couple already.

Myron appears carrying a large cardboard packing box. Betty is trotting happily behind him, like a good servile wife. Maybe that's why Myron owns him. (Wives do come in all sexes.) But when Myron sees me, he's not too pleased.

"Back already, doll-face?" he says.

"I just couldn't keep away."

"It looks like you couldn't keep quiet either," he says. "I saw you over there."

"I saw you too," I say. "And Thorin told me something happened between you and Tim at the Home Show last fall, and it might be related to his death."

"Really?" says Myron. "Is that what Thorin said?"

He sets the big box on the counter, then bends down toward

Betty and roughs up his ears a bit. He and the dog exchange big wet sloppy kisses, and I'm slightly revulsed. I prefer my kissing drier, like a cat's. As if sensing my reaction, Betty runs around to my side of the counter and starts licking my hand. I pull away ever so cautiously, for my experience with dogs, no matter how friendly and well-trained their owners claim them to be, is that after the tongues generally come the teeth.

Then with a single command and gesture, Myron sends Betty to the back room of the store. "Bed!" he says, and off scampers the dog, pathologically eager to do his master's bidding. And yes, from this angle, Betty is definitely a boy.

I say, "He certainly knows who's boss."

"Sometimes," says Myron. "That breed is very intelligent. They love to test you and keep you on your toes. You'll never get bored with a Portuguese water dog. But the best thing is, Porties don't shed. They don't have fur."

"No?" I say, wondering what that stuff is all over his body.

Myron sets about unpacking a gleaming chrome coffeemaker from the box on the counter. He brushes away bits of excelsior that adhere to shrink-wrapped plastic around the appliance. Then he holds it up and admires it.

"Isn't it gorgeous?" he says. "A Sunbeam fully automatic vacuum coffeemaker." He slits open the plastic film like he's doing ophthalmic surgery. Then he peels it down off the top half of the machine. He removes the coffeemaker's spring-loaded chrome top and peers inside, then sniffs at it.

"Oh, my, my!" he says. "This one has never been used."

He fishes around in the excelsior and finds the instruction book, also sealed in a plastic pouch. He opens it and examines it, then waves it at me.

"Look, look! It's barely been opened. Oh, what a find! I know someone who will beg for this."

I remind him about Timmy at the Home Show.

He says, "Why should I tell you about that?"

"You're going to have to tell the police anyway."

"Yes," says Myron, "and you'd like to tell them first so you can earn a merit badge. Is that it?"

How dare he understand the psychodynamics between Branco and me!

Myron says, "But what if I turn the tables, doll-face, and tell you something about Thorin? Something that—as you so dick-officially put it just now—something that might be related to Timmy's death? How about that? Will that get you two badges? Or are you going to bounce back and forth across Tremont Street like a Ping-Pong ball?"

"I was always more partial to badminton."

"You mean shuttlecock, don't you?" says Myron.

"I'll play whatever game you want if it gets a straight answer from you."

"Well, Pie-O-My!" says Myron. "Aren't you the dedicated little dick."

"I told you, I'm not a dick."

"We'll see about that," he says. "But here's the lowdown on Thorin and Tamantha." He takes a deep breath, holds it a moment, then says grandly, "They were lovers." His breath follows the pronouncement like the Wind of Truth.

"That's not exactly a Delphic oracle, Myron."

"You knew?"

"Thorin told me."

"He *what?*" screeches Myron.

"And he maintains there was nothing sexual between them."

"Oh, of course not," says Myron. "Thorin is just an innocent photographer doing art photos of naked young men."

"They're not naked, Myron."

"They might as well be!"

"I don't see how any of this implicates Thorin in Tim's death."

Myron shakes his head. "Oh, doll-face, are you really as obtuse as you seem? I'd guess that Tamantha was blackmailing Thorin. Maybe he was going to expose the whole damn cottage industry of porn in the South End. And Thorin wouldn't have that, so he killed poor young Tammy."

I ask, "Is there really a porn industry in the South End?"

"What do you think?" says Myron.

"I'm asking *you!*"

"Temper, doll-face, temper. You lose your temper a lot."

"Only with you."

"Maybe that's a sign of something."

"It's a sign that I've had enough, Myron. Anyway, the score is even now. Thorin said you and Timmy had a big blowup at the Home Show, and now you've retaliated by telling me that Thorin is a pornographer. Thanks for nothing, Myron."

I head for the door, but Myron stops me.

"Just a minute, doll-face. You know," he says, "you really ought to do some yoga or something, try to control that temper of yours. Now just settle down and listen to me. I don't want you going off to the police half-cocked and misinformed. That's why I'm going to tell you the truth about what happened at the Home Show. This is the unexpurgated version, the whole truth. Isn't that what you want?"

Is there enough time left in the universe?

"And when I finish," he says, "maybe you can run back across the street and tell Thorin too. Then he'll have at least one story straight, or as straight as someone like him can get anything."

"Can you just tell me what happened, without the filigree?"

Myron glares at me. "No finesse, doll-face. That's your problem." He lays down the coffeemaker like some archaeological treasure, then proceeds with his story.

"Tamantha called my things fakes. He did it right there at the Home Show, told every prospective buyer that my goods were fakes. I was mortified. Do you know what that kind of thing can do to your reputation? But he was clever about it. He did it quietly, so I couldn't convince the security people to remove him from the premises. He claimed that everything I sold was a Taiwanese knock-off. And do you know, that was the first show where I had a loss. Well, I can prove that everything here is the genuine article, or else a specially authorized reissue edition. Look for yourself. Nothing in this place is imported, including the glaze on that anniversary set of Fiesta Ware. Now I ask you, does that sound like a good reason for me to murder Miss Tamantha?"

He's right. It's a ridiculous motive, too extreme. But then, Myron is an extreme kind of person. Could an offhand remark about his precious things drive him to kill someone? Better let the police figure that one out.

I shrug. "You can't go by me, Myron. I don't care much about stuff."

"Stuff?" he says with a shudder, as though I've uttered blasphemy.

I thank him for his time and head for the door again.

He says, "Are you going to see Thorin now?"

"For what?"

"To tell him what I just told you."

"First off, Myron, I'm not a shuttlecock for either you or Thorin. Second, nothing you've told me is that important. Sorry."

Myron looks disconsolate.

I tell him to cheer up, that he's got a big treat in store.

"I see a tall, dark, and handsome Mediterranean stranger coming your way."

"Really?" he says.

I nod. "I can guarantee it."

Oh just you wait, little man, when you come face-to-face with Mr. Vito Branco. Which is exactly where I'm going next.

Outside I pass by Salena's realty office again—Gateway to Paradise—and notice that it's closed up already. Last train for heaven just left. Or maybe she's got her own steam room and sauna out back. Or maybe she's out for a late afternoon drive, running down unsuspecting pedestrians.

I walk down Tremont to Berkeley Street, turn left, and head toward police headquarters.

11

By the time I get to headquarters, a plump orange sun is setting in a glorious turquoise sky. This morning it was snowing with near white-out conditions. Now it's just wet everywhere, as if all that happened in Boston was a day of bountiful springtime rain. The weather doesn't seem to care that a young man was killed.

I tell the front-desk cop that I'm there to see Lieutenant Branco. The cop starts to give me directions, but I tell him I know where I'm going. I get up to Branco's office, where I'm told that the lieutenant is unavailable and I should have a seat. I explain that I'm there about the Tim Shaughnessy case, and it's kind of urgent. The sergeant says he already figured that, and he tells me again I should sit down and wait.

So I sit down and wait.

The phone rings a lot, and the sergeant takes a lot of messages. After about ten minutes I ask him if he knows how long Branco will be. He shrugs. His is manly too. Maybe if I'd made it through police school I would have learned how to shrug like that.

Then I ask him if Branco is actually in his office.

He says, "Oh, he's in there all right."

So I go back to my seat and wait.

Finally the door to Branco's office opens a crack, allowing the murmur of his distinctive baritone to slip out, along with a woman's laugh. It's a pretty laugh, tinkly and bright, like she's hearing something funny in a cocktail lounge. (Police headquarters is not generally known for party banter.) The door opens farther and the laughing stops. Then it opens all the way, and Branco comes out escorting pretty Salena Hightower from his office. She sees me and smiles, but it's not a very pretty smile. It's the kind of smile people make when they've just grabbed something from your reach.

Branco sees me and his forehead creases.

He escorts Salena to the elevator. He even waits there with her until it arrives. Once she's gone, he comes back to his office and walks by me with nary a glance, then signals for his sergeant to follow him. They go into his office and close the door. Five minutes later the sergeant comes out and closes the door behind him. He looks at me blankly and goes to his desk. I wait there another ten minutes, and finally Branco opens the door. He says, "Okay," then disappears back into his office, leaving the door open. I look at the sergeant for a cue. He jerks his thumb toward the open door. I get up and go inside.

The big boss cop is sitting behind his desk, methodically writing up some report. Branco is the kind of person who can write two thousand words a minute by hand and it comes out looking typeset. He doesn't look up when he says, "Close the door."

I close it and stand there. The packing boxes have multiplied since this morning. Maybe that's what Salena Hightower was laughing about. Even cops have real-estate traumas. Yeah, the joke must have been about moving. Ha ha. Why else would Salena be laughing in Branco's office? All I know is, her story stinks, and I'll make sure Branco knows it too, along with the rest of my South End exploits. But I don't quite get the chance.

"Sit down," he says, still writing quickly. Then finally the Holy Writ is finished. He caps his pen, lays it down, and folds his hands on the desk in front of him.

"You're doing it again," he says. "You're making problems."

"What problems?"

"For me!" says Branco. His hands clench each other in a vise grip.

I say, "I'm not making any problems."

"Quiet!" he says. He takes a breath, as though he's trying to calm himself. Then he says, "I'm going to say this to you—once— and I'm going to keep the emotion out of it. I'm going to state the facts as I see them, and you're going to listen. There will be no interruptions."

Is Branco doing affirmations? Doesn't he know they don't work?

"Do you understand?" he says. "Don't answer me! Just nod."

How can I nod when I don't agree?

Branco continues. "Not only have you been running around in public against my advice—I'm assuming that you purposely ignored my warning. Do you remember I said you might be in danger? Don't answer! Just nod!"

What else can I do?

"Right," he says, satisfied with my response. "So not only have you knowingly endangered yourself—"

"But you said it might be an accident."

"Quiet!" he yells. "I said no interruptions!"

See? Those affirmations don't work.

Branco takes a deep breath, then continues.

"With God knows how many social calls you made today, you managed to alert every person that my crew was trying to question. I don't know how you did it, Stan, but you got there before we did every single time. And that put us at a big disadvantage." He pauses. "I call that a problem."

I'm about to speak when up flies his hand.

"Don't!" he says, then takes a moment to collect himself. "You see," says Branco, "if people don't know the details of a crime, especially the identity of a victim, then they're very likely to answer our questions differently than if they do know. You get what I'm saying? *Just nod!* That's right. But today, thanks to you, Stan, everyone already knew about Tim Shaughnessy. We might as well have called in the media."

"I didn't mean to—"

"Don't talk!"

"I didn't think of it."

"Enough!" says Branco.

"I'm sorry."

"It's too late for that," he says. "Next time you might listen to me, or at least try a little discretion."

"You mean let you go first?"

Branco's eyes blaze at me. "I mean shut that flapping hole you call a mouth!"

The air in his office goes suddenly still except for a buzz from the overhead fluorescents. Maybe that constant hum has finally got to him. That's probably what made him snap just now, and he doesn't even realize it. All those years of fluorescent buzzing have finally taken their toll.

Branco says, "That's all I'm going to say about it."

The overhead lights flicker momentarily and the buzz stops for a second.

Branco says, "Now you can tell me why you're here. And just the facts, no filigree."

Jeez, I said the same thing to Myron, about the filigree. If I can say the same things Branco does, maybe I can get myself on the road to dickdom after all. Despite the cop's harshness, I can feel myself do an about-face, like a dog who's been kicked and is then allowed to lick his abuser's hand.

I start out telling him about Salena Hightower.

"That's the woman who just left here," I say.

"I know that!" snaps the cop.

"What did she want here, anyway?"

"No, no," he says. "I ask, you talk."

"You won't tell me why Salena was in here?"

The cop shakes his head, then moves both his brawny hands in a beckoning gesture toward me.

"What?" I say.

"Talk," he says.

"So this cooperation between us is one-way."

"It's two-way," says Branco. "You talk and I listen, as long as I can stand it. Now if you have something to say, say it!"

I start out with the near miss by Salena in her big Mercedes on Newbury Street. Then I tell him about seeing her at XuXuX, arguing with Angie. I stumble over the name of the salon, and Branco gets impatient.

"There's more," I say.

"Go ahead," he says with a big puff of his manly chest.

"Whatever Salena told me today, it started out one way and ended up another."

"For example?" says Branco.

"She made it sound like she was a regular customer at that South End salon I saw her at, but then she said she wasn't."

Branco's mouth twists into a smirk.

I say, "And she dyes her hair."

"So?"

"Did your lab examine that hair that was on Tim Shaughnessy's collar?"

"They're working on it," says the cop.

"Did they take a sample of Salena Hightower's hair?"

"Why should they?"

"How else will they know if it's the same hair?"

"There's time for that," says Branco, "if it's necessary."

I go on. "Then how about this? First Salena claimed she didn't know Timmy, then it turns out she's his landlord."

"All right," says Branco, and now he's almost listening.

"And then she acted like the guy across the street from her office might be interested in me, and he turns out to be her husband."

"That would be Thorin Hightower," says Branco.

"So you know about him?"

Branco's jaw tightens. "I told you, we've been working on this case too. Now have you got anything else?"

I tell him about Thorin's "pure love" for Timmy. Branco is stoney silent about that. I also tell him Thorin is a photographer.

"How do you know that?" says Branco.

"His photos are all over his store."

"You mean those big cutouts?" he says. "He did those?"

I nod. "They look like store display, but Thorin uses the store like a gallery for his own photography."

"How do you know this?" says Branco.

"I asked him."

"Just like that?"

"Sure," I say. "Why?"

"What made you ask him about the photos?"

"It just seemed an obvious thing. Why? What's the problem?"

"Nothing," says Branco. "It's a point in your favor."

"What do you mean 'in my favor'?"

"I mean we missed that, okay?" he says. "Just go on."

Next I explain Myron's possible motive, based on the crisis at the recent Home Show, but I tell Branco I think it's too weak.

Branco says, "Let's go back a minute." Then he asks me—Branco asks *me*—"What do you think about Thorin Hightower's love for Tim Shaughnessy?"

"What do I think?"

"Is that a motive?" he says.

"It might be a motive," I say, "but not for Thorin."

"Why not?"

I explain, "Why would you kill someone you love if he's single and you're married? Either you'd kill your spouse, or your spouse would kill you, or else *he'd* kill your spouse, or your spouse would kill him. But *you* wouldn't kill *him*, since he's the one you want to be with."

"Or maybe *he'd* kill *you*," says Branco, "with thinking like that." He shakes his head and blows another massive chestful of air through his pursed lips. The papers on his desk ruffle. "Anything else?" he says wearily.

"Just one more thing," I say. "It's about the owner of that salon who was arguing with Salena."

"Go on," he says.

"She's a young woman named Angie. She considered herself Timmy's girlfriend. She talked as though they were getting married."

Branco's face has become stern. His hands are lying palms-down on the desk, fingers drumming restlessly.

I continue. "Angie's not convinced Timmy was gay, and I guess she was hoping things would turn in her favor."

"And why exactly were you talking to her?"

"She's a hairdresser," I say. "We're of the same tribe."

Branco looks at his watch, then he stands up. "You've been a busy little bee, Stan. And you covered pretty much the same ground that my crew did."

"I wonder why I didn't bump into any of them."

"Because we do our work with discretion." The pride of Boston—that's Branco's crew. "But I'll also grant that you managed to gather one or two details we missed. It's probably thanks to your resemblance to the victim."

"Not because I'm good at my job?"

Branco's eyes flash at me. "You don't have a job, not here, not with me, not until you finish school."

"The police academy isn't the only measure of a person's worth."

"Here in my department," he says, "it's where we start. Now as far as this case goes, I'm telling you again, you've got to be careful."

"So you think it's homicide?"

"I don't know yet," says the cop.

"But it can't be an accident, not with all these suspects."

"I said I don't know!"

"Lieutenant, it's one or the other."

He says, "If it's an accident, the case will be closed shortly. If not, then your resemblance to the victim puts you in possible danger. Now I'm telling you again, stay off the streets."

"What, I should go hide?"

Branco says, "I know you better than that. But you don't have to advertise yourself either. That's all for now."

He punctuates this final sweet nothing with one of his trademark grunts.

I take my cue and leave his office.

As I'm waiting for the elevator, I sense that someone has slipped quietly into Branco's office. I turn to look just in time to see his office door close without a sound. I go back to the sergeant and ask him if someone just went into Branco's office.

The sergeant smiles and says, "Thanks for your time, buddy." He points toward the elevator. "That's the way out."

12

The tiff with Branco has got me feeling a bit down, so I head over to Snips Salon to see Nicole. A chat with my adopted big sister usually lifts my spirits. And if she can't help, I know something that definitely will, since Nicole keeps a small well-stocked bar in the back office of the salon. Why do you think they call them spirits?

It's around six o'clock, and the place is humming with clientele who are in for a long evening. It's Spa Night at Snips. Spa Night happens once a month. It's aimed at the high spenders who want to celebrate, say, a recent raise or bonus or a Dow Jones spike with a complete beauty makeover. Spa Night is also for the high spenders who believe their lives are too stressful and therefore they *deserve* a complete beauty makeover. And Spa Night is for the high spenders who simply *want* a complete beauty makeover. It's basically a cash cow for Snips Salon.

My arrival is perfectly timed, since the receptionist tells me Nicole is on break out back. I find her sitting in the small office, holding a styrofoam cup. I can smell the vapors, the spirits, of cognac. Also in the air is the scent of expensive, imported, aromatic tobacco smoke. Nicole sees me and smiles, then extinguishes her pastel-colored cigarette with surgical precision. (She never leaves a smoldering stub.) She tells me to sit as she pours me a snootful of cognac. She looks tired. I ask her if she's all right. She says she's had a difficult day.

"When you're my age, darling, you'll understand."

"Is that why you're smoking again?"

"Actually," she says, "something quite awful happened. I went to see Mr. Peretti today and asked if he could make my special blend with 'lite' tobacco, and the poor man collapsed and required emergency resuscitation. So I decided to keep smoking my usual blend and ordered five extra cartons. What else could I do? And how was your day?"

"Not as sensational as yours, doll. I'm only involved in a murder case."

"Is that official?" she says, sounding perkier. "Has the lieutenant assigned you to work for him?"

No wonder the sudden pep. Nicole is curious about Branco—again.

"No," I say. "I'm not working for him. Just the opposite in fact. All he does is cut me down."

"Well, of course he does, darling. What else can he do after you failed him?"

"Failed him?"

"When you quit the police academy."

"Nikki, I didn't quit. I took a leave of absence."

"It's the same thing, Stanley, especially after he pulled those strings to get you in. That kind of thing is very hard for a man like Vito to do. And then it turns out that all you wanted was some kind of hobby to occupy yourself, now that you have enough money to avoid working."

"Jeez, Nikki, whose side are you on?"

"Yours, darling, of course. But you have to admit, from the lieutenant's point of view, you look like anyone else with high-flown ambitions. No sooner do you find out how much work it's going to take than you up and quit."

"It's a leave of absence!"

Nicole says, "But what's the difference if you have no intention of going back?"

"Nikki, you know I can't."

"Yes, *I* do, darling," she says. "But I'm not sure the lieutenant understands your sensitive nature. He sees what he sees."

"Men!" I mutter.

"If you want my opinion," she says, "and I'm certain you don't, I think you should come back to the salon."

"Doll, you've sung this tune before."

"Yes, Stanley, and I maintain that you need the work, even if you don't need the money. How can I make it more attractive for you? I'm thinking of offering you a full partnership."

"A partnership? Nikki, you've never wanted a partner."

"I know, but maybe it's time. If it's ever going to happen, Stanley, there's no one else but you. What's to become of this place if anything happens to me?"

"What do you mean 'if anything happens'?"

Nicole says, "I'm just trying to be practical, to make arrangements before they become necessary. Isn't there a word for that?"

"Contingencies," I say.

"Yes," she says. "That's it. I want to prepare for contingencies."

"Nikki, are you keeping something from me?"

"Like what, Stanley?"

"This is sounding awfully morbid. And you look tired."

"Well, darling, I might as well tell you. I've been talking to my lawyer, about my estate."

"Your estate? Nikki, are you ill?"

"Why?"

"For one thing, you're smoking more than ever, as though time is running out. And now you're making a will."

She says, "I simply think it's time to plan for the future."

"What future? Death?"

"Not quite that far, Stanley."

"What does your doctor say?"

"My health is fine!" she says. "What has gotten into you?"

"Sorry, doll. You know how I get with estates and inheritances."

"Yes," she says. "You don't enjoy your money very much."

"I'm thinking about giving it all to charity."

"Charity?" says Nicole. Like Branco, she doesn't know Sanskrit.

"The money has only created problems for me."

"What problems?" she says.

"I never felt so aimless as when I became rich."

"Stanley, you are a very fortunate young man."

"But it's all blood money, Nikki. I can't really enjoy it."

"Nonsense!" she says. "Money has no life or soul of its own. It just is."

"Listen to you talking about souls!"

"Stanley, if you don't know what to do with your money, then just spend it as quickly as possible."

"On what?"

"Travel, clothes, nice things." The words roll off her tongue.

"I can spend it by giving it away."

"*Giving* it?" she says. More Sanskrit.

"I'm thinking of adopting a life of voluntary simplicity."

"A what?" she says.

"It's where you give up the quest for more things, bigger things, newer things. Lots of wealthy people are doing it. They claim it's a very liberating experience."

"So is a lobotomy," says Nicole. "If you pursue these absurd ideas, Stanley, you will no longer be my sole beneficiary."

"Your what?" I say. I guess my Sanskrit's not so fluent either.

"You heard me," she says.

"Are you getting tacky with your will, doll?"

"I did not amass my fortune through charity, Stanley, and I won't have it thrown to charity when I'm dead. If you don't know how to enjoy money and property that falls into your lap, then perhaps I should arrange for someone else to get it."

"Like who, doll?"

"Don't you mean *whom?*"

"I'll be the grammarian."

"I'm not so sure," she says. "But one thing I do know— Ramon won't give my money away."

"He doesn't know how, doll."

As though his ears are attuned to the sound of his name mentioned anywhere in the world, Ramon appears at the door to the back room. His hips gyrate slightly, marking time until the next bestowal of sex, money, and power on his oh-so-deserving self.

"Neekee," he says, "yure costumer is here."

"Thank you, Ramon," says Nicole, smiling sweetly at the little simp.

Ramon grins vapidly at me and I grin back, just as vapidly.

When he's gone I say, "He'll blow the wad in six months, a year at most."

Nicole says coolly, "You obviously don't realize how much I'm worth, Stanley."

"I'll bet Ramon does."

"He knows how to enjoy himself too."

"Maybe I enjoy giving to the needy."

"That's very noble of you, Stanley, but you won't be doing it at my expense." Then she stands up and announces a little too self-righteously for my taste, "Some people have work to do." And she leaves me alone in the little office.

The same cold treatment, first from Branco and now from her. Am I really less lovable with my millions?

13

That night, with no man or feline with which to occupy myself, I dial into Hairnet, the intersalon gossip network—also known as the telephone. I ring up Benjy, a former colleague who used to work in a neighboring salon on Newbury Street, and who just landed a plum job as Neighborhood Events Editor at the *Boston Examiner.* I don't ask Benjy how he got the job, and he doesn't tell. All I know is, he's got a lot of connections—and he met a lot of them horizontally.

He answers his direct line, "Neighbor Watch. Dish the dirt!"

"Benjy?" I say.

"Penny!" he squeals back, using his nickname for me, inspired by my coppery hair. "I hear you got that house."

"Thanks for giving me the lead, Benjy."

"What are friends for?" he says. "But that place is so big,

Penny. Aren't you going to need, like, a *spouse* or something?"

"I have other plans."

"Too bad," he says, "unless you're thinking of a brothel. That's what Boston really needs—a good male brothel."

"Benjy, I need a little information."

"This is Dirt Central, Penny-Poo, and your timing is perfect. I just fanagled unlimited Internet access. Do you know what that means?"

"Nope."

"It means I've been logged on since yesterday morning. Penny, this is the Telequeen Network times ten! Now what do you need?"

I tell him about finding Tim Shaughnessy this morning, on my property.

"Oh, Penny! The Welcome Wagon has slipped."

"For Timmy too," I say.

"This sounds like police work," says Benjy. "Speaking of which, how is that hot Italian cop of yours?"

"The same," I say.

"Sounds like you don't want to talk about it."

"There's nothing to talk about, Benjy, not on that front. But I could use some information, anything related to Tim Shaughnessy."

Benjy says, "Information is a piece of cake, Pennykins, just like you."

Then I hear the clickety-click of his fingers at the keyboard. There's a pause, and he says, "Hey dumpling, how come we never hit it off, I mean, romantically?"

"It would be like dating ourselves, Benjy."

"What's wrong with that?" he says. "I'd make a great wife."

"But we both want husbands."

"Not you, Penny. You had a husband, and look what happened. He was sexy and you were three steps behind, like chattel. That's not you, Penny. You're latent butch."

All gay men have a pal who makes them feel manly.

"Besides," says Benjy, "when was the last time you shopped for tableware?"

Dare I tell him about Myron's store?

"You'd be surprised, Benjy."

"Yes, Penny, but did you enjoy it? You hate to shop, and that's what a wife lives for." Suddenly Benjy is all business. "Okay," he says, "here we go. We've got search results on Tim Shaughnessy." A few moments pass as Benjy makes soft cooing sounds, like he's eating candy. "Oh," he says, "very interesting. Penny, you ever hear of Gardenia and Sons?"

"They're that big construction firm, right? Everything from high-rise monoliths to library tea gardens."

"Monoliths?" he says. "Penny, you have such a big vocabulary! But, that's them, all right—Gardenia and Sons, Boston's one and only. Thanks to the expert search tactics of your devoted Benjamin, we have uncovered a link to the late, adorable Tim Shaughnessy."

"A link?" I say. "What is it?"

"Patience, Penny-dearest. I have only just begun." Now Benjy types while he talks. "Am I chattering too much as usual? But if I can't express myself freely with you, Penny, why should I go on living?"

"It's okay, Benjy. Do what you have to do."

"But are you listening?"

"I'm all ears."

"Not quite, Penny, not according to what I've heard on these chat lines. But anyway, here we go. As you probably know, the Gardenias, those self-proclaimed blossoms of Italian nobility, have always kept our crowd out of the Columbus Day Parade, and you know it's just because we do better costumes. But then last fall they went and did an about-face, and they underbid every other construction company for the contract to renovate the recreational center."

"Recreational center?"

"Lovething," he says, "what time zone are you in? Oh, that's right, you were burnishing your buns in Key West when all this happened. Anyway, the South End Community Alliance, of which I am a director, in case you didn't know—"

"I pledged a wad of money, thanks to your groveling."

"I did not grovel, Penny. Anyway, SECA, as we are known to those in the know, did manage to secure a building in the South End to convert to a recreational center. Read gym, sauna, steam bath. You get the gist?"

"Oh," I say.

" 'Oh,' said the man reading yesterday's news. Anyway—so! Gardenia and Sons got the contract to rebuild the place, but they just about bulldozed *us* under with broken schedules and faulty budgets. It was scandalous!"

"What's the connection, Benjy?"

"You really did miss all this, didn't you? I guess it's time for Brenda Starr." Benjy drops his voice from coloratura to mezzo to sound more authoritative. "It is not clear exactly how it happened, but apparently one of Tony Gardenia's workmen was cruising another guy while this humongous I-beam was in flight. The I-beam veered slightly out of its intended path and broke the boss's neck."

"Did he die?"

"Did he *die?* Penny! Did Mary have a hymen?"

"So you're telling me the Gardenia clan hates gay men because their beloved scion Tony Gardenia was killed while working on the site of a gay recreational center?"

"And because one of the workers was momentarily distracted by the glistening physique of one of his colleagues. Let's not forget the cruise factor, my little Slavic dumpling."

"Who's little?" I say.

"Just testing your attention, Penny. With all this background it might have lagged."

"Background? Benjy, you mean there's more?"

"Oh, Penny, I know it's a long way to the altar, but it's worth the trek. Here's where it gets juicy. Despite all the accusations, the guy with the googly eyes was acquitted because the crane he was operating was found to be faulty. Those naughty Gardenias don't keep their equipment in tip-top shape. Supposedly that I-beam would have conked the boss even if the great, straight Tom Selleck had been manning it."

"I'll bet the Gardenia clan wasn't too happy with the verdict."

"There's more, Pennydrops. The very hunk whose vision was

momentarily taken with one of his compadres—allegedly causing the death of Crown Prince Tony Gardenia—was none other than—small fanfare please—Tim Shaughnessy himself."

"Oh, no!"

"Yez, cherie, I zink I zee zuh connection too."

"You're telling me that Tim Shaughnessy accidentally killed Tony Gardenia?"

"No, Penny. I'm telling you he was accused of it. The charge didn't hold."

"No wonder Tim didn't give the Gardenias as a reference."

"Would you?" says Benjy.

Then it hits me.

"Benjy, do you think . . . ?" I can't quite say it. Benjy helps me.

"That maybe the Gardenias killed Timmy? Is that what you're thinking, Penny?"

"They couldn't!" I say. "It's too extreme."

"Penny, have you ever heard the word *vendetta?* These are Italians we're talking about. You know, the opera people?"

"But Benjy, if they killed Tim, they must know that I hired him to work for me."

"And so by association . . . ?"

" . . . I'm guilty too?"

The line is quiet for a moment.

Then Benjy says, "I think Penny did a boo-boo."

New mantra: I will not panic. I will not panic.

I ask him, "What happened after the accident?"

"Nothing," says Benjy. "Work on the recreational center came to a dead halt. Oh, sorry, Pen. My inner editor must be dozing. But after that the Gardenias refused to lift a shovel. They were too busy spreading the 'bad word' about gays."

"Benjy, can you check on something else?"

"If you think it will save your neck."

"Does your magic box tell you who sold that property to SECA?"

"I don't have to look that up, Penny, because I know it. As a board member of SECA I was there. Oh God, was I there! Anyway, the former owner was a family-owned bakery."

"Italian?"

"Nope. French."

"Okay then, who handled the sale?"

"That would be Gateway to Paradise."

Clink, chunk, go the pawls and ratchets in my Slavic data bank.

"I know it well, Benjy. There was a bitch named Salena, right?"

"Penny! Is that a nice thing to call a realtor? Are you feeling bitter?"

"No, Benjy, I'm trying to feel clever. By the way, where are you finding all this stuff?"

"Oh, here and there, anywhere I can. Why?"

"Is it reliable?"

"Reliable, Penny?"

"Is it true, Benjy?"

"Oh, Pennypie, what is truth?"

I sigh. "Never mind."

"Tuppence, you really have to get online. The chat rooms alone are worth it. It's like having your own talk show. Oops, gotta run. Here comes the boss."

And the phone line goes dead.

Breathless chats with Benjy can be partially offset by a total immersion alcohol bath, or something as extreme. This time I decide to run my own version of Spa Night at Snips, but instead of a complete beauty makeover, I settle for a self-inflicted dip-and-clip. First I dye my hair mousy brown to conceal my redhead identity from any killers-at-large. Then I get out the electric clippers and trim the hockey hair down to a uniform one-half inch length. I consider shaving my mustache too, but the last time I did that I looked like a camel. So I dye it to match the hair, then trim it close. The new me shows little resemblance to the late Tim Shaughnessy. I look more like a cute, cuddly teddy bear. Or else a gargantuan shrew. But hey, I'm a Gemini. That means two personalities, minimum.

14

Next morning I'm out bright and early. It's springtime again, no blizzard conditions, lots of sunshine. I put on the sunglasses and visor cap I wore yesterday. Those, along with my new mouse-brown brush-cut, should provide near perfect camouflage among the other lads strolling the South End. First stop is police headquarters to tell Lieutenant Branco about the link between Gardenia and Sons Construction and Tim Shaughnessy.

As I get off the elevator on Branco's floor, I see someone vanish into the adjoining elevator. A smallish person, I think, with dark curly hair.

I get to Branco's office. His greeting?

"What happened to your hair?"

I explain the dip-and-clip.

He looks dubious.

Then I relate what I learned from Benjy about the Gardenia clan and the South End Community Alliance, about the big contract to build a recreational center, and about the accidental death of Tony Gardenia at the building site. I explain to Branco how bigshots like the Gardenias know how to get revenge when one of their own is killed, even if it was an accident. So it's very possible that they killed Tim Shaughnessy.

Branco takes it all in without any reaction. At the very least he should be defending his Italian heritage. I've implied some awful things about vendettas. Instead he sits there with a little bitty Buddha smile on his sensual lips.

"And now," I say, "what if the Gardenias decide to come after me? I mean, I hired Tim Shaughnessy. There's no telling how far people like the Gardenias will go to avenge their oldest son."

Branco speaks quietly. "You obviously don't understand these things, Stan. It's not like some gangster movie. Even vengeance has its ethics." He talks as though he's privy to such codes of behavior. Maybe he is. Maybe all Italians are. He says, "The people you mention might have considered taking further action—legal action—against young Shaughnessy, but only if they were absolutely certain he was responsible for their son's death. As for going after you, well it just proves how wild your imagination can get. Now, I've got plenty to do without getting tangled up in one of your wild, straw-grasping, harebrained—"

I finish the sentence. "Baroque flights of fancy."

Branco grunts.

"Back here on earth," he says, "we have to look at things more simply."

"But you admit that Tim Shaughnessy's death wasn't an accident, right?"

"I don't admit anything," says Branco.

"But this business with the Gardenias is a solid lead."

Branco heaves a sigh. "What's the source of your information?"

I give him Benjy's name and work number.

Branco says, "He works for the *Examiner?*"

"Yes," I say.

Branco grunts.

I remind myself to call Benjy and warn him of Branco's call.

As he writes it all down he says, "If I can find the resources, maybe I'll get someone on it. Right now I want to get that photographer in here."

"Thorin Hightower?"

"That's right," says Branco. "You liked the guy's work."

"I noticed it," I say.

"Turns out he has a record—convicted and served time for drug dealing. So much for your innocent artist theory."

"Hey, I said he was a good photographer. I never said he was innocent."

Branco says, "If things go the way I expect, we should have a wrap on this case today."

"You think it's Thorin?"

Branco disregards my question. "I want to thank you, Stan, for your good intentions. I hope you'll understand when I tell you that I really don't want or need your help anymore, in this or any other case. Is that clear? I know you mean well, but frankly, the ratio of your help to the problems you create is pretty low. In fact, this time around it's negative—no help, all problems. So let's just break it off now while we're still on good terms. Okay?"

He looks at me expectantly, as though I am to nod silently—perhaps even to genuflect—then crawl out of his office.

Instead I tell him it wasn't Thorin. "It couldn't be," I say. "He might have a record, but he didn't kill Tim. He loved him like a . . . like a nephew!"

"I don't want to get into it, Stan."

"You don't have anything against Thorin except his record."

The ends of Branco's mouth curl into that know-it-all smile.

"We have a lot more on the guy than that," he says. "Now as far as you're concerned, I think maybe it's time for a vacation. You ought to leave town until we clear this whole matter up."

"You said you might close the case today."

"We might," says Branco.

"Are you worried that the Gardenias might come after me? Is that really why you want me out of town? You can tell me, Lieutenant. I can handle the truth. I'm stronger than you think."

He laughs briefly. "It's a good thing you're really not in any danger."

"Last night you thought I was."

"Last night we didn't have a suspect. Look, why don't you go somewhere nice and warm. Relax. Forget all about this business. Work like this isn't for people like you, Stan. Your talents are better utilized . . ." He pauses before proclaiming my manifest destiny. "Your job," he says, "people like you are cut out to . . . well, to have a good time. That's really what you're good at. You should leave the dirty work for people who can handle it."

So goes the art of the well-tempered put-down.

Now, two things bother me. One, why is Branco suddenly so eager to get me out of town? And two, why does he think I don't know what dirty work is? Has he ever shampooed someone whose only contact with water is during a weekly wash-and-set?

"I'll think about it," I say. "The vacation, that is."

Then I leave the station.

Outside headquarters, the late morning sun is still shining brightly. Looks like the weather is going to try for springtime again. I head toward the South End.

15

Thoughts of shampoo and dirty work lead me to XuXuX. Since Angie the hairdresser was so close to Tim Shaughnessy, she'll certainly know something about the fatal accident at the SECA site. But today is not the day I find out. XuXuX is closed up tight. I peer through the window and see all the signs of a small startup salon. Two styling stations face one of the side walls, the one that's completely covered with high-grade industrial mirror, the kind used by major ballet companies. Against the back wall of the shop is a shampoo sink and a curtained doorway to a storage area. Against the other side wall are a sit-down dryer, a radiant-heat dryer, and a reception desk. But the place is dark inside, no sign of life. Then I see a sign taped on the inside of the door: FAMILY EMERGENCY.

Well, it's time for my second breakfast anyway, so I head over to Members Only Café. With that sexy espresso puller and his charming smile, it was fertile terrain on my first visit yesterday. Maybe if I keep my cap and sunglasses on, the guy will forget he ever saw my real face, and he'll find me appealing again. Or maybe somebody else will.

The café is bustling with festive energy. The topic du jour is Cartier rings and Patek Phillipe watches. Two of the boys are showing off their bounty like young princes who've just received regal baubles from Dear Mama to mark the real arrival of springtime. Myself, when I landed the cash from my lover's death, I did the same thing, but in reverse, which seems to be my usual mode of operation. I bought those very same trinkets for my parents, and they didn't have the foggiest notion of their value, intrinsic or otherwise.

I look for the espresso boy from yesterday, but he's not around. I discreetly ask a young guy behind the counter about him. He smiles knowingly, then replies in a voice loud enough to reach around the block. "You looking for Chip?"

I nod bashfully.

"Chip's not here," he says with his built-in megaphone. "Did you want some coffee?"

"Uh, sure," I say. Meanwhile all conversation in the café has come to a halt. They all know it now: I'm there for Chip. I'm just another damsel smitten by his charm and his fastidiously wrought body. To break the silence, I casually ask if anyone has seen Angie the hairdresser. No one has. The espresso machine begins pumping its elixir, and the café chatter resumes.

"Is yours eighteen or twenty-four carat?"

"I don't know. Isn't twenty-four too soft?"

"Honey, there's nothing soft about twenty-four!"

Since there's no place to sit in there, I take my coffee to one of the small outdoor tables. Besides, the weather is beautiful and it's actually much quieter out on the sidewalk. No sooner do I sit than I sense someone standing beside me. His cologne is expensive, probably Cartier or Patek Phillipe.

"Taking the waters, doll-face?"

It's Myron, and he's got his dog, Betty, with him. The pooch sniffs at my hand, and I pull away. Myron—I'm not kidding—is wearing pink pedal pushers.

He asks, "What did you do to your hair?"

"I needed a change."

"There's change and there's utter ruin, doll-face. That's going to take months to grow out."

"I've got time," I say. I decide not to reject Myron's endearment today. Maybe it will foster trust. His, not mine.

He asks, "Did the police talk to you yet? They questioned me yesterday and it was awful—almost humiliating."

"You must have seen Lieutenant Branco."

"I think that was his name," says Myron. "For some reason I couldn't think clearly. The room felt too small."

"That's the guy," I say.

"Then, after all those personal questions," says Myron, "came the ultimate indignity. The police want me to take Betty in to their lab for a hair sample."

"The dog?"

Betty's tail thumps in reply.

"Imagine!" says Myron. "But we haven't submitted yet." He pats Betty's head. "Have we, baby?"

Betty whimpers and wags his tail.

Myron says, "I'm conferring with my lawyer to see if it's a privacy violation." He plays with the dog's ears a moment, then says to me, "Have they talked to you yet?"

"I found Tim, remember?"

"That's right," says Myron. "And you own the house too."

"Who told you that?"

Myron shrugs. His looks just like mine, all girly. "You did," he says.

"I don't think so."

Myron says, "Well, somebody did."

"Who?" I say.

"Oh, doll-face, who knows? In this neighborhood you hear so much you can't keep track of it all."

Or any of it.

I say, "Were you around when that accident happened at the SECA recreational center?"

"Eh?" says Myron.

"A guy on the construction site was killed, and the company blamed the accident on Timmy."

"When?" says Myron.

"Last fall."

"I don't think so," he says doubtfully.

"Oh, it happened all right, but the charge didn't hold."

Myron huffs noisily. "I *meant* that I don't recall being in town when it happened."

"But you must know about it."

"Oh, doll-face, forgive and forget, that's my motto."

"What's there for you to forgive?"

"Nothing," says Myron. "So I just forget. It's even simpler that way. Too bad about your hair, though."

I explain that I wanted to erase any similarity between myself and Timmy.

"You certainly did that, doll-face. Well, I'm seeing someone inside." He heads toward the café entrance.

I say, "Chip's not here."

Myron turns back. "Who said I'm seeing him?"

"You were mooning over him yesterday."

"Mooning?" says Myron.

"Showing keen interest. Gaping, actually."

"And you weren't?" he says.

"Me?" I say. "I'm here for the coffee."

Myron looks skeptical.

"If Chip's not here," he says, "then he's probably pumping up that bubble-butt of his." Myron swallows noisily, and I am appalled to share yet another trait with him—this time an appreciation of Chip's callipygian gifts.

As offhandedly as I can, I ask him, "Do you know where Chip's gym is?"

Myron pouts his lips, which gives his face a piggy look, and he moves his jaw as though he's ruminating my question. "His gym?" he says. "Why, I believe he goes to that old church on Albany Street."

"His gym is in a church?"

"It's not a church now, doll-face! Look," he says, "would you like a bit of advice from your aunt?"

How am I supposed to answer that?

"I guess you don't," he says, "but I'm going to tell you anyway, for your own good. I wouldn't plan a trousseau for Chip. Not that you don't have a certain appeal, which I'm sure some people appreciate. But don't waste it on Chip. He likes to charm people. It's a compulsion with him. But it doesn't mean anything."

"I'll remember that."

"I mean it, doll-face. Chip doesn't ride your bus."

Another shared image! I had said roughly the same thing to Angie yesterday, about Tim Shaughnessy. And now here's Myron saying it to me about Chip. What must I do to deliver myself from becoming this man?

Oblivious to the threat he creates to my sanity, Myron says, "Chip is complete unto himself. He isn't interested in men or women. He doesn't want anybody. The only attraction he feels is for himself. The only person he really enjoys is himself."

"You seem to know a lot about him."

Myron says, "I know things about Chip nobody else does."

"Thanks for the lowdown," I say. "I'll keep it in mind."

"Doll-face, I'm just trying to keep you from getting hurt."

My coffee is done, so I get up. Partly I want to get away from Myron, and partly—dare I admit it?—I want to find Chip's gym. I want to see this self-sufficient muscle monster in action for myself. He couldn't be as awful as Myron says. I think Myron is jealous that I have a better chance of a date with Chip than he does. That's what "auntie's concern" is really about.

I wave good-bye to Myron and start walking away, but he and Betty are suddenly walking alongside me. I feel a warm wet tongue lick my hand. It's actually kind of pleasant—but only kind of. I know there are many, many teeth where that soft tongue comes from. Myron assures me that he's not following me, that I'm free to go chase after Chip all on my own, and good luck, don't say I didn't warn you.

"I just want some company," he says. "I have a big day ahead, and I'm feeling a little anxious."

"Trouble?" I say.

"No, no," he says quickly. "Actually I'm going to be, er, receiving something I've been wanting for a very long time. And if I can talk to someone beforehand, well it might help calm me down, put me in a better frame of mind to savor the moment." He pauses on the sidewalk. "Oh, I like that," he says. "Savor the rare moments of grace in an indifferent universe. Isn't that nice?"

"Sounds like a fortune cookie," I say.

"Oh, doll-face," he says. "Here I thought you were secretly a nice person, which is so rare these days."

"Not like the fifties," I say.

We start walking again and pass by XuXuX, which is still closed up.

"Oh, too bad," says Myron. "I wanted to pay her for trimming Betty's hair the other day."

"Betty?" I say. "You take Betty to a hairdresser?"

"It's not a disease," says Myron.

Hey, that's my line, bitch.

Myron says, "Portuguese water dogs have hair, not fur. That's why they don't shed. It's almost like human hair."

"But humans do shed," I say. Especially if their hair is damaged by dying or perming—like Salena Hightower's.

But why should Myron believe me? He's basically bald.

I ask him how well he knows Angie.

He replies, "How well does anyone know their hairdresser?" He looks at the sign on the door and laughs. "Family emergency?" he says. "I shouldn't wonder."

"What do you mean?"

"Doll-face, were you born yesterday? It's a faghag's duty to profess love eternal to her chosen idol. Now that Tamantha is dead, of course Angie would say something like that. They all think that way, the lady-friends of the fairies. They consider themselves our salvation. It's how they've always relieved their own guilt, in the name of mercy, tolerance, and forgiveness. And now they use 'family' as well."

"I never thought of it like that."

Myron tries to look wise. "Maybe you've stayed a little too nice for your own good."

"Some would disagree."

Myron says, "If you're looking for people who were close to Tammy, I mean really, truly, intimately close, then you'd do better with Thorin."

"Then the police are on the right track after all."

"The police?" says Myron.

I tell him, "The police are looking for him now."

"For Thorin?"

I nod.

"They think he killed Tamantha?"

"I don't know," I say. "Thorin claims he loved Tim—I mean, really loved him—so who knows?"

"Yes," says Myron. "Their pure, pure love. Frankly, I suspect the only thing pure about it was that they played priest and acolyte together. And you say the police are looking for him?"

I nod.

He chuckles. "Do you know what's happened?" he says.

"No," I say.

Now Myron laughs out loud, and Betty begins squealing and whimpering as if he wants to join in. "They've got the wrong person," says Myron. "Again!"

"You mean you know who killed Timmy?"

"No, no!" says Myron. "But really, the police ought to know better by now. They've been down this path once before." He's quite agitated now, and Betty is growling softly, getting revved up to bark. "If the police suspect Thorin, they should go after Salena."

"His wife?"

"Doll-face, those two are a matched pair when it comes to crime."

"You mean Salena is an accomplice?"

"Accomplice?" says Myron. "She's the bad egg! Did you know that Thorin was in jail once?"

"You mean the drug charge?" I say.

"That's right, doll-face. Well, get this," he says. "Thorin didn't do anything wrong. Salena was the one dealing drugs and she got caught, stupid thing! Thorin just happened to be in the house. But when the case came to trial, who is the defendant? Thorin. And he took the rap for her too."

"Thorin went to jail for his wife?"

"That's right."

"But didn't the police reports show—"

"Doll-face, do you think the police really care? Someone breaks the law, they find someone who looks guilty, and justice is served. End of story. But if you want the truth, you have to talk to the people in the neighborhood, the ones who bought drugs from Salena. Then you'll hear another whole story, the real one."

"How can that happen?" I say.

"Doll-face, are you really as naive as you act?"

Myron has a way of asking questions I can't answer.

He says, "Is Thorin at the police station now?"

"I don't know. But why are you so concerned? I thought you and Thorin were enemies."

"Enemies?" he says. "I never said that!" he splutters. "I never used those words. Don't you go misquoting me now. We are friendly rivals, nothing more." Myron checks his watch. "Oh, doll-face, now look what you've done! We've been jabbering away and I've got to go get ready. Well, I suppose our paths must part—I to my appointment and you to your assignation. Just don't forget what I told you about Chip."

Myron's face is smug, as if he knows it's doomed between me and the body-beautiful Chip. Hell, even I know it's doomed. In fact, why am I even going to find him? Is it just my DNA in action? I see a firm, round butt that's fairly screaming for attention, and thither I go? Whatever the reason, I head off down the sidewalk. Then I hear Myron call out to me.

"Just one more thing, doll-face!"

I turn.

"If you do find Chip, would you give him a message from me?"

"Sure, Myron."

"Just tell him what time it is."

"You want me to tell Chip the time?"

"That's right," he says. "He'll understand."

At least now I have a real reason to find the guy.

Myron and Betty cross the street, and I watch them walk off together. With that dog on a leash, Myron seems different, and it's not the pink pedal pushers. He holds himself straight and doesn't waddle so much. Maybe it's Betty. Maybe Betty is the pal who makes Myron feel manly.

16

Most people have a special place of fear, a locale or a situation that causes sweats, nausea, anxious hallucinations. Doctors have diagnosed these symptoms as Adult-Onset MIDFG, a recurrence of the pediatric syndrome known as Mommy-I-Don't-Feel-Good. My own place of psychic darkness is that dubious hallmark of civilization known as The Gym. Having spent my later school years dreading or avoiding gym class, I assumed that as a so-called adult I would be free of the humiliating arena. But here in the last moments of the twentieth century, hordes of people are defining their very beings by their choice of gym. No self-respecting gay man can afford *not* to belong to one. You might as well have leprosy. It's true. Go to any gym, and you'll find every sissy who couldn't climb rope in seventh grade is now preparing feverishly for the Greased-Up Gwendolyn Decathlon and Beauty Pageant.

So, is it excruciating peer pressure that drives me to seek out Chip the coffee boy's gym? Or is it Chip himself? One thing is certain—I am not looking for love. I've had my fill of that. I'm not even looking for friendship. But that's not saying, given a proper invite, I couldn't lose myself in temporal and corporal pleasure with Chip's meticulously cultivated body. The worst he can do is reject me. In fact, it's a sure bet he will if I even bother to try, which I won't. So with nothing to lose, there is nothing to fear. I tell myself that no one will laugh at me either. That's all in the past. Besides, today I am only a visitor, a civilian in civilian's clothing.

I walk and walk and finally find the old converted church in the deepest part of the South End. It's so far south it's almost in

North Dorchester, which as far as I know isn't even on the map. The building is huge, no mere ex-church. Maybe it was a cathedral once, or even a basilica. There's a hand-carved plaque at the main entrance apparently to maintain the spiritual quality of the place. It reads: SOUTH END KINESIOLOGICAL SOCIETY, or SEKS for short.

Inside, the stairway goes down, down, down, all the way to subterra. Down there are two heavy plate glass doors that open onto a vast underground cavern. What was once a vacant foundation for the towering edifice above is now a boundless workout floor for SEKS. I go in.

The lighting inside is all indirect, which gives the place a soft, spooky, secret feeling. It's quiet down here too, almost silent, yet the largeness of the space stirs the air about my ears. The stillness is broken by the occasional whoosh of a controlled exhale, or the quiet clang of metal plates allowed to graze each other, or a languorous and painfully subdued moan somewhere far off. This is a place of ritual, of worthiness, of death-or-transfiguration. Those are the only choices: Become a god or die. There's no bulletin board announcing high-step, low-step, or twelve-step aerobics here. No slimnastics, no Jazzercise, no bun-burning, pec-popping, ab-crunching specialty classes. No lunchtime express sessions. No one is in a hurry here. You have your whole life to transmogrify. All that's wanting is a cloud of incense or maybe a fog machine and halogen spots, for this is Boston's temple to the body. This is where Chip the coffee boy prepares himself for those espresso-pulling floor shows at Members Only Café.

A big muscular hunk with a shaved head sits behind the reception counter. He asks quietly, reverently, if he can help me. I tell him I'm just looking, thanks. I survey the workout floor and see that the obscure object of my desire is out there. He's sitting on a bench and wearing his familiar garb: black sweatshirt and black sweatpants. Black sneakers too. The only skin visible is that of his head and hands, which is further emphasized by his dark hair. He's almost completely covered up, and I wonder if it's modesty, which would confer a kind of sweetness on him; that far from being an exhibitionist, this bodybuilder is shy. Or is Chip's concealment of flesh an expression of puritanical severity? Or, worse, is Chip simply withholding from public view that which the public is not worthy to see?

He runs one hand slowly up and down his other arm, pausing during each pass to feel his forearm, upper arm, and shoulder muscles. Then he switches and does his other arm the same way. He executes the movements lovingly. The actions are familiar, yet each one is imbued with meaning far beyond touch and motion. Removed from the mundane surroundings of the café, Chip is no longer a coffee boy. He appears to be someone else, the way a movie star looks different onscreen, or a dancer onstage.

He looks toward the counter where I am standing, and even from that distance I can see his cool blue eyes. He seems to regard me with a cold judgmental gaze: "I am young and beautiful, and you are not. I am lithe and muscular and you are not. I am erudite and you are not." Erudite? No, wait. That's me. Chip's eyes are saying, "I eat only what is good for my body and you do not. I am God and you are not. I disapprove of you." Hell, everything he's thinking is true, which I suppose gives him the right to scorn mere mortals like me. But doesn't he have just one little flaw, something hidden maybe, like the fact he enjoys reading clinical studies on intrafamilial bloodletting?

But all my imaginary flagellation is for naught, for when Chip sees me he smiles broadly and waves to me.

Oh joy! Oh bliss! He recognizes me!

I take these signs as an invitation. True, I may be hopeful for that invite I mentioned earlier.

"Yesterday," he says, pointing his big, beautiful manly forefinger at me. "At the café, right?"

"Right," I say.

"I almost didn't recognize you with the new hair."

I run my hand over the bristles. "I needed a change."

"You sure got one," he says. "So, are you looking for me?"

Isn't the whole world?

"Kind of," I say.

"Well here I am. What did you want? Are you thinking of joining up?"

With a quick down and up motion of his eyes Chip checks out my body, then makes a little smile that implies I'd better say yes.

"Maybe," I say.

"You found the best place," he says. "You won't bump into a lot of people you know here."

My mind projects an X-rated film of shower-room antics you might not want your noted colleagues to witness.

"But if I joined," I say, "we'd know each other."

"Hell, we don't know each other!" says Chip with a broad smile.

Does this anonymity improve our chances of shower-room antics?

I blurt, "Gee, you don't even sweat!" What am I saying? What am I thinking? Have I lost my mind? Does it show that I want to bury my face in this guy's flesh and become anaerobic?

Chip keeps that easy smile on his face. "I'm not working out now. I just finished with a client. She's getting ready for a competition."

"She?"

"This is a mixed gym." He's still smiling.

I look around, and sure enough, the guy is right. There is an occasional female body, though little if any estrogen in the place. Even the doors to the rest rooms are marked "girls" and "boys," as if to expunge any reference to gonadal hormones. Then again, maybe the designations are supposed to lighten the prevailing atmosphere, like small talk at a wake.

Chip is still smiling at me, and I realize I'm filtering my vision to see only what I want. And one thing I definitely should *not* want is to be attracted to this guy. It would be too shallow, too meaningless. But how can I not be attracted? It's like telling yourself not to like chocolate. Nutritionists and cardiologists admonish you, but your resolve melts as easily as that wafer of Swiss bittersweet on your tongue. Dietary restraint is overwhelmed, and your mouth can only say, "More, more!"

Chip says, "Come on. I'll show you around."

Not the shower room! Anywhere but the shower room!

The god walks away from me with the slight limp he had yesterday. Oh merciful heavens, there is a flaw! Maybe there's even a heart in there somewhere, and my attraction can be based on an inner beauty as well as the superficial miracle of his body.

"Hurt your foot?" I say.

"It's nothing," he says. "Pushed a little too far on my last set of calf raises."

Like I thought he was doing pointe work.

"Does it hurt much?" asks Flo Nightingale.

"No pain, no gain," says Chip.

I ask him how long he's been working out.

"You mean here?" he says. "Or in my life?"

Who cares?

"Here, I guess. In Boston."

He seems to forgive my blundering efforts at small talk.

"I came to Boston last fall, from California."

"Last fall," I repeat. "So you missed all that trouble around the SECA recreational center."

"The where?"

I explain, "SECA is the South End Community Alliance. It's a gay organization that was building a state-of-the-art gym. Actually, it was going to be just a few blocks from here."

"Is that so?" he says.

"You didn't hear about it?"

Chip says, "Must have been before I came to town."

"Still, with your work at the café I thought maybe you heard something about it."

Chip smiles. "I don't pay much attention to what people say there."

See? He has depth.

"Did you ever know a young guy named Tim Shaughnessy?"

Chip thinks a moment, then shakes his head. "Doesn't sound familiar."

"He worked on that project. He was real cute, a construction worker, had red hair like me. I mean, like mine was."

Chip smiles, and once again the judges vote him a winner. "Can't say I ever knew him."

We move on to more important matters.

I ask, "Which part of California are you from?"

"Which do you think?"

"Southern," I say. "You have that look."

"Which look?"

"The good look."

He smiles again. It's no wonder he does it so much, with such nice big white teeth. He probably has a special workout for them too. "You're right," he says. "I lived in West Hollywood, the best place in LA."

And the best shower rooms too.

I say, "So if things were so good out there why did you come to Boston?"

"I needed a change," he says, "just like you with your hair."

"But I didn't move three thousand miles."

Chip says, "I wanted my life to feel new, and the easiest way to do that was to move. That is, unless you're into drugs." We pause in our stroll around the floor and he asks me, "Do you do drugs?"

I'm not sure how to answer him because—it's pitiful to admit this, but—I want him to like me. And I know that drug use can mark the first and last boundaries of a friendship. Chip doesn't wait for my answer.

"Well, I don't," he says. "They mess up your body. I don't even take protein powder. If you can't nourish yourself properly with food, then examine your diet. If you need to change your headspace, then move."

So there is a bit of puritanical severity in the god after all.

"What do you do?" he asks.

"I, uh, I'm between jobs," I say.

"You got some money?"

"A bit."

"How much?"

His directness stalls me.

"Sorry," he says, and once again flashes that smile, as if to cloak the nakedness of his question. "In LA when you ask someone how much money they have, they tell you. It might not be the truth, but they tell you something. See, I want to open a restaurant, and I'm looking for backers."

"That should be easy for someone like you."

He says, "I've got to learn how to cook first."

"I meant the money part," I say. "It should be easy with your looks and ambition."

102

Chip smiles again, as if to acknowledge the facts of life.

"Trouble is," he says, "everyone wants sex in return."

"It could be worse, Chip."

"How?"

"They could want their money back."

For some reason Chip thinks this is funny, and he laughs. It's the first time I see and hear him laugh. It looks like something else he cultivates along with his muscles. Maybe in LA you have to know the right way to laugh too.

Once he stops laughing he says, "You know something? I like you. What's your name anyway?"

I resist a moment, for to tell him will bring us closer to knowing each other, and further away from those shower-room antics you can do only with strangers.

"I'm Stan," I say. "Stan Kraychik."

He puts out his beautiful right hand and says his name.

"Chip Holton. Glad to meet you."

I shake his hand. Of course it's strong. It's perfect, like everything else about him. But I don't care about that. I don't care at all.

Chip says, "So how did you find me here?"

"Someone told me."

"Who?"

I can't say it was Myron. That association will kill any hope of a future with Chip.

"It's all right," he says. "You don't have to tell me. But if it was one of my clients, I'll give him, or her, a free workout."

It's too hard to resist this guy. "It was Myron," I say.

"Oh," says Chip.

"But we're not friends."

"That's all right," says Chip.

"No, honest. He's not my cup of tea."

Chip laughs. "Not mine either. People like Myron . . . I guess they're harmless. But he sure likes to ogle the guys."

"Maybe some guys are ogleable."

Chip smiles. "The first time I caught him staring at me, I stared back. He took that to mean I was interested."

"Silly man!"

"Next thing I know, he's giving me things."

"Things with strings?" I say.

"Not me," says Chip. "There's no strings on me."

No flies either, not on those sweatpants.

He says, "So you're thinking about working out?"

"Maybe."

"You might have some great potential there."

"Really?" I say.

Suddenly he lunges at my body and starts feeling it through my clothing.

"Do you mind?" he says. "This is the only way to tell."

It all happens so fast I find myself giggling coquettishly. His hands are experienced, expert even. They know exactly where to find things—things that belong and things that don't. But his touch doesn't convey interest. It's clinical and cool. And though my body is happy for the attention, however analytical, I know that Chip Holton will be repulsed by his findings. So much for shower-room antics.

Finally he steps back and delivers his report.

"Once you get your body-fat ratio down, you've got a lot of natural muscle and bone tissue in your favor."

"That's thanks to my mother."

"I'm a damn good trainer," says Chip. "I have excellent references, and they can show you their results."

"I'm not sure I'm ready to sign up—"

"The only thing is," he says, "I always tell a new client right off, just so there's no misunderstanding. I'm straight."

"Oh," I hear myself say. Then comes the throbbing haze of embarrassment, and I force myself to sound blithe and cheery. "That's okay with me." Damn that Myron! He warned me. And no wonder Chip's touch is so remote. It really *is* business to him.

Chip says, "Most gay guys get the wrong idea when I start touching them."

Silly gay guys!

Chip goes on. "But in this business you're working with the body, and you have to touch it. Sometimes it gets a little personal. You've got muscles everywhere, and they all have to be worked."

"And touched."

"Right," says Chip.

"But it's strictly business."

"Absolutely," says Chip. "With me, business is business."

Just like that other profession, the world's oldest one.

He says, "I like gay guys though. They're interesting."

So are aardvarks.

I tell him I'll think about it, bodybuilding that is.

"No problem," he says. "I'm pretty much booked solid anyway."

"Is this the only gym you work at?"

"Only here," he says. "You want me, you join this gym. And if you do become a client, just remember, I'm not gay."

"You've made that perfectly clear."

"Sometimes people forget," says Chip. "Gay guys can get fixated on their trainer, and then they start hoping he's gay too, because he represents how they want themselves to be."

Oh, those silly gay guys!

"Not me," I say.

"That's good," says Chip, "because it shouldn't be a problem. I'm straight, you're gay. What does it really matter?"

"When you put it that way, it doesn't."

But how does he know about me? Oh, hell—how else? Because it shows!

Chip says, "Just let me know when you want to start and we'll set up a date for your first workout. That first one's on me. Then depending on how it goes, we can sign you up for a six-month intensive."

"After which," I say, "I'll look just like you."

"Not quite," says Chip with a patronizing smile. "And you understand that my services are not included in the gym membership, right?"

Are God's services included in church offerings?

"I never thought otherwise, Chip."

"See ya 'round then, buddy."

"See ya 'round," I echo.

As I swagger toward the exit I remember the most important aspect of my mission, the whole reason for my being there at all.

"I almost forgot, Chip. I have a message for you."

"For me?"

"From Myron."

"Myron?" he says.

"He said to tell you the time."

Chip looks at his watch and says, "Oh, shit!"

So the god says naughty words too.

The next thing I know, he's dashing past me like a horse out of the gate. He bounds up the stairs and out of the building. Gone, just like that, and still in his priestly workout garb too. But the final image of Chip's firm and bountiful butt taking those stairs two at a time has imprinted itself on my psyche. I leave SEKS feeling stronger, more supple and virile than before, and I haven't even done my first rep. All because some straight hunk is willing to give me his time and some very personal attention in exchange for my money.

17

When I get up back to the street, Chip Holton is nowhere in sight. That limp hasn't slowed him down much. Gods heal quickly. I glance down Albany Street and spot a big black Mercedes-Benz sedan. Even from this distance I can see gold lettering shine in the rear window. It turns at the intersection of Union Park Street and heads toward the South End business district. Looks like Chip Holton maybe got a lift to his urgent destination.

I walk back to Tremont Street. By the time I get there, Salena Hightower is already in her office, talking on the telephone. As I enter the place, she ends the call quickly.

"Well, well!" she says, flashing her pretty smile at me. "If it isn't our neighborhood watchdog making his rounds."

"Good day to you too," I say. And speaking of dogs, bitch . . . "How's your hair these days, Salena? Sometimes the change of season can make it a little dry or brittle. Sometimes it even breaks off." In strands about five inches long.

"My hair is fine," she says prettily, "but yours looks like a disaster area. You certainly don't look like Timmy now."

So much for being incognito. But how does Salena know that's why I did it?

I ask her, "Did you just give Chip Holton a lift back here?"

"Who?" she says.

"A good-looking guy in black workout clothes. He's a personal trainer. In your quest for fitness I thought you might know him."

Salena says, "Do you have business to transact? Or are you just bothering me again?"

"Actually," I say, "I'm house-hunting for someone else today. Chip Holton wants to open a restaurant, and I was wondering if you have any good properties available."

"Are you backing him?"

"Why?"

Salena says, "Chip Holton has already approached me about a business site, but the boy has no money." She laughs. "In fact, as far as I know, he can't even boil water."

"That won't stop him," I say.

"He's straight, you know."

"I know."

"And will that stop you?" she says.

I look out the window at Domestic Tech, which belongs to Salena's husband.

"How's Thorin doing?" I say.

"He's straight too," says Salena.

"His store looks closed."

She says quickly, "I believe he has an appointment."

I recall Branco telling me he wanted to question Thorin. That's probably where Thorin really is, down at headquarters, being charged with Tim Shaughnessy's murder. Some appointment.

I say, "Did you enjoy your visit with Lieutenant Branco last night? It sounded like you two were having a jolly old time together."

Salena says, "What I told the police is certainly none of your business. And I don't appreciate you tattling on me either. That lieutenant called me out of the blue this morning, just to ask if I was at XuXuX yesterday."

She pronounces it *zoo-zoos*. It's so easy when you know how.

"Why do you think I'm the one who told Branco?"

"Because you were at the station last night and you're the only one who saw me at the salon yesterday."

"Angie saw you too."

"Yes," says Salena, "but why would she tell the police about our argument?"

"I thought you two weren't arguing."

"We weren't," she says. "And that's exactly my point. This morning the lieutenant assumed that Angie and I were arguing, the same way you did. Interesting coincidence, wouldn't you say?"

"I know what I saw, Salena. Besides, maybe Angie isn't so determined to conceal that argument. She was Tim Shaughnessy's friend, after all. Maybe finding his killer is more important to her than some argument with you. Or was that argument related to Tim's death?"

"How could it be?" says Salena. "We didn't even know Timmy was dead at the time."

"So you say. But if that's true, then what's so secret about the argument? Yesterday you denied any argument at all."

"It's a personal matter!" says Salena. "It doesn't concern you or the police. Now if you don't mind, I have work to do." And as if to give credence to her words, Salena sets up her workout chair. *Up!* spring the two long arms of high-tensile steel with the stirrups dangling loosely at the ends. She grabs them and begins her routine—pulling, holding, counting, exhaling. She looks at me between reps, then shifts her eyes toward the door. "You can go now," she says.

I tell her, "You know, I might want to buy one of those things myself. Did you get it around here?"

Pull, hold, count, exhale.

"Mail order," she says. "They send you a video too."

"I don't need that," I say. "I can just watch you."

She glares at me, but there's also a part of her that likes being watched. It's that old exhibitionist gene. Some people have it, some people don't, and there's nothing you can do to change it. She continues showing off a while, so I talk.

"I hear you handled the original sale of property to the South End Community Alliance last summer."

Salena's workout suffers a breach of rhythm. Then she says, "I suppose every gay man in the city knows about that sale."

"It should have helped your business, right?"

Salena smiles her pretty smile. "It doesn't hurt to know your demographics."

Pull, hold, count, exhale.

I say, "I've heard that realtors often work closely with certain favored contractors."

"It's a professional courtesy," she says. "Part of the business."

"Including the little kickbacks?"

No answer to that from the body beautiful.

I ask her, "Is that how it was between you and the Gardenias?"

"What are you getting at?"

"I wonder how much business a one-girl shop like yours can refer to a giant company like Gardenia and Sons."

Salena says, "I provide enough referrals to make it worth their while."

"So Gardenia and Sons paid you some money for recommending them to build SECA's recreation center. Fine. Like you say, it's a professional courtesy. But then Tony Gardenia gets killed on the site, and that's not so fine. Maybe things got a little sour between you and the big company. Maybe the accident put a strain on your relationship with the Gardenias."

"Nothing is strained," says Salena.

Except maybe the quality of mercy.

"And that's not how it happened," she says.

"Then why don't you set the record straight?"

Pull, hold, count, exhale. Pull, hold, count, exhale.

"Okay," says Salena. "I did handle that sale for SECA, and I worked hard to get them a good contract with Gardenia and Sons.

In fact, I put myself on the line for SECA. No one seems to recall that part of the deal. The Gardenias didn't want any part of it at first, but I convinced them it would be good for future business, and finally they agreed."

"Then the accident happened."

"Yes," says Salena. "That fool Timmy went and destroyed all my hard work, just because he couldn't keep his damn eyes on his job."

"It was an accident, Salena."

"Was it?" she says. "Silly little gay boy!"

"His being gay didn't kill Tony Gardenia."

"A straight man wouldn't have done that."

"Straight men cruise plenty, Salena. But none of this matters, because the equipment was faulty."

"So the court said."

"That's right," I say. "But I wonder if maybe the Gardenias had a contract out on him. To hell with what the court said. People like to get even."

Pull, hold, count, exhale. Pull, hold, count, exhale.

When Salena realizes that no amount of exercise is going to make me vanish, she abruptly stops her workout.

"Who have you been talking to?"

"The information is all out there, Salena. You've just got to know where to find it." Thank you, Benjy. Thank you, Hairnet. "Someone like you is very good at that."

"What's your point?" she says.

"My point is that maybe the all-powerful Gardenias wanted to eliminate the guy they considered family enemy number one. But maybe they didn't want to get their hands dirty. It's bad for big shots to have dirty hands. Maybe they asked you to do them a favor."

"Me?" says Salena. "What kind of favor?"

I shrug. "Maybe they convinced you it would make up for their tragic loss at SECA. Maybe it would put you back in their good graces to . . . well, to rid them of a thorn in their side."

"You think I killed Timmy?" says Salena.

"Why not?"

"Are you out of your mind?"

"Didn't you just tell me how lovely-dovey you were with the Gardenias? There's no telling how far you'd go to maintain good business relations with a company like theirs. Maybe your whole future as a realtor hinges on it. Maybe your life."

Salena glares at me. "And maybe it's time you faced some facts. Like, for example, what do *you* really know about Tim Shaughnessy? You knew the sweetie-pie, the cherub with the smiles, right? The chorus-boy act?"

I resist a nod. Tim was damn cute and appealing. *Another opening, another show!*

Salena goes on. "Well, it was all lies. Timmy was no cute, dumb boy. He was a clever, conniving businessman. I didn't like him and I'm not afraid to say why. That little crook got hold of my client list. He went through it name by name and called every person on the list. Then he offered each and every one of them a lower quote for the same exact work that my recommended contractors had already bid on. Now how do you think that made me look?"

"Like a rip-off artist."

Salena glowers at me.

I say, "It's called competition, Salena. You ought to know about that."

She says, "It's not competition when your records are stolen."

"Did you report the theft to the police?"

"No," she says.

"Why not?"

"Because the original records were never missing from my office."

"So then how do you know they were stolen?"

Salena says, "Because I found copies."

"Where?"

I wait.

She glowers some more.

I say, "Were you someplace you weren't supposed to be?"

She says, "It was my client list that was somewhere it wasn't supposed to be."

"You claim that Tim got this list of yours, and it's a fact you were his landlord."

Salena glowers. "I am not a landlord! I am a property manager."

"Whatever you call yourself, doll, it doesn't take much to figure that you were at Tim's place without his knowledge or consent, and that's how you found your list there. I think it's called breaking and entering."

"I didn't break in," she says.

"It's against the law even if you have a key."

"Look," says Salena, "I did not kill Timmy! And I did not help the Gardenias do it either. The one thing I do know is that the South End is a finite property base. It cannot tolerate newcomers edging in on the business. There are already too many qualified contractors for the available work."

"That may be so, doll, but the last I heard, the free-enterprise system doesn't grant someone the right to kill the competition."

"Tim Shaughnessy wasn't competing with me!"

"Maybe not in real estate."

"What do you mean by that?" says Salena.

"Maybe the competition was more personal."

"Meaning?" she says.

"Meaning your husband seems to have very strong feelings for Tim."

"God!" she says. "You have a filthy mind!" Salena Hightower's indignation is not as pretty as the rest of her. "You think I'd kill Timmy because of that?"

"Maybe he knew about that drug rap your husband took for you. They were pretty close, Thorin and Tim. Maybe your husband told him everything, and maybe you weren't comfortable with that. If the truth about your drug dealing got out, it might damage your reputation."

"Where are you hearing these things?"

"I keep telling you, it's all public information. The sources vary"—thank you, Myron—"but it's all out there."

"I'm too busy for this nonsense," she says. "Would you please leave now? Or do I have to call the police and have you escorted out?"

"Call Branco," I say. "Maybe you two can continue that laugh riot you started last night."

Salena lets go of the stirrups on her workout chair, and they fly up every which way. She grabs the phone on her desk.

I say, "It's all right, doll. I can see the door."

I leave Gateway to Paradise and go next door to Myron's place, Domestic Art. If Salena is the keeper of heaven's gate, then I'd rather face the alternative, even if that means putting up with Myron. At least he's eager to gossip, and you never know what scandalous tidbit will fly from his bitchy bouche.

But Myron's door is locked, as though the store is closed. Oddly though, the lights are all on. Maybe he's just gone out for a minute. As I peer inside, Betty comes trotting out from the back part of the store. He's wagging his tail and squealing softly, like he wants to come out and play. "Sorry, pooch," I say. "You gotta ask your mommy first."

I cross the street to confer with Thorin at Domestic Tech, maybe pull his chain a while. Exactly how much does Salena Hightower know about her husband's relationship to Tim Shaughnessy? And why was Thorin willing to go to jail for her? Or did Myron fabricate that whole story just to make life in the South End seem more exciting than it really is?

But I forgot that Thorin's place is closed. Some South End retailers really do keep bankers' hours. Maybe because they're at the bank so much, or else at police headquarters.

While I'm peeping into Thorin's store and admiring all the soft-core photo displays, there's a sudden commotion behind me, across the street. Out of nowhere three Boston police cruisers have arrived, lights blinking and sirens blaring. They arrange themselves to block all outbound traffic on Tremont Street. I see Salena in her office. She springs up from her desk and goes to the window to look out. She appears alarmed by all the noise and the nervous, flashing lights. Maybe she called the cops and complained about Betty's whimpering? But then, why would she be alarmed?

Two cops go to the door of Myron's store. Someone is unlocking it from the inside, but I can't make out who it is because of the gathering crowd and the cops and cruisers all around the place. The door opens slightly and the two cops slip inside. A few moments later two more follow them. Minutes pass, and the first two cops come out escorting Chip Holton between them. He's still in his priestly workout clothes, but his head is hanging down, like he's really sad about something. The cops put him in a cruiser and take him away.

Then an emergency medical van pulls up. Two medics emerge and rush into Myron's store. Moments later they come out, supporting Myron between them. His face is bloody, and he's howling incoherently. Betty is behind them, barking loudly. The medics try to get Myron into the van, but he seems more concerned with making a scene on the street than cooperating with them. They finally get him into the van, and Betty bounds in after him. One of the medics drags Betty from the van and shoves him back into Myron's store. He secures the door, but Betty's barking is still audible.

I head over to police headquarters.

18

At the station I go up to Branco's office. I was all set to tell him about Salena Hightower and her connection to Gardenia and Sons, but that can wait for now. I want to know about the sex-and-violence between Chip "the god" Holton and Betty Crocker's long-lost twin, Myron the shopkeep.

Branco's assistant tells me he's tied up downstairs and probably won't be free for a few hours. The appealing imagery does not escape me. I head back downstairs and manage to catch Branco just as he's entering the locked corridor that leads to the interview rooms.

"No visitors today," he says coldly and closes the door in my face.

I consider waiting for him, but even if I hole myself up in that moldly place for the rest of the day, there's no guarantee Branco will talk to me. I might as well wait outside, where the weather is playing at springtime again. On my way out, I see someone I recognize from the police academy, a fine-boned Hispanic woman named Tina. We became good friends during the time I was at the academy. I even did her a big favor back then, and here she is now, an official rookie.

"Tina!" I say.

"Stanny!" she cries out. She gets up from her desk and gives me a big hug. "Look at you! What happened to your hair?" She runs her hand over my head. "You look like a teddy bear."

"And here you are," I say. "A big-time cop."

She rolls her eyes. "They put me on inside detail for a while. I'd rather be on the street, and instead I'm transcribing interview tapes."

Oh, propitious fate!

"Say, Tina, do you know if they brought a guy named Chip Holton in just now?"

Tina nods toward the door Branco just slammed in my face. "He's in there with the lieutenant."

"What's going on?"

"You know I can't tell you," she says.

"Please?" I say. I give her my warm, sincere look. "Just pretend I'm a cadet."

"Oh, you!" says Tina. "And those eyes!" Then she gives me a rundown of the situation. Chip assaulted Myron in the back room of his store, then he called the cops. They don't know what prompted the attack yet.

A light goes on at the control panel on Tina's desk.

She says, "Looks like they started."

"Any chance I can listen in?"

"Listen in?" she says. "In your dreams, Stanny. You know better!"

"But this case involves me."

"All the more reason," she says. "If we're going to question you, your story has to be straight." She smiles. "You know what I mean."

"But it's connected to the Tim Shaughnessy case."

"The kid who died yesterday morning?"

I tell her, "That happened on my property."

"No kidding!" says Tina.

"And since Myron knew Tim, maybe there's some connection to what happened now with Chip, and if I could just listen in . . ."

"Oh, Stanny," she says, "I don't think so. You know how it is."

"Yeah," I say, relenting. "You're right, Tina. I understand." Fact is, she's a cop and I'm not. "Say, that was some fun we had at the academy, though, eh?"

"Stanny," she says, "when you were there I had the best time."

"Remember how I showed you how to fire a gun?"

I flap my limp wrist in front of her, and we both laugh the way we did when I showed her my unique technique on the academy's firing range. Tina may have excelled in all the manly, phys-ed-type aspects of being a cop, but I was the all-out champ in shooting.

"Of course I remember!" she says. "Right after you showed me that trick with your wrist, I passed my target-practice test. Finally! If it wasn't for you, I probably wouldn't graduate."

"Hey, what are friends for?"

I cast my eyes toward the interrogation rooms.

I say, "I wouldn't mind a little help myself right now."

Tina says, "What?"

"Maybe we could do a trade. A color and cut for, say"—I nod my head toward the interview room—"a little listen?"

Tina says, "Huh?" Then, "Oh, I get it."

She considers the situation, runs her hand through her hair.

"I don't know, Stanny."

I give her my pleading look.

"Stop it," she says.

I touch her hair. "A nice highlight will bring up all those natural flecks of gold."

Tina says, "You did such a good job that other time." She mulls the situation a while, then she says, "Maybe we should have a coffee later, catch up on things, you know?"

"Sounds great," I say.

She tells me she gets off work at four, and we arrange to meet at a pushcart coffee bar a few blocks away. Then I leave the station like a bigshot dick with inside connections.

I've got a few hours to kill, so I take Branco's advice and go see a travel agent about a vacation. But as I'm sitting there talking about cruises and island holidays, inside cabin, outside cabin, sundeck, promenade, blah-blah-blah, I know I'm just killing time. So I leave the travel agent armed with a pile of brochures.

Then I head off to XuXuX, hoping maybe Angie has resurfaced from her family emergency. But the place is still locked up like a drum. Absolutely dark.

Four o'clock rolls around, time for the rendezvous with Tina, my secret correspondent. The pushcart coffee bar is at one end of an enclosed courtyard. I take a table removed from the others and wait. When Tina arrives she looks around to make sure no one recognizes her. Then she comes over to me.

"Sorry I'm late," she says. "I almost forgot your gift."

"Gift?" I say.

She hands me a small brightly colored paper sack with handles. It's from a bonbon boutique on Newbury Street called Aubarde. The chocolates are flown in daily from Geneva. The prices are astronomical, and the experience is just as cosmic. As I look inside Tina says, "Happy Birthday!"

My birthday's not for two months. Then I realize she's trying to cover her criminal actions. Inside the bag, under a gaily wrapped box of candy, I see the edges of a bunch of cassette tapes.

Tina leans close to me and murmurs, "Stanny, you were right. After you left the station, things really started jumping. Tim Shaughnessy's name was everywhere. So what I did, I copied the interview tapes for you. I didn't label anything, so you'll have to figure it out. But they're numbered in the order they happened. Some of the subjects got questioned twice, so it might get a little confusing. But do me a favor after you hear these, okay? Just put the suckers under a broiler until they're one big pile of melted plastic."

"Tina, I owe you."

"You owe me nothing," says Tina. "But here's one more thing that's not on the tapes. They brought this woman in for fingerprinting, real fancy type, dressed to kill, everything was money-money."

"I think I know who you mean."

Tina says, "Well, did she make a stink! Claimed her personal rights were being violated. She was ready to call in the Supreme Court. But through all that noise I saw that she was flirting with the lieutenant."

"No!" I say.

"Some dumb broad, eh?"

"So what happened?"

"What do you think?" says Tina. "The boss put her in her place!"

"Branco's some guy, eh?"

Tina beams. "I'm very lucky he picked me to work for him."

Would Branco have picked me if I had finished police school?

Tina says, "So he tells this dame, 'Sometimes people have to yield their rights in a homicide case.' "

"Branco said *homicide?*"

"Yeah," says Tina. "Why?"

"Last I knew he wasn't sure."

"The man said *homicide.*"

"This is good," I say. "Now maybe we'll get somewhere."

Tina says, "So listen! This dame is moving her tits and ass all over the place, fluttering her lashes, and she says to the lieutenant, 'Am *I* a suspect?' " Tina manages a very good impersonation of Salena Hightower. "So Lieutenant Branco looks right at her and says, 'We can't exclude anyone, ma'am.' Stanny, you should've seen her face! All that dancing around for nothing!"

"Tina, I owe you big-time."

"I told you, Stanny, you owe me nothing. You helped me, now I help you. You're the brainy one anyway. I belong on a beat, not inside typing up reports."

"Thanks, Tina. I promise you personal hair care as long as we both shall live."

"Sounds like we're married."

"Don't tell your husband."

19

I rush home with my bag of goodies and hunker down for some serious homework. Turns out the box of candy from Tina is real, so I even have a half pound of imported bonbons to keep my jawbone busy during the show. It's going on five o'clock, and I should have some real food first, but I'm too eager to hear the tapes. So I slap cassette number one into the player and slap a cream-colored truffle into my mouth.

Branco's voice comes on the tape, and I'm almost ashamed to hear it in my own living room, as though it's absolute proof that I'm doing something forbidden. He starts out with the formalities regarding the date and time, along with the names of the other cops present in the room. Then Branco's voice says that he is interviewing Chip Holton. He reads the guy his rights, but Chip says he doesn't want a lawyer. Branco asks him if he is ready to make a statement, and Chip agrees. I'm not surprised. When you're in a small space with Branco, you are overcome by a willingness to tell all.

In a quiet, repentant voice Chip begins to explain that he had visited Myron earlier this morning to pay a debt.

Branco interrupts him. "That's Mr. Kratz, right?"

"Yes," says Chip.

Kratz? Betty Crocker's family name is Kratz?

I get my attention back to Chip's statement. Apparently Myron told him he didn't want money for this debt, and Chip was so disgusted by what happened after that, he began to hurt Myron. He stopped just in time. When he realized what he had done, he called the police.

Branco says, "Could you be more specific about how you hurt Mr. Kratz?"

Chip says in a soft voice, "I had my hands around his neck. I was choking him."

"Did you hit him?"

"No," says Chip.

"When we got there Mr. Kratz was bleeding. Can you explain that?"

"No."

"You're certain you didn't strike him?"

"Not unless I blacked out," says Chip.

Branco says, "Do you have blackouts?"

"No."

"Then why do you think you might have blacked out?"

Chip's voice sounds fragile. "Because it was so awful."

"What was?" says Branco.

"What he wanted to do."

"Can you tell me?"

"It was disgusting," says Chip. "See, I lied to Myron, told him I felt confused, that maybe it would be all right if he put his mouth on me. I was trying to tell myself that it didn't really matter what he was doing down there, as long as I didn't want to do it back. But it was disgusting! He was really enjoying it."

And what about you, Chip-doll?

Branco says, "Did you at any time before this meeting with Mr. Kratz suspect that he would ask you for sex as payment?"

"No," says Chip, once again settled in his quiet little victim's voice.

"What exactly was this payment for?"

Chip hesitates. "Myron has something I wanted."

"And what is it?"

Another pause. "It was something that belonged to me."

"So Mr. Kratz has something of yours that he wanted you to pay him for?"

"Yes," mews Chip.

"That's odd," says Branco. "Why would he do that?"

"Because he knew I wanted it back."

"How did he manage to get hold of it?"

There's a pause, then Chip says, "He found it."

"And how did he know it was yours?"

Chip is silent.

"Please answer the question," says Branco. "If Mr. Kratz found this thing, how did he know it was yours?"

"Because it's something he gave to me."

"Gave to you?" says Branco. "You mean it was a gift?"

Another pause, then a barely discernible "Yes."

"So Mr. Kratz gave you something, which you then lost, and which he subsequently found and then wanted you to pay him for. Is that right?"

"Yes."

Branco takes a deep breath, then lets it out in a big he-man kind of sigh.

"And you were agreeable to that arrangement until Mr. Kratz wanted a sexual favor as his payment."

"Yes," says Chip.

Branco says, "Mr. Holton, would you please describe this thing of yours that Mr. Kratz has possession of?"

Chip says, "It's a nail file."

"A nail file. Could you be more specific?"

"It's a diamond-dust file, sterling silver with an onyx handle. It's in a black leather case and has an inscription on the handle. I think it came from Shreve's."

I can almost see Branco's mouth puckering up on that.

"Can you tell me what the inscription says?"

There's a pause. Then Chip says, "I'd rather not."

"Can you explain why Mr. Kratz would give you such an expensive item?"

Chip gulps so loudly that it registers on the tape. Then he says, "Myron says my hands are perfect, and it bothers him that I use toothpicks to clean under my nails. He says it's a sign of low-class breeding. I guess he gave me the file so I wouldn't use toothpicks anymore."

Branco says, "And where is this file now?"

Chip says, "I guess Myron still has it."

Branco says, "And do you want the file back?"

"No. I mean, what's the point, if I'm here talking to you?

That's what I was afraid of in the first place, that he'd go to the police."

"And why is that?" says Branco.

Another pause. Then Chip says, "I think there's something else I'd better tell you. If I don't, Myron will."

"And what is that?"

"Myron found that file in the house where the accident happened yesterday morning."

"Accident?" says Branco.

"The kid who fell down the stairs."

Long pause on the tape. I'm holding my breath too.

Branco says, "Are you telling me that you were in that house yesterday morning?"

"Yes, sir."

Oh ho! Now we're in "sir" territory! I quickly stuff a bonbon in each cheek, not quite prepared for the apricot-mint melange that results.

Branco says, "Was Mr. Kratz in the house as well?"

"I guess so," says Chip. "But we weren't there at the same time."

"What time were you there?"

"In the morning."

"Please be specific."

"I can't," says Chip. "I don't remember."

Another blackout, probably.

Branco says, "When you were there, Mr. Holton, was anyone else with you?"

Chip is silent.

"Please answer the question," says Branco.

More silence.

"Mr. Holton, would you please explain what you were doing in that house?"

"Oh, Jesus!" says Chip. He makes a loud groan, and then he starts crying.

A few moments later Branco's voice says, "I am stopping the tape while the subject collects himself."

I stop the tape too, as though I must respect Chip Holton's

masculine pride, just as Branco has done. I chomp on another bonbon, thinking how Branco is pretty good at getting the Real Dirt. I'd have to have someone in a styling chair to get the same results, and even then I've never made a straight guy break down. Not yet.

When I start the tape again, Branco is restating the formalities. Then he says to Chip, "Please explain what you were doing on the property at 101 Waltham Street the morning of April first."

Chip says, "I was meeting Thorin for a photo shoot."

"Thorin?" says Branco. "You mean Thorin Hightower?"

"Yes," says Chip.

"And he was going to take photographs of you?"

"Yes."

I have an unsettling feeling that there won't be enough bonbons to get me through all the tapes.

Branco asks, "What was the nature of this photo shoot?"

Chip explains. "We have a deal. Thorin takes pictures of me and splits whatever he gets by selling them."

"I see," says Branco.

Chip says, "He's going after the greeting card companies right now, but he's planning to branch out."

"Meaning what?"

"Specialty magazines, things like that."

"Meaning what?"

Chip says, "All the photos so far were mood shots, romantic kinds of things."

Branco pauses before asking the next question.

"Were you clothed for these photos?"

"Oh, yeah!" says Chip. "Wow! Don't get the wrong idea. It was always jeans and a sportshirt. I might unbutton the shirt a little, and roll up the sleeves. But there was nothing sexy or porno about the photos. You could give them to your grandmother. I mean, I'm not gay or anything."

Exactly what does "or anything" mean?

Branco says, "Go on."

"I know Thorin wanted to try some sexy shots. He made comments about it all the time. But I told him I wasn't interested in that. I don't mind flexing my muscles, but I'm not going to drop my pants in front of a camera. Would you?"

The question elicits no comment from Branco.

Chip says, "I think some things should be kept personal. The only time I'm naked with other guys is at the gym, but this would be different. I mean, the whole world would see me. So I told Thorin no."

"And that was the end of it?"

Chip says, "He told me to keep it in mind, that there was no hurry. But then he always brought it up again, so I know he wanted to do it. Anyway, we talked about it when we set up the photo shoot for yesterday, and I told him no again. But that's what I was thinking about while I was fixing my nails. Thorin always likes to get my hands in the frame—I have really nice hands—"

There's another pause. Chip is probably showing his hands to Branco.

Chip says, "I was giving them a touch-up. I mean, even straight guys like to look good."

There's another pause. Maybe Chip is waiting for a compliment, or some grunt of agreement from Branco. He's got a long wait.

Branco says, "Please continue with your statement."

Chip says, "So there I was, thinking about the photo shoot and I started having second thoughts. Like what if Thorin forces me to do something sexy?"

"Forces you?" says Branco.

"Not physically. But Thorin can be very convincing. He has that way about him, and the next thing you know, you're doing exactly what he wants."

Does Branco recognize a similar talent in himself?

Chip continues. "And the more I thought about it, the more I worried that Thorin would want me to do something sexy for him. Then, I don't know, I got feeling kind of weird about it. I couldn't stop thinking about it. I was afraid that people seeing the shots would get the wrong idea about me. They'd think I was gay, and I'm not gay."

Branco says, "Please go on."

"So I decided to get out of that place before any trouble happened between us."

"Trouble?" says Branco.

"I wasn't sure how Thorin would take it if I backed out of our business deal. I think he sees me as his meal ticket. Well, I'm sorry, but I've got my own reputation to think about. I figured I'd call him and make excuses about the bad weather, and maybe we could just forget the whole thing. I'm sorry I ever got involved with him at all."

"Is that what you did?" says Branco. "You called him?"

"Yes," says Chip. "I phoned him at his store as soon as I could get somewhere quiet. Thorin wasn't there so I left a message on the machine. You can hear it yourself, unless he erased it. I told him I wasn't going to make it for our session on account of the weather, and he shouldn't bother going either."

Branco says, "And where does Mr. Kratz fit into this?"

"Myron must have showed up after I left."

"And that's when he found your nail file, the one he had given you as a gift."

Chip replies, "When you say it like that, it sounds awful. Myron gave me that file because he thought my hands deserved good treatment. You can make a lot of money modeling hands. That's really what I should stick to. None of that bare body stuff."

"So you *have* posed without clothing?"

"God, no!" says Chip. "I already told you, never. I keep my body to myself."

Theoretically speaking, Chippo.

Branco says, "And you dropped the nail file on your way out."

"Yes," says Chip. "I left there in a hurry, kind of worked myself into a panic I guess, and that's when I must've dropped it."

"Was anyone else in the house at that time?"

"No," says Chip. His voice is firm and strong this time. "But it's obvious Myron was there after me if he found the file. Look, I'm sorry I hurt him, but I was really disgusted by what he wanted to do. That's kind of how I feel about Thorin now too. I don't want to be involved with people like that anymore."

"Are you saying that Mr. Hightower wanted to have sex with you too?"

"No, no, no!" says Chip. "Thorin is definitely straight. But he wanted to do some sexy shots of me."

I hear the sound of a door opening. Branco announces the entrance of another cop, and that cop informs him that Myron Kratz is ready to be questioned.

Branco tells Chip that he's going to hold him for further questioning.

Chip asks why.

Branco explains that he has just admitted to assaulting Myron Kratz, and if Mr. Kratz presses charges, he'll have to arrest Chip, pending bail.

Chip's response to that is, "Shit!"

So ends cassette number one.

Forget the commercial break. I go straight for cassette number two.

20

The second cassette begins as the first one did, with Branco's formal remarks. This time the subject is Myron Kratz. Even before Branco reads him his rights, Myron says, "I reserve the right to terminate this interview at any time and call my lawyer."

Branco says, "I was just about to read you your rights." He does, and then asks Myron if he wants his attorney present.

Myron declines, then adds, "But if things get touchy in here, I won't say another word without my lawyer."

"Certainly," says Branco. "And we appreciate your cooperation, Mr. Kratz." Then Branco asks him, "How are you feeling now? Better?"

Myron replies, "I could use a tranquilizer."

"We'll see about that shortly. Our doctor promises me that

you are in no health danger, so I thought it would be better to get these questions out of the way now. Then you can concentrate on recovering."

Myron says, "How does it look? Has the bleeding stopped?"

A pause.

"Yes, it's stopped," says Branco. "It doesn't look too bad, actually." His voice is warm and reassuring, a tone I've never heard before. "You might have a nasty black eye, though."

"My badge of courage," says Myron.

Branco laughs. He actually laughs, and I wonder if this is standard police procedure, to treat a victim with compassion. I can't even get the time of day out of the guy, and here he is being *nice* to Myron. Branco laughed with Salena too. Is his perpetual coolness toward me a sign of special regard? Or does he simply dislike me?

"Would you like some water?" he says.

There's a silence. Then Branco says, "Your nod doesn't register on the tape, Mr. Kratz. Please answer yes or no."

Myron says, "Yes," and I know it's a real interview after all.

A few moments pass. Presumably someone is getting Myron some water.

Branco says, "Better?"

Myron says, "Yes, thank you."

Branco says, "I'd like to proceed now, if you don't mind. Just let me know if you become uncomfortable, and we can resume the interview another time."

Why doesn't he send out for tea and crumpets?

Then Branco says, "Are you ready?"

Another pause.

Branco says, "Mr. Kratz, I remind you that your nod doesn't register on the recorder. Please answer yes or no. Are you ready?"

"Yes," says Myron.

And Branco begins. "We have a statement from an acquaintance of yours, a Mr. Chip Holton."

"He's no acquaintance of mine," says Myron. "This is gay-bashing pure and simple. You've arrested him, of course."

"We're holding him here," says Branco, "and we're trying to determine exactly what transpired between the two of you."

Myron says, "He came into my store and beat me up. That's what happened."

Branco says, "Mr. Holton has told us that he did not strike you at any time."

"Obviously the boy is lying," says Myron. "Or do you think this is stage blood?"

"You maintain that Mr. Holton did strike you?"

"Many times!" says Myron. "Many, many, oh how many times!"

Branco says, "Was this meeting between the two of you previously arranged?"

"What?" says Myron.

"Did you arrange to meet Mr. Holton at your store?"

"I did not!" says Myron. "I told you, he just walked in, dragged me to the back room, and started beating me."

Branco says, "Mr. Holton claims that the two of you had arranged this meeting today."

"That's a lie."

Branco waits a moment, then asks, "Mr. Kratz, where was your dog during this incident?"

"My dog?"

"Yes. You have a dog, don't you?"

"Betty," says Myron. "Betty was . . . resting."

"Where?"

Myron hesitates. "Back in the storage area."

"Is Mr. Holton familiar with your dog?"

"I believe he's pet Betty once or twice on the street."

"And what was your dog doing during this incident?"

"What?" says Myron.

Branco says, "Did your dog attempt to protect you at all?"

Myron says, "Betty wouldn't hurt a baby!"

"But Mr. Holton is not a baby. Can you explain why your dog did not try to protect you?"

"Well, no," says Myron.

After a moment Branco continues. "Mr. Holton also states that you are in possession of something that belongs to him, and that you demanded very specific payment terms for its return. Is that true?"

"No, it is not," says Myron.

"You deny that you have something of Mr. Holton's?"

"Absolutely."

"Mr. Holton claims that you once gave him a very expensive nail file as a gift. Is that true?"

"Why would I give *him* anything?"

Branco says, "Please answer yes or no."

"I never gave that muscle-head a thing," says Myron. "The answer is no."

Branco says, "Did you ever purchase such a nail file?"

"I have owned many nail files in my lifetime, Lieutenant."

"I'm talking about a very specific file, diamond dust on sterling silver, with an onyx handle, in a leather case."

"That sounds very nice," says Myron. "Quite luxe."

"Did you ever buy such a nail file?"

Myron pauses before he says, "No."

"From Shreve, Crump and Lowe?" says Branco.

"Not even from Wal-Mart," replies Myron.

Branco's questions seem to invigorate Myron, while they made Chip docile and repentant.

Branco says, "Mr. Kratz, can you tell me your whereabouts yesterday morning between the hours of nine o'clock and ten-thirty?"

"What does that have to do with Chip beating me up?"

"I'm trying to determine his motivation."

"I was in my store," says Myron.

"Did you leave your store at any time during those hours?"

"Lieutenant, have you forgotten what the weather was like yesterday? Who would go out in a mess like that?"

Branco says, "Not even to walk your dog?"

Myron pauses. "Betty didn't need a walk."

There's an interruption, and Branco announces the entrance of one of his men bearing a large manila envelope. The two men whisper to each other. Then Branco continues to Myron.

"Mr. Kratz, we have just found this object on the premises of your store."

I hear the crumpling sound of a heavy manila envelope and then of something sliding out of it and landing with a soft thump onto the tabletop. Branco describes it as a sealed evidence bag containing a narrow leather case. Protruding from one end of the leather case is an onyx handle. Branco says, "Mr. Holton told us about an inscription on the handle, but he declined to say what it is. I'm willing to have the lab take a look—"

"That's not necessary!" says Myron.

"Would you care to amend your statement?"

Myron says, "First tell me if you have a search warrant."

Branco says, "We can produce one."

There's a pause.

Myron says, "I wish to state that I am continuing this interview voluntarily, and without legal representation. However, I have just suffered a severe assault to my body from which I have not completely recovered. Therefore, I reserve the right to amend or retract any and all statements I make here."

Branco sighs heavily. "Shall we postpone this interview until your attorney is present?"

"No," says Myron, "but I want to have it on record that I am cooperating with you, and also that I am not waiving my rights by staying here and talking."

"Everything you say in this room is on record."

"Fine," says Myron.

"So you recognize this item?" says Branco.

"First of all," says Myron, "it's from Tiffany's, not Shreve's. Typical of Chip not to know the difference."

"So this was a gift from you to Mr. Holton?"

"Yes," says Myron. "At the time I gave it to him he seemed to appreciate my attention."

"Go on," says Branco.

"Well, there's nothing to go on with, is there?" says Myron. "You buy a boy an expensive trinket, he makes suitable sounds of gratitude, and that's it."

"Did you hope for something in return?"

"Something?"

"A favor?" says Branco.

Myron says, "If you're implying that I expected sex, then you're absolutely wrong."

"What did you expect then?"

"I thought he might show a little more friendliness toward me."

"And did he?"

"He showed nothing!" says Myron. "In fact, after I gave Chip the file, he became more distant. Funny thing though—he kept the file, didn't he?"

"And then it came back into your possession."

"Yes," says Myron. "It did."

"Exactly how did that happen?"

"I found it."

"Where?"

Myron pauses, a long pause.

Branco repeats the question. "Where did you find this file?"

Myron remains silent.

Branco says, "Mr. Kratz?"

Finally Myron speaks. "I think it might be time to call my lawyer."

So ends cassette number two in the strange affair between a faded queen and a hetero narcissist.

Onward to cassette number three.

21

From Branco's introductory remarks on the third cassette, I know that Thorin Hightower's attorney is present during his interview. Having been churned through the justice machinery once before, Thorin understands an unsubtle truth about the legal system: no lawyer, no law.

Branco begins by asking Thorin, "What were you doing inside Tim Shaughnessy's place in South Boston, where my crew apprehended you a short while ago?"

There's a pause, during which I hear barely perceptible sibilants, probably passing between Thorin and his law-tron.

Then Thorin says, "I was retrieving some property."

Branco says, "What is the nature of this property?"

"Electric trains."

"Electric trains?"

"Yes," says Thorin. "Timmy had a rare set of electric trains."

"And who do these trains belong to?"

More susurrous sibilants.

Thorin says, "They belonged to Timmy."

"Do you mean Tim Shaughnessy?" says Branco.

"Yes," says Thorin.

"You were in Shaughnessy's place retrieving some of his property?"

"That's right," says Thorin.

Branco says, "This may sound old-fashioned, Mr. Hightower, but I believe that's called theft."

Another voice, presumably Thorin's attorney, says, "I object!"

"Duly noted," says Branco. "You're on the record." Then he asks Thorin, "Why were you taking this property?"

"I owed somebody a favor."

"Who?"

Psss, psss.

Thorin says, "Myron Kratz."

Branco says, "So you were stealing these trains for Mr. Kratz?"

Again the lawyer yelps, "I object!"

"Good for you," says Branco.

Thorin says calmly, "It wasn't theft. Myron is a collector, and he assured me that Timmy had promised the trains to him."

"And you believed him?" says Branco.

"I had no reason not to," says Thorin.

Branco asks, "How did you get into Shaughnessy's place?"

"I have a key."

"And how is that?"

Pssss, pssss, pssss.

Thorin says, "I like having something personal of Timmy's."

Branco takes a deep breath.

"Where did you get the key?"

"I copied it," says Thorin.

"From whom?"

Pssss, pssss.

Thorin says, "I am advised not to answer that."

Branco says, "Are you aware that even with a key you were committing an illegal act?"

Psssssssss, psss-pss, psssst!

Again Thorin says, "I am advised not to answer that."

"Mr. Hightower, why did you agree to do this deed for Mr. Kratz?"

Thorin explains. "Myron has something that belongs to me, and he agreed to return it if I got Timmy's trains for him."

Sounds like Myron's special collection agency runs twenty-four hours a day.

Branco says, "What is this thing of yours that Mr. Kratz has?"

"A lens cap," says Thorin.

"For a camera, you mean?"

"Yes."

I hear the noise of an envelope being opened. Branco describes the contents of an evidence bag as a Nikon lens cap. The edge is engraved with Thorin Hightower's name.

Branco says, "Is this it?"

Thorin says, "Yes."

Branco says, "We found this at Mr. Kratz's store this morning."

Thorin says, "Well, now you know I'm telling the truth." He sounds relieved.

Unmoved, Branco says, "So Mr. Kratz was blackmailing you?"

"Yes."

"Do you know how Mr. Kratz got possession of this?"

"He says he found it."

"Do you know where?"

Pissssy, pss, pss.

Thorin says, "At 101 Waltham Street."

Hey, no big deal. That's my house. Everybody goes there.

"Were you ever there yourself, Mr. Hightower?"

"Yes."

"When?" asks Branco.

"At various times."

See? The place is goddamn Squatter Central.

Branco says, "When was the most recent time?"

"Yesterday morning," says Thorin.

"Can you tell me what you were doing at 101 Waltham Street yesterday morning?"

"I was waiting for Chip Holton to arrive, but Timmy showed up instead."

A long pause follows. Branco is probably reordering his strategy. I need a moment to regain my senses too. Thorin, Myron, Chip, and Timmy, all of them were in my house yesterday morning. Probably Betty too! I only hope the foot traffic continues when I'm open for business. I fish around in the chocolate box for another bonbon.

Branco says, "So you and Mr. Holton had an appointment at the property on Waltham Street?"

"Yes."

"For what reason?"

"I sometimes take photographs there. The place is really rundown, but there's a room in back with some very interesting light against the exposed brick."

I'll have to remember that when my customers ask for a room with atmosphere.

Branco asks Thorin, "Are you aware that you were trespassing?"

"It seemed harmless," says Thorin. "I wasn't doing any damage to the place, not that anyone could."

Hey, watch it buddy! That's my future homestead.

Branco says, "So yesterday morning you arranged to meet Mr. Holton there."

"That's right," says Thorin.

"And what happened?"

"I snapped a candid shot of Timmy when he came in."

"Why did you do that?"

Thorin says, "I thought it was Chip. I thought it would help get him in the right kind of mood."

"Mood?" says Branco.

"We, uh . . ."

134

Pssss, pssss, pssss. Pss-pss.

Thorin says, "We were going to try something new yesterday."

"New models?" says Branco.

"That's right," says Thorin.

Branco says, "Please explain."

Thorin says, "Up to now it's been mostly muscle shots, clean and aboveboard. No nudity. We're about to introduce a line of greeting cards. It's all G-rated."

"But you say you wanted Mr. Holton in the right mood yesterday."

"Yes." says Thorin. "Yesterday was different. I had suggested to him once about doing something a little more sexy, but Chip balked at the idea. He thinks if he does sexy shots he might be perceived as gay. I don't know where he gets that idea, but it partly explains why he's the kind of exhibitionist who keeps his clothes on."

"Are you saying that Mr. Holton is an exhibitionist?"

"There are many variations of the word, Lieutenant."

Always wise to know the rank of the cop who's questioning you.

Thorin continues. "Exhibitionism can range from something as simple as a charming smile for the camera, all the way to exposing your most secret and sacred taboos."

"And where does Mr. Holton fit in?"

Does Branco care?

"He's very modest," says Thorin, "but I think the idea of erotica intrigues him."

"And why is that?" says the cop.

"Because I only mentioned it to him once. Yet he brought it up every single time we talked after that. So we agreed that we might try for something a little more sexy in yesterday's session."

"You agreed?" says Branco.

"In a way," says Thorin. "That's why I snapped that candid shot of him, or who I thought was him. You've got to be playful and spontaneous when you're doing erotica or else it comes off completely lifeless."

Branco says, "So you're saying that Chip Holton agreed to do sex photos?"

"No, no," says Thorin. "Not sex photos. *Sexy* photos. There's a big difference. This was strictly soft-core stuff. You see it all the time—magazine ads, greeting cards, book covers. I promised Chip that nothing would show, not even pubic hair—that is, if he even got around to undoing his pants."

"And did he?" says Branco. *Sprong!* goes my brain until Branco finishes the question.

"Did he agree to do those photos?"

Thorin explains, "He said it would depend on how he felt when he got there. Like I said, that's why I snapped the candid shot, to get him in the mood for more surprises. But taking that candid shot was a big mistake."

"In what way?" says Branco.

"Because it wasn't Chip who came in," says Thorin. "It was Timmy. And I wasn't ready for the way he reacted. That poor kid really freaked out. It was probably the flash that did it. It can startle you, especially when the light is low, the way it was in that old house yesterday morning."

"So you were alone at the property when Tim Shaughnessy arrived there," says Branco. "Is that correct?"

"Yes," says Thorin.

"What happened then, after you took the candid shot?"

Thorin says, "Once Timmy calmed down a bit, he told me that he'd looked at the films I'd entrusted to him."

"Films?" says Branco.

"Yes," says Thorin. "I'd previously given Timmy some negatives and prints of mine."

"I see," says Branco. "And what was the nature of these films?"

"They were duplicates of the ones I'd sent to the greeting card company."

"So the subject of the photos was Mr. Holton?"

"Yes," says Thorin.

"And why did you give them to Tim Shaughnessy?"

Thorin says, "Now I wish I hadn't. It was a big mistake. But I wanted to build Timmy's trust. That's part of what love is to me, to be able to trust a person. I'm not ashamed to say I loved that boy."

"Go on," says Branco, sounding mildly uncomfortable.

Thorin says, "Unfortunately Timmy looked at the photos and

he jumped to conclusions. Some people get the wrong idea when they see my work. I suspect it awakens something in them, even though nothing is explicit in the photos. Timmy told me he was ashamed that I was doing that kind of stuff. I explained that it was completely innocent, there was never any sex involved, not even nudity, but he was thinking the worst. Like I said, some people jump to conclusions. I told him not to panic, to take it easy, that I'd stop the whole business right now, if only he'd forgive me."

"Forgive you?" says Branco.

"Yes."

"For what?"

"For betraying his trust."

Branco says, "It sounds as though Mr. Shaughnessy betrayed *your* trust."

"No," says Thorin.

"Perhaps you had a secret hope that he would look at those films?"

Thorin's lawyer pipes up. "I object!"

Thorin says, "It was all a big mistake. I loved Timmy. I'd do whatever he said."

"Loved him?" says Branco.

"Like a . . . a son, almost."

"So there was nothing sexual between you."

"Jesus!" says Thorin. "I just told you."

"Please answer yes or no."

"No, goddamn it!"

Branco says, "Then what happened?"

"I told Timmy he could come with me and I'd destroy everything in front of him—prints, negatives, everything. But he said he was meeting a client there at the old house, and that he'd come by my store later and we could work it out. That was a relief."

"Why?" snaps Branco.

"I assumed everything was going to be all right between us."

"Is it possible that Tim Shaughnessy was planning to blackmail you with the photos you had entrusted to him?"

"No," says Thorin. "Timmy would never do that. Besides, there was nothing serious in them, nothing to blackmail me with."

Branco's voice is edgy. "Then why did you go and take the photos from Shaughnessy's house?"

Pssss, psssss, pssss.

Thorin says, "I never did that."

The tape player nearly explodes with the sound of a heavy envelope being thrown down onto the table.

Branco says, "We found these in your store. Are these the films you entrusted to Tim Shaughnessy?"

There's a pause, then some shuffling sounds as the contents of the envelope are examined. Then Branco tells Thorin to answer verbally.

"Yes," says Thorin. "These are mine."

"And how did you get them?"

"I didn't."

Branco yells, "Then how did they land up in your store?"

A pause.

Thorin says, "I don't know."

"I think you went to Shaughnessy's place and got them," says Branco.

"I didn't!"

"You just admitted you have a key," says Branco, "and my crew found you there this morning. Maybe you went back today to make sure you'd got everything yesterday."

Thorin says, "I didn't take these."

Branco says, "You were afraid that poor kid was going to report you as a pornographer, so you went yesterday and got the films yourself."

"No!" says Thorin. "And they're not porn! Look for yourself. There's more sex in the Sunday paper."

"That's highly subjective," says Branco. "And who knows how that young man felt about it? Maybe these photos bothered him very much. Didn't you say they awakened things in people? Maybe it was *your* sensitive, high-strung nature that was betrayed, not Tim Shaughnessy's. And your *pure love* for him was shattered, so you killed him in a blind rage."

Thorin cries, "That's not true! Not true!"

Branco says, "When did you get these films back? Just after you killed Tim Shaughnessy yesterday morning?"

"I didn't kill him!" says Thorin. "When I left him in that house he was alive."

Suddenly there's a lot of *pssssss*ing going on between Thorin and his lawyer. Then the lawyer says, "Are you prepared to charge my client?"

"I will be," says Branco.

More *psss*ing between lawyer and client. Then the lawyer says, "My client would like to amend his statement regarding the retrieval of these films from Tim Shaughnessy's house yesterday morning. He hopes you will take this information as a measure of his willingness to cooperate with you in resolving this matter."

"What has he got to say?" says Branco.

"Is his willingness to cooperate understood?" says the lawyer.

"It's on the record!" snaps Branco.

Thorin says, "I'll tell you, but first I want to make sure you understand that I didn't kill Timmy. We had a bad argument and he had hard feelings about that, but I didn't kill him."

Branco says, "So you've said and so I've heard. Now what else do you want to tell me?"

"Okay," says Thorin. "I did go to Timmy's place right after I left him at the old house yesterday. And yes, I wanted to get the films. Timmy was upset, and I wasn't sure what he'd do. These are my only copies, and I can't afford to lose them."

"Didn't you just say you were willing to destroy these films in front of Shaughnessy?" "Yes," says Thorin. "But I always hoped it wouldn't come to that." "So you went to his place to get the films." "Yes," says Thorin. "But when I got there it was a mess. Someone was there before me, and the films were gone."

Branco says, "We found no sign of forced entry. Whoever it was must also have a key."

There's a pause.

"Do you know who that might be?" says Branco.

Another pause before Thorin speaks.

"I'd rather not spell it out, Lieutenant."

"This is no time for what you'd rather do or not do! Just tell me what you know."

Thorin says, "My wife is Timmy's landlord. She has keys to his place."

So much for spousal immunity from incriminating testimony. Branco says, "So what? She's his landlord, and she has a key."

Thorin says, "Maybe she took the films and planted them in my store."

"And why would she do that?" says Branco.

"That," says Thorin, "that I don't know."

There's a long pause.

Finally Branco says, "Mr. Hightower, I am holding you here for further questioning."

The lawyer says, "But my client has shown he wants to cooperate."

"That doesn't exonerate him from suspicion," says Branco.

My pal Benjy would like that "e" word, which also reminds me to warn him that Branco is going to call sometime.

The lawyer says, "There's a limit on how long you can hold my client without a charge."

Branco replies, "I know the rules!" Then he says to Thorin, "Have you anything more to say?"

Thorin is mute.

Branco ends the interview.

What began as an assault of Myron Kratz by Chip Holton has developed into a baroque menage à quatre, of which the fourth member, Tim Shaughnessy, is dead, and another member, Thorin Hightower, appears to be the prime suspect.

Three tapes down, two to go.

And I'm out of bonbons.

22

It's almost a relief that cassette number four is a continuation of the interview with Myron Kratz, whose attorney is now present. I'm not ready for any new players at this point.

After his opening comments, Branco repeats his last question to Myron just before the previous interview was stopped. He sounds sterner now. Maybe he's getting tired, or maybe it's the presence of Myron's lawyer.

"Where did you find the nail file you had previously given to Chip Holton as a gift?"

"I found it in the old house at 101 Waltham Street."

For his part, Myron sounds blithely relaxed and confident, which may also be thanks to the presence of his lawyer, or perhaps to a happy handful of tranquilizers taken since the last session.

Branco says, "And what were you doing there?"

"I was walking Betty, and we ended up following Chip from the café where he works."

"So you did leave your store yesterday morning," says Branco.

"Yes," says Myron. "And now I'm telling you the whole truth, Lieutenant. As I was saying, Betty needed a walk."

"At what time was that?"

"I don't recall exactly," says Myron. "I didn't think to look at my watch. I had other things on my mind."

"What things?"

"Haven't you ever followed someone, Lieutenant?"

Branco says, "Do you often do that, Mr. Kratz? Follow people?"

Myron's lawyer interrupts with some remark about relevancy, but Myron says it's okay. He wants to talk to Branco. He wants to tell him everything the way it really happened. He wants to be a good, responsible citizen who cooperates with the police.

"Yes," says Myron, "I do sometimes follow people, depending of course on who the person is and where they might be going."

"Did you know where Mr. Holton was going that morning?"

"No. But I did see him go inside that old building on Waltham Street."

Branco says, "And you followed him inside?"

"Oh, no," says Myron. "I had no idea what he was doing there. There are times, Lieutenant, when it's not a good idea to drop in on people unannounced."

"Then what happened?"

"Chip was in there, oh, ten minutes or so. And when he came out he was looking around suspiciously."

"Could you be more specific?"

Myron says, "He wanted to make sure no one saw him."

"Did he see you?"

"No," says Myron. "I pulled myself into a doorway. And it was snowing, remember? It was a goddamn white-out. Oh, excuse me for saying that on the tape. Can you rewind it? I guess not. But—oh, wait! This is important. This is very important. This is probably the most important thing I can tell you. When Chip came out he was limping."

"Limping?" says Branco.

"Yes," says Myron. "He was limping."

"Why do you think that's important?"

"Because he wasn't limping when he went in there."

"Are you certain?" says Branco.

"I followed him, didn't I?"

Damn that Myron! That's exactly what I did the day of Timmy's death—follow Chip's grinding butt to Members Only Café. And the limp was absolutely there. Wounded warrior indeed!

"Go on," says Branco.

"This is the part where I thought my lawyer should be present," says Myron. "I did go into that place myself, and that's when I saw Tamantha sprawled out on the stairway."

"Tamantha?" says Branco.

"Oh, sorry," says Myron. "I mean Timmy."

Branco grunts. "And what do you mean by 'sprawled out'?"

"I mean he was dead," says Myron.

"How did you know that?"

"I just knew."

Branco asks, "Did you touch him?"

"No," says Myron. "But I could tell."

"How?"

"Oh, Lieutenant, you know by looking when someone is dead. You don't have to touch them."

"Mr. Kratz, are you experienced in these matters?"

"No."

"Do you realize it is possible that Tim Shaughnessy was still alive at that moment? That he might have been saved?"

"Well how would I know that?" says Myron. "He looked dead to me. And I wasn't about to go and touch him."

"Where was your dog during all of this?"

"You mean Betty?"

"Did you bring her into the house with you?"

"Betty is a he, Lieutenant. And yes, he came into the house with me."

Branco says coldly, "Go on."

"Well," says Myron, "I suppose I ought to tell you about this too, although I'm not very proud of that naughty boy's behavior. Betty and Tamantha were best friends, just like two young buddies. You've heard the expression 'A boy and his dog,' Lieutenant? That was Betty and Tam. And that morning Betty was very naughty. He ran up the stairs to where Tamantha was lying."

Branco snarls, "His name was Tim!"

"I know that, Lieutenant," says Myron. "I know his name was Tim . . . when he was being butch anyway. There's no need to lose your patience. It's just a form of endearment."

"So you and Tim Shaughnessy were friendly?"

"Of course," says Myron.

What about that incident at the Home Show?

"It was Betty's reaction that assured me that Tam—er, Tim was dead."

"What reaction?" says Branco.

"Betty went up to lick him. He always did that, and Timmy used to like it. But this time when Betty licked him, he started growling and barking. Betty was extremely upset, and I knew something was wrong. When I called him back to me, he was literally crying. I knew we should get out of there and call the police. That's when I found the nail file, on my way out of the building to call you."

Branco says, "Is that also when you saw the lens cap belonging to Thorin Hightower?"

"You know about that too?"

"Yes, we do," says Branco.

Myron says, "Well, I thought these things might be useful. You can see that I was very careful to keep them both clean."

"I'm sure the lab will appreciate that," says Branco. "So then you called 911 to alert us about Timmy's body."

"Yes," says Myron.

"But you didn't leave your name."

"I didn't see the need."

"You certainly are able to remain calm in stressful situations, Mr. Kratz."

"With the kind of life I lead, you have to."

"Were you able to stay cool with Mr. Holton?"

Myron's lawyer pipes in again, quibbling about relevance, and once again Myron shushes him.

"No, no," he says. "Let me talk. I want to explain everything to the police. I'm not ashamed to discuss anything I do." Then Myron says to Branco, " 'Mr. Holton,' as you insist on calling Chip, turns out to be a very dangerous character. I had no idea he would become so violent. He seemed very agreeable when I laid out the terms of our, er, transaction."

Branco says, "He may have seemed agreeable because he was scared."

"Scared?" says Myron. "Of what? Of me? What could I do to him?"

"You had the nail file."

"Lieutenant, are you defending him? He attacked me!"

"Maybe Mr. Holton didn't know what else to do when you changed the terms of your transaction."

Myron says, "I did not change the terms."

"Then there was a misunderstanding."

"Well said, Lieutenant!"

Branco says, "So you arranged to meet with Mr. Holton to return his nail file, in exchange for which you expected certain favors. Is that right?"

Myron says, "It sounds so Victorian when you say it like that—certain favors. But yes, I did hope that Chip and I could reach some friendly truce. I mean, I didn't really expect anything of him beyond, as the French say, 'making the plank.' "

"Would you care to explain that?" says Branco.

"Certainly," says Myron. *"Faire la planche* is very popular with straight men. I suppose it's because they don't actively participate in the, er, intimate act, and therefore they can feel absolved of any guilt. The term implies lying on one's back, but you can do it just as well standing up, or even sitting down. One person makes the plank, and the other one does all the work. It's that simple. Being the plank is as passive as anyone can be and still be alive. Some men barely make a sound when they—"

Branco clears his throat. "Thank you, Mr. Kratz."

"Certainly, Lieutenant."

"Are you intending to file charges against Chip Holton?"

A long pause follows, and now I wish I had a videotape of this interview as well.

Finally Myron speaks. "Do I have to decide that right now?"

"No," says Branco.

Myron's attorney makes noises, but Myron shushes him again. Then he says, "I'll let you know what I intend to do, Lieutenant, very soon. Now, would you please ask one or two of your burly men to escort me to the hospital? I believe I have the right to a complete medical workup, including an MRI, and I want everything I'm entitled to."

Branco says, "You certainly know your rights."

"It pays to," says Myron.

"Just one more thing," says Branco, "and then you can go. Does this dog of yours—this Betty—does he ever lose hair?"

Myron answers proudly, "That breed doesn't shed."

"Not even in the springtime?"

"Never," says Myron.

"Do you mean to tell me that your dog has never lost one strand of hair from his body in all the time you've owned him?"

Myron says, "Well, I couldn't say that, Lieutenant. Once in a while you'll find a stray hair, but it's a rare thing, hardly matters."

After that the interview ends quickly. I think film buffs call this kind of thing a "short subject."

Just one more cassette and my afternoon's work is done.

23

The fifth tape is a continuation of Branco's interview with Chip Holton. Branco's opening remarks inform Chip that he is entitled to an attorney, but Chip declines again. Brave boy!

Branco's voice sounds very supportive now, and I have my first doubts about the objectivity of this second round with Chip.

Branco says, "You stated earlier that you were at 101 Waltham Street yesterday morning to meet with Thorin Hightower."

"That's right, sir."

Chip is still making with the "sir" business, so he must be aiming for extra points.

Branco says, "Is that where you injured your foot?"

"Yes, sir," says Chip. "Sorry I forgot to mention that earlier."

"You can explain it now." Branco sounds like an archetypal nurturing dad.

Chip explains that he hurt his ankle when his foot crashed through one of the rotten stair treads in the old house.

Branco asks him why he was walking around the place.

Chip says he was restless.

Meanwhile I'm wondering if he can sue me for injuring himself on my property. Just let the little trespasser try it!

"Restless?" says Branco.

Chip explains, "Like I said before, I wasn't sure what was going to happen with Thorin."

Branco says, "We've spoken with Mr. Hightower, and he states that he was in the house yesterday morning, and that he did speak with Tim Shaughnessy."

Chip says, "Thorin wasn't there when I got there."

Branco says, "We also have a statement by Myron Kratz, who

146

claims that he was at the old house too, and he found Tim Shaughnessy's body on the stairs. That's when he found your nail file."

A pause follows.

Branco continues. "If Mr. Kratz's statement is true, that implies that you were in the house before he was."

Chip says, "So what if I was?" His voice is a little shaky now.

Branco says, "But you've stated that no one else was in the house with you."

"That's true," says Chip, but he sounds uncertain.

"No one?" says Branco.

"No," says Chip. "I told you. No one."

"Well," says Branco, "at some point between the time you went in and the time you came out, Tim Shaughnessy's body appeared in that house. Now how do you explain that?"

Another pause. Then finally comes Chip's faint voice.

"I can't."

"It's your word against Mr. Kratz's. Is that why you beat him?"

It's about time Branco accused Chip of his crime!

"But I told you," says Chip, "I didn't beat him. I . . . I . . . just put my hands around his neck, and I tried to hurt him that way. But I didn't hit him. I know I didn't hit him."

Branco presses him. "What are you hiding? Who are you trying to protect?"

"Look," says Chip. "Look, I think I'd better tell you. Thorin was definitely there before me."

"How do you know that?" says Branco.

"I just do."

"You have to be specific," says the cop. "Tell me why you know that Thorin Hightower was there before you."

I scream out loud, "Because he saw the lens cap!" But no one hears me in my living room.

Chip says, "I think I might need a lawyer now."

"Do you want to stop the interview?" says Branco.

"No, no," says Chip. "I'll tell you now. I don't think I can wait any longer. It's been bothering me for two days. I want to get it off my chest."

His nicely sculpted, well-developed chest.

"Go ahead," says Branco, the comforting dad.

"The truth is," says Chip, "that kid was already in there when I went in."

And me out of bonbons.

"So you weren't alone?" says Branco.

"No," says Chip. "I lied before. And he was already dead."

"Are you changing your original statement?"

"Yes, sir. I'm telling you the truth now. You'll ask me why I didn't tell you this before. And I'll ask you, would you have admitted something like that? Would you have said that kid was already dead when you walked in there? How does that make me look? It makes it look like I killed him. But I didn't even know him, so why should I kill him? When I saw him lying on the stairs, I went up there to see if I could help him. That's when my foot went through the stairs. I got to where he was, and I felt his neck for a pulse, but he was dead. That's when I hightailed it out of there real fast. I was afraid Thorin would come in and think I did it."

"Why would he think that?" says Branco.

"Just from how it looked," says Chip. "With me there and the kid lying on the stairs. I had to run. It was bad enough that I wanted to break away from Thorin and the photography. I was really nervous that morning. I wasn't sure what would happen with Thorin, and I didn't want to find out. I'm sorry I lied about finding the kid. I just didn't know what else to do."

Branco says, "How long were you in the house?"

Chip hesitates. "About ten minutes."

"And what were you doing during that time?"

"I . . . I . . . Like I said, I was walking around, thinking about the photo shoot. Then I saw the kid on the stairs." After a moment, Chip adds, "That's how I know Thorin was there before me."

A long pause follows.

Then Branco says, "Mr. Holton, at this time Mr. Kratz has not filed a formal charge against you. I've taken your statement, and the fact is, I have no other reason to hold you here at this time, so you're free to go now."

What? An admitted fag-basher goes free?

"Just don't leave town," says Branco.

No, that's for me to do.

Branco says, "You'll still have to answer any charges brought by Mr. Kratz."

Chip says, "I'm really sorry about that. I'm sorry about everything. I was wrong to hurt Myron. But he made me feel so ashamed, what he wanted to do. I'm just not that kind of person. I guess I lost control. I'll face whatever punishment I deserve for hurting him."

Branco terminates the interview, but somehow manages to leave the tape running a few seconds longer, creating a moment much like Citizen Kane's boo-boo, where he believes the microphone is off and no one else can hear.

Branco says to Chip, "It takes a lot of courage to admit things you might be ashamed of."

Then the tape goes silent.

Nice way to end the show, with typical macho logic.

I'll listen to the tapes again later on, before broiling them as Tina instructed me to. Right now I want to get outdoors and catch the last rays of evening light, so I head over to Snips Salon to see Nicole.

24

It's seven o'clock and Snips Salon is still busy. The shop is always busy. Sometimes I wonder if it's busy even when it's closed. Maybe being the sole beneficiary of Nicole's estate isn't such a bad idea. But I don't want to linger on that thought.

Nicole has a client. I go and dawdle near her manicure table. She glances up briefly from her work to greet me. Then, with her attention focused intently back on her customer's hand, she says to me, "You look a bit washed out, dear."

"I feel like I just saw a bad movie."

"You spent this beautiful day cooped up in a dark theater?"

"I was at home, doll."

"Not watching those videos again?"

"No!"

"Well," she says, "daytime television is just as bad. I still say you need a job, dear."

"Nikki, I wasn't watching TV."

She looks up at me again, and this time she actually sees me. "Something's on your mind."

I nod.

She says to me, "We're almost finished here." She smiles generously to her client as if to assure her she's not getting the bum's rush. Then Nicole tells me to go wait in the back office for her.

Back there I pour myself some bourbon and wait. Five minutes later Nikki comes rushing in. She pours herself some coffee, then sits down and lights a cigarette. So much for the nonsmoking Nicole. But nondrinking? At night? I mention it.

Nicole says, "I'm working, Stanley."

"Since when did that stop you?"

"Just tell me what's on your mind, dear. I'm booked solid tonight, and I really can't afford to take a break."

"Since when are you a model of workplace efficiency?"

"We can't afford two laggards in the family."

I tell her I spent the last two hours listening to police interviews.

She says, "That's very good news. I'm glad that you and the lieutenant are cooperating again. Now I really must get back to—"

"Nikki, these tapes I was listening to—they're police tapes, the real thing."

"I understand, darling, and I'm happy for you. I knew Vito would come round."

"Not quite," I say. "They're copies."

Nicole arches an eyebrow. "Copies?"

"Someone owed me a favor."

"Well, well," she says. "So we're on the other side of the law now."

"Business as usual for gays."

"Don't start that with me, Stanley. You have a very good life, better than most people in fact. Just because the law doesn't explicitly provide a separate bill of rights for people like you doesn't mean—"

"Nikki! You sound like Branco now."

"And you're revving up like some activist. Frankly, dear, it doesn't suit you. Now, what is the problem?"

"The problem," I say, "is on those tapes. It's obvious that Branco is siding with the one straight white male suspect."

"Well, can you blame him?"

"Nikki! Whose side are you on?"

"Yours, of course," she says. "And it sounds to me as though you're just having your usual problems with the lieutenant."

"No, this time it's different. Branco's job, any cop's job, is to uphold the law, not to show favoritism to someone who shares the same socio-sexual corral."

Nicole's eyes cross slightly. "When you talk like that, Stanley, I think I'm against higher education. I wonder what you'd say if Vito showed favoritism to *you.*"

"There's little chance of that."

"That's where you're wrong, Stanley."

"Nikki, why are you taking his side?"

"I am not taking sides!" She gets up, grabs a styrofoam cup, and pours herself a generous portion of bourbon.

I say, "I'm driving you to drink."

"Don't flatter yourself," she says, then downs a good solid shot from the cup. She sits down again and takes a long, slow drag from her cigarette.

"Now I recognize you, doll."

She says breezily, "Who cares that my customers are waiting for me? It's more important that you tell me what that big horrid brute did to you this time."

"Branco didn't do anything."

"Then what?" she says.

"He's going to arrest Thorin Hightower for killing Tim Shaughnessy."

"Why does that upset you?" says Nicole.

"Because Thorin is a sensitive, artistic man who happened to love Tim."

"And you think the big bad lieutenant should not arrest him because of that?"

"Well . . ." I hesitate. "Thorin does look pretty guilty."

"Stanley," she says, "is it possible that the lieutenant is right this time? Maybe you're upset because things aren't quite turning out the way you expected."

"I am not upset!"

"Of course not," she says calmly. "But am I on the right track?"

"Kind of," I mutter.

Nicole takes another long, deep drag from her cigarette. As she exhales a big cloud of smoke, she makes a pronouncement.

"The truth, Stanley, is often unpleasant."

I feign a cough.

Nikki continues. "I'm sure the lieutenant has good cause for his actions."

"He's basing the charge on evidence that was found at the crime scene."

"There, you see?" says Nicole. "Despite your cynicism, Stanley, the police do know their work."

"Don't be too sure, doll. It's all circumstantial, and the police aren't even the ones who found this so-called evidence."

"Then how do they know about it?"

"There was a little matter of blackmail."

I give her a condensed version of the purloined tapes.

"Goodness!" she says when I finish.

"Right," I say. "There was a lot of foot traffic in my place yesterday morning."

"I wonder if any of them were in there more than once."

"Nikki, let's not even consider the possibility."

"And it all comes down to Thorin killing Timmy?"

"That's what it looks like."

"But you don't believe it."

"Would you, doll?"

"But why not him, Stanley?"

I hesitate. "Thorin seems too sensitive."

She says, "But darling, that's just your *opinion*, and that could be exactly the kind of thing that Thorin tries to portray, that a sensitive soul like him could never do anything against another person. But you never know who might be hiding under a veneer of sensitivity."

"Like what? A serial killer?"

"Then you tell me, Stanley. Who would you accuse?"

"It's *whom*, doll, and I'd nab Myron. He's obviously lying about everything."

"How do you know that?"

"I don't," I admit sheepishly. "It's more of a feeling again."

"And perhaps *that* feeling is influenced by your dislike for this Myron person."

"Who said I dislike him?"

"Your face, Stanley. Your face twists up just saying his name."

"Isn't that what Branco is doing to Thorin, basing his judgment on an emotional response? Isn't that what juries do? Why shouldn't I?"

"Well, darling," says Nicole, "this seems like just another repeat performance. I'm sure things will work out. They always do. You have to focus on the brighter things."

"Like what?" I say.

"Maybe you should take a trip somewhere, clear your mind."

"I already tried that, Nikki. Remember?"

"Yes, Stanley, but this time you should do it for fun."

"Yeah, well, Branco wants me to go on vacation too."

"With *him*?" Her eyes blaze brightly.

"No, doll. Our universe doesn't have physics like that."

She exhales a fluffy cloud of smoke. "You never know, Stanley. You just never know about these things."

"Nikki, I don't need a vacation, and I don't want a vacation."

"Well then," she says, "come back to work. We can set things up here at the shop exactly how they were before you got all that money. You can be Vannos again. Then at least you'll have a social life."

"Vannos is dead, doll."

"Then pick a new name," she says. "The important thing, Stanley, is that you'll have a creative outlet. You know how important that is to you. And your clients will bestow gifts and compliments on you. It can be wonderful. Why do you want to turn your back on all that?"

"There's someone I wish would turn his back on me."

She ignores that remark. "Why, just this morning one of my clients brought me a huge box of truffles from Aubarde—you know, that place down the block."

Nicole takes the box from the desk drawer and holds it toward me. My stomach lurches at the sight of the gaily decorated *ballotin*. I hold up my hand to keep the box at bay.

"No?" she says. "I thought you loved these things." She opens the box and smells them. "Heavenly!" She offers the open box to me. This time I put up both hands.

"Really?" she says. "You're not dieting again, are you?"

"No, doll. I'm just not in the mood."

She smells the chocolates again. "You know, you could probably die from these things, although how can anyone eat more than one?" She puts the open box on the table in front of me.

As if on cue, the half pound of fresh-cream chocolate truffles I devoured at home begins dispensing its peptic consequences.

Nicole says, "You have that washed-out look again, dear. Maybe you'd better go home and lie down."

"Maybe I'd better," I say.

"And don't worry about the lieutenant," she says. "I'm sure everything will work out fine between you. It always does."

She puts out her cigarette and leaves her bourbon unfinished. When she's out of the office, I cover the chocolates and put them away. I have to avert my gaze as I do it. Then I down the rest of her bourbon. No sense wasting good liquor. Besides, it might help settle my stomach.

I leave the shop by the back door.

Back home, I'm lying in bed. It's around ten o'clock, and I'm tossing and turning, trying one side then the other, then on my back, then my stomach, then with my head elevated, then legs elevated.

But nothing helps. The fact is, a few hours ago I consumed about two million grams of fat in one sitting, and now the piper must be paid.

I've listened to the interview tapes again too, and those final seconds between Branco and Chip on the last tape are really bothering me now. Partly I'm furious that the cop just about condones Chip's assault on Myron. But I'm also feeling a little jealous. Branco treats Chip with compassion and understanding—like a whole person—and it's only because they're both straight. It probably works that way in the Marines too. If some drunken night a lonely recruit finds himself in a dark alley with his pants around his ankles, taking it up the butt, well, as long as he makes suitable sounds of regret to his commanding officer, then all is forgiven—no court-martial—and he's still a man. But if he bathes first and does the same deed on clean sheets—come on!—the guy's a fag.

The phone rings. I heave the fifty-pound receiver to my ear.

"Huh?" I say.

"Penny?"

"Oh, hi, Benjy."

"Penny? You sound like Debbie Doom."

"I ate something that didn't agree with me."

"Those things work out one way or another."

"Thanks, Benjy."

"Hey, I hear you changed your hair."

"Who told you that?"

"Someone on a backroom chat line."

"A what?" I say.

Benjy explains. "I logged onto a local chat line and someone was saying that Stan Kraychik looks like a Marine now."

If that's how the Gospel According to Hairnet perceives me, maybe all I need to get a date is a dark alley and a uniform: I'm sorry, Colonel. I was drunk. He forced me.

"Penny, you have secret admirers on the Internet."

"I don't know if that's good or bad."

"There is no 'good or bad' in cyberspace."

"Benjy, some real person is punching real keys somewhere out there. Is it possible to find out who it was?"

"One of the benefits of the Net is that you're relatively anonymous."

"But someone must know who's on there. I mean, people pay to do this, right?"

"Penny, I only told you because I thought you'd be flattered. That's not even why I called. I'm calling because I got a phone call from a cop."

Oops.

"Sorry, Benjy. I meant to warn you about that."

"No problem, Penny. Actually we had a very nice chat, very impromptu, you know, the kind I like best."

"It was Lieutenant Branco, right?"

"Is he the one who gives you wet dreams?"

"I never said that!"

"You don't have to, Penny-Pop. You hear that voice and you're ready to do whatever it tells you."

"The effect wears off, Benjy."

"I hope not."

"So what did Branco ask you?"

"He wanted to verify the sources of the information I told you—you know, about the SECA deal and Gardenia Construction and all that. He seemed to know all about it. Did he take notes on you or something?"

"Branco is very methodical."

"So what's his story, Penny? Closet doors? Or beaded curtains."

"Neither," I say, but I'm wondering why Branco would bother to call Benjy if he already has his suspect in Thorin Hightower. Is he just confirming what I told him? Doesn't he have better things to do?

Benjy says, "And that voice of his. I can still hear it."

"You ought to see the rest of the package."

"Please tell me he's a troll, please!"

"He's a troll, Benjy."

"You lie."

"I lie."

"Well that voice of his piqued my interest, so I did a little research on Mr. Branco. Wait till you hear what I found. Penny, this is capital H-O-T, hot! And you're hearing it directly from me, right now, before it hits the papers."

"Okay, Benjy. You've got my attention. Shoot!"

"Ooh, I love it when redheads talk dirty."

"I'm not a redhead anymore, remember?"

"Too bad," he says. "Anyway, by now you are probably too familiar with Gardenia and Sons, the molto homophobico construction company."

"Yes, Benjy, yes."

"Well, they just applied for a change of name, and it's been approved, and I thought you'd want to hear about it. *That's* why I'm calling. Oh, Penny-pence, online snooping is so much fun!"

"Benjy, the envelope please."

"Okay, Penny, okay. Here we go. Gardenia and Sons Construction is soon to be redubbed—are you ready? Drumroll, please!—Gardenia, *Branco* and Sons. Isn't that something? Penny? *Penny?* Are you there?"

"I'm here, Benjy."

"I thought the line went dead."

"Something did."

He says, "It's going to be in all the papers tomorrow, but I thought you'd want to be the first to know, especially considering, if I may say so, dearest Penny-thing, your peculiar liaison with a certain member of the newly extended Gardenia family."

"Does the article actually say that the Gardenias are now linked to the Boston police through Lieutenant Branco?"

"No," says Benjy. "It's just a notice of a corporate name change. I'm the one who made the connection. For all I know, it could be another Branco altogether, not yours."

"He's not mine," I say.

"Too bad, eh?" says Benjy.

"And you found out about this on the Internet?"

"Yes," he says. "I'm telling you, you've got to get online. Of course, you have to know where to look, which I do. I have that nose for news. That's how I got so far so fast in this new job."

"And I thought it was your excellent gag control."

"Penny!"

"Legend has it you never come up for air."

"Where did you hear that!"

"The old-fashioned way."

"Who? When? Where?" says Benjy.

"One of your ex's was talking in the styling chair."

"It should've been the electric chair."

"Benjy, it's a compliment to be known for breathless blow—"

"Penny, please! I'm blushing."

"And I'm getting a Ph.D. in Bible Art."

"Uh-oh," says Benjy. "Here comes the boss."

Then he hangs up quickly, just like the other time.

One good thing: Benjy's effervescence has magically cured my heartburn.

Then, since there's nothing else to occupy me, now that Branco has his prime suspect in the murder of Tim Shaughnessy, I haul out the vacation brochures I got earlier today. I might as well do what Branco says I do best: have fun.

The guy obviously doesn't know me from Adam.

Or a Marine.

25

First thing next morning I go to police headquarters to see Lieutenant Branco. I'm still not convinced that Thorin is guilty. Besides, with all the hustle and bustle over Myron and Chip's apache dance yesterday, and then the ensuing hours spent listening to the interview tapes, I never got a chance to tell Branco about Salena Hightower's chummy relations with the Gardenia clan. And since her husband, Thorin, implied that she was at Tim Shaughnessy's place sometime the morning he was killed, I'm certain that Salena Hightower is just as involved with Tim's death as

Thorin is—more so, probably, with her connection to the Gardenias. Speaking of which, so is Branco now, at least according to Benjy's Hairnet update last night. As I enter the station I feel as though I'm armed with state's evidence.

On the way up to Branco's office I pass Tina at her desk outside the interview rooms. When she sees me she averts her gaze. Has Branco found out about the tapes she copied for me? I go to her desk and tell her I tried that recipe for broiled pigeon last night.

"I did just what you told me," I say, "but somehow I burned the whole thing to a crisp. Couldn't even tell what it started out as."

"That's too bad," she says coolly.

I tell her I'm on my way to see Branco.

She says, "He's not upstairs. He's down here."

She nods her head toward the locked door that leads to the soundproofed interview rooms.

"Who's he got in there?"

"I shouldn't be telling you," she says.

"Why not?"

"Stanny, I don't want to get in trouble."

"What trouble?" I say. "You're just talking to me. There's no law against that."

"But it's against procedure."

"Tina," I say, "I'm not someone off the street. You know me. I was at the academy with you. Doesn't that count for something?"

"Maybe," she says.

"Come on," I say. "We're on the same side. Just tell me who Branco is talking to."

Tina says, "Salena Hightower."

Good timing! Just the girl I want to tell him about.

I ask, "Do you know what's up?"

Tina says, "The lab boys found her fingerprints all over Tim Shaughnessy's place. She was supposed to be checking up on the plumbing, but her prints were everywhere *but* the kitchen and the bathroom."

I say, "You never know where those damn pipes are going to lead you."

And things are looking up for my case against Salena.

Suddenly Tina makes a minuscule shake of her head, warning me to shut up.

Moments later Salena Hightower emerges from the locked corridor where the interview rooms are. She's escorted by two cops, and she's not so giggly and chatty as after her first date with Branco, that time in his office. She sees me and just about spits at me.

"Blabbermouth!"

Whatever happened to the pretty South End realtor?

The cops lead her away.

Then Branco emerges from the corridor.

"You again?" he says.

"I have something on that woman, Lieutenant, the one who just left."

Has Branco registered the fact that I'm standing near Tina's desk? Would he believe that we are simply old school chums from the police academy?

Branco says, "I can give you a minute, no more."

He takes me into one of the interview rooms. We sit down. It's obviously not official, since there are no other cops in there with us, and Branco doesn't turn on the recorder.

"Go ahead," he says.

I tell him I talked to Salena Hightower yesterday. "And it turns out she is very well connected to Gardenia and Sons Construction Company."

"And?" says Branco.

"And she just about admitted that they're involved with Tim Shaughnessy's death."

"She said this to you?"

"In so many words."

"How many words?" says Branco.

I fumble.

Branco says, "Stan, I've got work to do and you have a vacation to take. I don't know where you're getting your information, or even why you're getting it, since I've already told you to stop."

"But Timmy is connected to Salena," I say, "and Salena is connected to the Gardenias. Did you check out her story why she was at Timmy's place two days ago?"

Branco's eyes flash brightly. "Yes, I did," he says. "But where did you hear about it?"

"Salena told me."

"Salena Hightower?" he says.

"The same," I say. "Tall, brunette, pretty. Just walked out of here. You know who I mean now?"

Branco says, "Exactly when did she tell you this?"

"Yesterday."

"Just like that?" he says. "She told you she was at Tim Shaughnessy's place the morning his body was found?"

"Not exactly," I say. "She said things that made it *obvious* she was there. I figure, why question the obvious? Don't you believe me?"

Branco says, "We had one hell of a time wringing the same information out of her just now—the fact that she was at Shaughnessy's place that morning—and then you come breezing in here telling me you already knew about it."

"Maybe it's my finely honed interview technique, Lieutenant. It took years at the styling chair, but I'd be glad to offer you a few pointers."

"I don't need pointers," says Branco. "The subject became very cooperative once we confronted her with fingerprint evidence."

"I don't have that advantage."

"That's right," says Branco. "You don't."

"So now you know that Salena was at Tim's place, and that she's also connected with the Gardenias. So, are you going after them?"

"Who?" he says.

"The Gardenias."

"For what?" says Branco.

"For Tim's death. It couldn't be Thorin."

"Thorin?" says Branco.

"Thorin Hightower, Salena's husband. Aren't you holding him?"

"Who the hell have you been talking to?"

"No one," I say. "I . . . I assumed it."

"I don't believe that!" he says. "You tell me where you got the idea I'm holding Thorin Hightower."

"You mean you're not?"

Branco's face is still, as though he's posing for some Roman sculptor to catch every perfect detail of his mouth, his nose, his forehead, his chin. But what's to be done about his eyes? You can't capture them in marble. You'd need some kind of rare gem that glitters with an icy-hot gray-blue light.

He takes a deep breath. Then he says, "Tell you what I'm going to do, Stan. We're going to have it out here, once and for all, just us two. Okay?"

"I don't understand."

"You will," he says. "I'm going to listen to you now, one more time. But that's the end of it. I've been very patient with you. I even took a few risks with you, went out on a limb. Okay, it didn't pay off. So now I think it's time to call an end to it."

"An end to what?" I say.

"To putting up with you and your antics. I'm doing serious work here, and you—you'll pardon my French—but you're just screwing around. Now for old times' sake I'm willing to listen. I'm even willing to answer you, because as far as I'm concerned, when we walk out of this room, it's over. You go your way, I go mine."

What am I supposed to say? That breaking up is hard to do?

Branco say, "Now, you tell me everything you know, including your . . . theories. I'm sure there's plenty of those. Then I'll explain to you in detail why you're wrong. Sound fair?"

So much for the blind eye of justice.

First thing, I ask him why Salena Hightower went to Tim Shaughnessy's place two mornings ago.

Branco says, "No, no, Stan. You don't ask. You tell."

"It's a theory," I say. "You said you wanted my theories too. So, theoretically speaking, why would Salena go to Timmy's place?"

Branco answers reluctantly, as though he'd rather fight with me personally, which is a guaranteed win for him. "She stated that Tim Shaughnessy reported an emergency plumbing situation that he had taken care of himself. She went to his place to make sure the repairs had actually been made, since he was claiming a rebate on his rent."

"But she made the whole thing up."

"That's right," says Branco. His anger has dissipated already. Maybe the way to his heart is to second-guess him, but with correct answers only. "She did make it up. And why do you think she did that?"

I say, "To give herself a reason to get in there."

"For what?"

"Timmy must have had something she wanted."

"Right again," says Branco. "What do you think it was?"

"Information of some kind. I think Salena found her client list among Tim's papers, which means that's where she was looking, not at the plumbing."

Branco says, "This is very good, Stan. It's odd how you know so much. I could almost swear you were listening to the interview just now."

"I wasn't."

"I'll verify that," says the cop. "But what you suspect here is exactly what Salena Hightower just admitted to."

"I told you, I talked to her yesterday."

Branco goes on. "She says she needed to see some contracting papers for one of her clients, and that it was very urgent, very critical. There was some big money hanging on it."

"Then why didn't she ask Tim to give them to her?"

"Because she couldn't find him," says Branco.

"Because he was dead," I say. "And Salena—"

"*And,*" interrupts Branco, "since Ms. Hightower had a very close and personal friendship with young Shaughnessy, she knew he wouldn't mind her going to his place, especially if he understood the urgency of the situation."

"Friendly?" I say. "She's his landlord. How friendly can they be?"

Branco says, "Don't you have a close friend like that, someone you trust implicitly with every aspect of your life?"

"Do I?"

"Isn't Ms. Albright close to you?"

"Nicole?" I say. "She's like my big sister. But Tim and Salena were enemies, not friends."

"According to who?" says Branco.

"According to Salena Hightower, at least when she's talking to me."

Branco says, "That's not how I interpret her statement."

I say, "Was it while Salena was looking for those documents at Timmy's that she found the photos taken by her husband?"

Branco squints his eyes. "Which one of your little helpers told you that?"

"Am I right?"

Branco says, "I don't know what you've been up to, Stan, but none of that matters now. The case is closed."

"Closed?"

Branco nods. "I just got the preliminary lab reports this morning. From all indications, Tim Shaughnessy's death was an accident."

"An accident? With all those suspects!"

Branco's eyes burn. "There are no suspects, not anymore. It was an accident."

"We've got Salena, we've got Thorin, we've got Myron."

"Who is we?" says Branco.

"What about that Angie girl? Where is she?"

"Who?" says Branco.

"That hairstylist who disappeared. She can tell you that Salena and Timmy were enemies. Have you got any news on finding her?"

"Why should I?"

I tell him, "Because Angie was Tim's friend, and she's been missing since yesterday."

Branco looks at his watch. "Well, Stan, your minute is long up."

"But you said we were going to have it out. You can't call time on me now."

Branco says, "I can do whatever the hell I want with you."

Whoah. Time out.

"Lieutenant, Tim Shaughnessy's death was not an accident.

Take Salena. I mean, her perfume is still polluting the air in here, so why not start with her? She had both motive and opportunity to kill Tim. If she heard his answering machine the other morning, she knew he'd be at my house waiting for me. So it was easy enough to go there and kill him."

"But she has no motive," says Branco.

"She's paying back the Gardenias!"

"The Gardenias?" says Branco. "The construction people?"

"I keep trying to tell you, they are key players in this case." I look into Branco's eyes. I want to tell him what Benjy told me last night, about the Branco name being newly joined to the Gardenia name. I want to ask him, Are you now linked to those construction people? Is that why you don't want to talk about them? But I can't do it. Branco has put up some kind of barrier that won't let me say it. Instead I remind him that Salena arranged the contract at the SECA site, where the Gardenias' crown prince Tony was killed. "And even before that, Salena Hightower had longstanding business ties to them."

"So?" says the cop. "What does any of this have to do with Tim Shaughnessy?"

"She was trying to pay back the Gardenias for a deal that went sour."

"I'm missing a connection here, Stan."

"Salena killed Timmy to pay back the Gardenias for Tony's death. Okay?"

"Jesus, are you off base!"

"Lieutenant, that was her hair on Timmy's collar."

"Was it?" says the cop. "How do you know that?"

"Because it was dyed."

"Is that so?" says Branco. "And how do you know that?"

"By looking at it. I am an expert colorist."

Branco says, "You didn't pick it up, did you? Handle it? Move it?"

"I know better than that."

"Do you?" says the cop. "Well, Stan, I've got bad news for you. That hair is not dyed. It's from a dog, a Portuguese water dog."

Gulp.

"Are you sure?" I say.

"The lab is one hundred percent certain."

"I guess my color perception is slipping."

Branco says, "From where I sit, that's not the only thing."

"And from where I sit, Salena Hightower still has the best motive for killing Tim Shaughnessy."

"Stan, if Shaughnessy's death was homicide, we have more evidence against the woman's husband than we do on her."

"And that's exactly how they planned it."

"Planned *what?*" says Branco.

"You know about Thorin's drug rap?"

Branco rolls his eyes heavenward.

I go on. "He took that rap for Salena. You probably already know this, but she's the one who was really dealing the stuff. Thorin took the rap because Salena's realty business was on a roll and he was out of work. That's why she set him up in that store, as payment for serving time for her. That's the foundation of their marriage. She does the deed and he takes the rap. And this is the ultimate crime—murder one."

Branco is shaking his head. Suddenly he looks dismally tired. "You know what I think?" he says. "I think you have too much time on your hands."

"But it's all true!"

"Who told you this?"

I hesitate, then tell him. "Myron Kratz."

"Kratz?" says Branco. "The guy who filed that bogus assault charge?"

"Bogus?" I say. "He had a bloody nose."

Branco stifles a laugh. "It's very easy to make your nose bleed, especially if your head is in the clouds."

"Well, I know something Myron Kratz didn't tell me."

Branco looks at me like, Who cares?

I say, "There's going to be a new name added to all those big construction trucks that are driving all over town."

"Which ones?" says Branco.

"The ones that say Gardenia and Sons on them. Gee, there's that name again."

"So what?" says Branco.

"I heard about an official change of name for Gardenia and Sons Construction Company. It's going to happen any day now." Branco's gray-blue eyes have gone black. "There's a lot of people named Branco in this town."

I say, "There's a lot of people named Gardenia too."

He says coldly, "The Gardenia family has no connection to this case."

"No connection?" I say. "They hate gay people ever since Tony Gardenia's death. Tim Shaughnessy was gay. The Gardenias believe he caused Tony's death. On top of that, Salena Hightower has close business ties to them. And you sit there and say there's no connection?"

Branco says, "The business matters of that family are no place for someone like you to be messing about."

"Of course you'll defend them, now that you're on their side of the door. It's no wonder you're shielding Salena Hightower too. She's almost part of the family."

Branco slams his two fists on the table.

"I don't have to sit here and listen to you shoot your mouth off! I'm warning you, Stan, any further interference on your part could be deemed an obstruction of justice."

"For what?" I say. "An accidental death? If I'm an obstruction, Lieutenant, then maybe the Boston police need a laxative."

"If you don't shut up, Stan, I'm going to file a complaint against you."

"What am I doing against the law?"

"You're courting a libel action, that's what."

"I'm just voicing an opinion that happens to be based on fact."

Branco says, "Now get this straight, okay? I'll say it in plain English, just in case your mind wanders. Your little pal Tim Shaughnessy died of an accident."

"No he didn't."

"He fell and broke his neck."

"If he did, he was dead before he fell down."

"Why won't you believe the facts?"

"Show them to me," I say. "Let me see the autopsy report."

"No way!" says Branco. "Now I'm telling you for the last time, you're not needed here. Got it?"

"Sure," I say. "That's simple enough even for me."

Branco says, "I want you out of town. Take that vacation."

"Duly noted."

"And, Stan, would you do me one last favor?"

"You mean for old times' sake?"

"Don't make me get a restraining order on you, okay?"

I look Branco straight in the eyes and say, "I thought those were for estranged lovers."

Branco stands up.

Maybe I went too far on that one.

"I'll call an escort for you," he says.

I start backing out of the interview room.

"I can find my way."

"Just don't stop to chat along the way."

"It's been swell," I say.

He says nothing.

Are these really our last words to each other? Will my final moments with the cop be those of anger and disillusion?

Once I'm outside the station things get worse. No matter how much I think it through logically, I sense that Vito Branco, upholder of Truth, Justice, and the American Way, is lying. I'm sure he's blocking the case because he's now part of the Gardenia mob that killed Tim Shaughnessy. The guy is gilded in guilt, and no matter how handsomely he carries the mantle of nepotism and corruption, I must expose him and this desecration of justice. I shall report the whole matter to the police commissioner. Though with my luck he'll be a Gardenia too, and I'll be slapped in irons. So maybe I should alert the media instead, even hire a ghostwriter for the story. I can see the headline now: FAG-BAITING COP EXPOSED BY ROOKIE DICK. I'll be on all the talk shows, surrounded by photo blow-ups of Branco hanging his head in shame. People will applaud my convictions. It will be a great day for sissies everywhere, for a gay hairdresser will have vanquished a corrupt cop. And once Branco has atoned for his crimes, I shall exercise tender mercy and let him go free.

26

I head over to the South End via Berkeley Street. When I reach Tremont Street I see Myron on the other side, walking Betty. Myron is wearing big Sophia Loren-style sunglasses, no doubt authentic fifties originals. He and the dog are about to cross Berkeley Street and head down Tremont to the commercial area. The walk signals are lit all around, and Myron and Betty start crossing, as do I on my side of the street. Myron looks my way. I smile and wave at him. Then, believing myself safe with the walk lights lit, I start crossing the intersection diagonally toward the same corner where Myron and Betty are heading. I'm almost there when suddenly Betty turns toward me, breaks free of Myron, and lunges at me. His teeth are bared and he's barking wildly. He grabs onto the leg of my pants and pulls at it violently. I'm terrified of those teeth, but there's nothing to do but go along with him. It all happens so fast, I can't make sense of it. Betty grabs more of my pants and yanks me to the sidewalk, pulling me to the ground. Here goes, I think. He's going for my neck. It's only then, from down on the sidewalk, that I spot a big black Mercedes-Benz tearing up Berkeley Street, running the light and careening onto Tremont Street. The horn blares and the tires squeal as the car zooms away. Through the car's windows I recognize hair-for-brains Salena at the wheel and Thorin in the passenger seat. His finely sculpted head is unmistakable. Nothing like a morning joyride to keep the conjugal fires ablaze, I guess.

Myron says to me, "Are you all right?"

"I think so," I say. As the shock of the moment passes, I see that Betty's teeth have torn my pants. "Damn dog bit me though."

"Bit you!" says Myron. "Betty saved you!"

"He didn't have to bite me."

"Ungrateful cow," mutters Myron.

I roll up my pants leg to assess the damage. Sure enough, the skin is broken, though only superficially—no blood. I pass my fingers lightly over the wound. It's no worse than a paper cut. I was lucky. The crisis over, I realize I've just uttered some heated words toward poor Betty. I'm almost ready to hug him for his Lassie-like feat of daring. But when I look up, Myron and Betty are already walking away down Tremont Street. Betty's head is hanging low. He even turns around and looks back at me with sad, sorry eyes, as if he regrets grabbing a bit more than fabric in those powerful jaws. I wave meekly, and Betty turns away.

I get myself back on my feet, brush myself off, then continue heading south on Berkeley Street toward Shawmut Avenue. I want to go by XuXuX Salon, in case Angie is back in operation. But her sign proclaiming a family emergency is still on the door, and there's still no sign of life in the place. Then I notice a light on inside that wasn't lit yesterday. But it's only a night-light, probably connected to a timer gone out of whack. I peer into the place. It's as still as a mortuary.

I head back to Tremont Street and the commercial district. Salena's Gateway to Paradise and Thorin's Domestic Tech are both closed up too, just like XuXuX, but with no indication why. After their mutual near-misses with the police, and the near-miss with me too, perhaps the happy couple has flown away in their death chariot. Maybe they plan to rekindle the urges that conjoined them in the first place, and to do it in a locale more conducive to their renegade personalities, a place like Hollywood or Key West. Thorin and Salena will embark on their new life, redefine their relationship, and settle down to a nice comfy home life with traditional family values. No more drug raps or centerfold escapades.

Myron's Domestic Art is open, so I go in. I can hear him shuffling around with something on the floor behind the counter. His head pops up briefly. The Sophia Loren-style sunglasses are still on. He sees me and becomes nervous, as though he's doing something naughty. Down he goes behind the counter again, and I hear the sounds of a heavy box being slid out of sight. When

Myron comes up again, he removes the sunglasses, and I see that Branco's prediction has come to pass: Myron has a black eye. It's a beaut, too—looks like bad Bette Davis makeup. (That's "betty," not "bet.")

I ask him how the real-life Betty is doing, after our skirmish with Salena's deathmobile.

"Why?" says Myron. "Are you thinking of suing me? Because if you are—"

"No, Myron, I'm not. Actually I want to apologize for what I said about the bite. Betty didn't hurt me at all. I guess I was shaken up by the incident, and I didn't realize what I was saying."

As if on cue, Betty comes out from behind the counter and sidles up to me, wagging his tail. He's still holding his head kind of low. I put my hand out to pet him, gently, gently.

Myron says, "I suppose I wasn't quite myself either, so your apology is accepted."

"And how is Betty?" I say, as I pet the dog's head. I look directly into his eyes. Betty returns my gaze and wags his tail. What is coming over me? Is this me, actually petting a dog? Talking to it?

Myron says, "We're probably more shaken up about it than Betty is. He's very resilient. He has to be, living with someone like me."

"Too bad about your eye," I say. "Walk into a door?"

Myron tells me it's nobody's business.

I tell him it might be mine since it all began on my property, with Timmy's death.

Myron says, "What began there?"

"Your trouble with Chip Holton."

"Trouble?" he says. "I have no trouble with Chip."

"No? There sure was a lot of excitement here yesterday. Police cruisers, ambulance—"

"We had a little misunderstanding," says Myron. "That's all."

"Are you going to file assault charges?"

"I told you," says Myron, "it's none of your business."

"Myron, you were among the many parties trespassing on my property two days ago when Timmy was killed. So, I'm sorry to tell you, but it is my business."

"Trespassing?" he says. "Who was trespassing? You have no proof I was there."

"The morning I found Tim's body, someone else called 911, just before I did."

"Who told you that?" asks Myron.

Do I tell him I heard his own voice admit it?

"I think that anonymous call was you."

He laughs. "Doll-face, you're grasping at straws. Look, let's make an agreement. The things that happen at your house are your business, and my relationship with Chip Holton is mine. Does that sound equitable?"

"Sure, Myron, especially since they coincide."

"Coincide?"

"Weren't you at my place two days ago?"

Myron eyes me suspiciously. "You must be a dick. You know too many things you shouldn't."

"You can think whatever you want, Myron."

"I will," he says, "and I don't need your permission, doll-face. Now, was there something you wanted to buy? Or are you here just to bother me again? You know, some people show their affection that way, by bothering the person they're attracted to. Is that how it is with you, doll-face? Hmmm? Because I don't think you want to buy anything."

"I'll leave the buying and selling to you, Myron. Especially the transaction known as blackmail."

"Oh, now don't judge me, doll-face."

"Isn't your relationship with Chip Holton based on blackmail? Too bad he's told it all to the police. Now you have nothing to hold over him."

Myron says, "You seem to know the answers to a lot of questions you haven't asked yet. The little dick has been busy."

Busy being banished by the big dick.

I tell him, "There's still plenty of answers I don't know. Like, for example, why are you fixated on Chip? He's straight."

"Straight, gay," says Myron. "Who cares when you're choking on a bone? Look, the boy has talent, so why not exploit it? It's just a matter of negotiating the terms. Chip Holton can put it up in klieg lights that he's straight, and that's fine with me. I'm not asking him to *do* anything. He just has to be there."

"A tableau vivant for your pleasure."

"He did it for Thorin. Why not for me?"

"Thorin didn't want sex."

"Is that so?" says Myron.

"It was strictly business between them."

"It was business with me too," he says. "You make it sound like Chip and Thorin are as pure as the new-fallen snow. Right! They're just two healthy South End heterosexual males making erotic photographs for the rest of us."

"But the photos aren't erotic."

"Not yet," says Myron.

Then I notice dark bruises on his neck, and I recall a discrepancy I heard on the police tapes.

I say, "Looks like you've recovered pretty well, Myron. Yesterday you were all bruised and bloody."

"You saw that?" he says.

"I saw the medics drag you out of here."

"Oh, oh!" says Myron, as though he's been perusing vintage editions of *Dick and Jane*. "I finally have a witness! Do you know— you probably do—that Chip denies he ever struck me? Can you believe that? Yes, he denies it! Yet there I was, just as you said, dripping blood everywhere yesterday. Say, doll-face, would you consider testifying for me?"

"Testifying?"

"I can't find anyone else who saw me."

"Myron, there was a whole crowd out there."

"Really?" he says.

Yeah, but no applause.

I tell him I saw him come out of his store with the medics. "But I don't know what really happened in here."

"Well," he says, "the police didn't do it, I can tell you that."

Do I hear a faint note of regret?

I ask him, "Have you filed charges against Chip yet?"

Myron hesitates. "There's still time," he says. "And if you help me I'll give you whatever you want—anything in the store. It's yours if you'll testify for me. I want to get that boy where he lives. I want to bring him right to the edge of social extinction and let him teeter there a minute. And when he realizes that I have his fate in my hands, then maybe I'll let him go free—depending on my mood, of course."

Oh, dear. This is too reminiscent of my recent fantasy to humiliate Branco. Is it my destiny to be—shudder!—Myron's soul mate?

I say, "That's an awful heavy burden to lay on one testimony."

"I'll get him," he says. "I'll hurt that boy."

"But why?" I say. "What did he do to you?"

"He rejected me!"

"Rejected? Myron, we all get rejected."

"But Chip rejected me as a person."

As opposed to what? A chipmunk?

Myron says, "I didn't want sex with him, not at first. I knew he was straight. I just wanted to be his friend. I wanted to get to know him. But it was just no, no, no."

"Maybe you came on too strong."

"What's too strong?" says Myron. "I met him right after he came to Boston. He was working at Members Only. All I did was ask him if he needed any extra help. He asked me what I meant, and I told him I often had tickets to the big theatrical events, and if he was interested he could accompany me, no strings, just some company to help him learn his way around town. He said he didn't really like theater, and that he was really busy with his clients."

"Maybe it's all true."

"Yes," says Myron, "but he never even thanked me for the offer. Would it have killed him to say thank-you? What do you call that?"

"Bad manners," I say.

"Well, doll-face, I call it rejection. No matter how many excuses you make, it's still rejection. Do you know what it's like to live in constant rejection? Probably not. Most young people don't. And you probably have it easy with all that money."

I say, "How do you know about my money?"

Myron says, "It works both ways, doll-face. You're not the only one who knows answers without asking questions."

"Didn't Chip accept a gift from you?"

Myron says, "Now I'm sure you're working for the police. No one knows about that except Chip—and the police. Or did Chip tell you? But why would he? Are you undercover, doll-face? Oh, I know you can't say. Then you wouldn't be undercover, would you?"

"I'm not, Myron."

"No, of course not," he says. "But you never really know who's undercover, do you? Well, I have nothing to hide. And your being a dick actually works in my favor, because now I know whatever I tell you will get back to the police."

"Now that we've cleared that up," I say, "what about the nail file?"

"Yes, the nail file," says Myron. "Well, naughty Chip lost it, and then I found it. And do you know where? Well of course you do! I found that nail file at your house. *Then* did Chip Holton's tune change toward me! He didn't say no so easily then. That's when I felt my power. That's also when I told him that I no longer wanted just a theater companion."

"Now you wanted sex."

"Oh, doll-face, you have a way of destroying illusions. I told Chip I wanted something less adorned and more honest."

"Did he understand that?"

Myron says, "He agreed to meet me, didn't he? Right here in my store yesterday? How could I know he had no intention of delivering on his promise?"

"But how could Chip promise you anything if you were negotiating in illusions?"

"They weren't illusions, doll-face, not for me."

"Did you tell Chip explicitly that you wanted sex in exchange for that nail file?"

"I don't see how he could have misunderstood me."

"And what happened once he got here and found out what you wanted?"

"That's when he . . . when he . . ."

Then Myron starts blubbering. Within moments he's wailing uncontrollably, like a child lost in a shopping mall. The poor thing really needs his mama. Still, I don't dare comfort him physically.

I know if I so much as touch the sobbing wretch, I'll catch whatever he has—emotional ailments are highly contagious—and what Myron's got ain't pretty. The situation reminds me exactly why I gave up on clinical psychology. I can't maintain a psychic distance from people in crisis. I lose objectivity and tend to absorb their pain, which in the mental health field guarantees early retirement. My defense against this foible is to ignore the crisis and talk about something else. Is it any wonder I quit the field?

I am rescued from Myron's crisis by his dog, Betty, who rushes to Myron, barking and wagging his tail, licking him and comforting him in a way I cannot.

Finally Myron regains enough composure to talk. Betty remains close-by.

"Do you know what Chip said to me?" he says. "It was awful. I didn't deserve to hear those words. No one does."

"What did he say, Myron?"

"He told me I was disgusting. That's the word he used—*disgusting!*"

Same thing Chip said on the police tapes.

Myron whimpers a moment. Betty joins in. Then Myron goes on. "Chip told me he'd rather strip naked in front of Thorin's camera than to let me even touch him. He told me he'd rather show himself off to every stranger who might buy Thorin's photos, that he'd feel real pleasure in doing things to himself for all the world to see, that he didn't care what people thought of him that way. But that even if someone held a gun to his head . . ." Myron has trouble going on. "Even if his life depended on it, Chip wouldn't so much as piss on me because it would make him feel dirty. Oh, the rejection! The *rejection!*"

He sobs again, and Betty licks his face again. But now I see there's something staged about it. Myron has performed this little skit before—different town maybe, and a different cast, but the same show.

I say it quietly. "Chip never struck you at all, did he?"

Through his sobs, Myron snivels, "No."

"So what did happen?"

"He squeezed my neck. I couldn't breathe. The room started going white. But all the time he was hurling those awful verbal assaults. I felt myself fainting, and that's when he finally let go of me. It was awful. He was completely in control, and I was humiliated. Then I heard him talking on the telephone—I think he was calling the police—and I felt so bad about what he said that I had to do something to hurt myself, just to cover the pain of those words. It was filthy what that boy did, absolutely filthy! Now do you see why I want to hurt him back?"

Dare I admit that I might?

"You can accuse me of exploiting them," says Myron, "those soft-eyed boys with brawny backs. But what am I supposed to do when they show up at my door with a sign that says 'Use me!'? What would you do?"

I can't answer that. Perhaps constant exposure to Chip's good looks and perfect muscles would erode my common sense too. Maybe they already have.

Myron says, "You're not going to help me, are you?"

"Not intentionally," I say. "But if finding the truth about Tim's death also serves your purposes, Myron, then so be it."

Myron wipes his nose. "You almost sound like a real dick now."

"Maybe I am."

His eyes become cold and sober. "Then why don't you whip out your license for me?"

"I don't have one."

"We all have one, doll-face. It's how you use it that counts. Some dicks follow rules, and some dicks improvise."

"And some dicks want answers."

Myron leers. "And some dicks are content to feed sheep."

I leave Myron's shop, and I begin to understand why Chip Holton said those awful things to him.

Because they might be true.

27

I decide to head over to Members Only Café for a late morning pick-me-up. Maybe that het-hunk Chip Holton will make my day and top my cappuccino the way I like it. And I can find out if the scandal sheet Myron just read me is true. Unlike Myron though, I'll accomplish my mission with impeccable decorum.

But Chip isn't working at the café today, so I decide to seek him out at his other performance arena, the South End Kinesiological Society. But no luck at SEKS either. However, I do set up an appointment for that introductory workout Chip mentioned yesterday. I make it for tomorrow afternoon. Who knows what the future holds for these Slavic limbs? Someday I may even have to get myself a Pec-Pouch.

On my way back through the South End, I pass XuXuX one more time. I peer inside again and notice all the essentials of a small, busy shop—still untouched. The night-light I saw last time is off now and, just as before, the place is deadly still.

Then an odd thing happens. As I'm looking in through the big front window, the night-light comes on again. A few seconds later it goes out. Then it starts blinking on and off randomly, like a pirate's semaphore. Within the gloomy confines of the darkened salon, I see the curtain to the back room pulled aside slightly. Behind it Angie appears like an apparition. Is she real this time? She signals with her hand for me to go around to the back of the building. I find my way through the alley and wait at the back door to XuXuX. Eventually the door opens and Angie admits me. She's real, all right. She closes the door behind us and locks it. The inside of XuXuX feels like a soundproof, lead-lined bunker.

"Took you long enough," she says. "I've been waiting here two days."

"For me?"

"I tried calling you," she says, "but I didn't want to leave a message. You never know who's going to hear it."

"I live alone," I say.

"I didn't mean that," says Angie.

"And how did you know my name?"

"You told me the other day," she says.

"I did?"

"Yeah," says Angie. "And I figured you'd come looking for me, so I hung out here."

"Why did you figure that?"

Angie whispers, "Because I have a feeling about you."

"A feeling?" I say.

"I think you want to know what happened to Timmy as bad as I do."

"We may have different reasons."

"Maybe," she says. "Maybe not. But I thought we could help each other."

"And so you waited here two days for me?"

"Not twenty-four hours a day," she says. "On and off. There was a wedding too."

"A wedding? The sign on the door says family emergency."

Angie shrugs. "People take you more seriously if you say emergency."

"So there was no emergency?"

"Not for me," she says. "But it looks like you had one. What happened to your hair? Y'know, you really ought to let a professional take care of you."

Her comment reminds me that I haven't seen her since the day I found Timmy's body. Curiously, her grief has disappeared as completely as my hockey hair.

Then I ask her, "So who got married?"

Angie hesitates. "A relative," she says. "But I don't know what the hurry was. I hope she's not pregnant."

"Who is it?" I say.

"Just a relative," Angie says quickly.

"And that's why you disappeared, for a wedding?"

"I didn't disappear," she says.

I ask her, "Do you run this place alone?"

"Yeah, why?"

"You don't seem very busy."

"I'm busy enough," she says. "Why? You need a job?"

"Not quite."

"You can make a lot of money doing hair."

"Is that so?"

"Oh, sure," she says. "Especially if you work for one of them fancy-assed Newbury Street salons. There's one down there called Snips. What I heard about that place you don't want to know."

"Tell me, Angie. I wouldn't want to make a mistake."

"All I can tell you is don't go there."

"Where'd you hear that?"

"It's general knowledge in the trade."

I say, "I heard it was one of the best places in town."

"Then you heard wrong. They're just a rip-off. But if you're interested in salon work, I could start you out here—nothing complicated, sweep up, maybe do some shampoo."

Is it time to come out of retirement?

"So," says Angie, "do the police know who killed Timmy yet?"

"They suspected Thorin."

"Thorin?" she says.

"The photos convinced them."

"Which photos?"

I explain to Angie what I know—though I don't tell her I heard it on those interview tapes—about how Thorin gave Timmy a packet of films and prints, and how Timmy opened the packet and supposedly "lost faith" in Thorin. And before the two of them could work it out, Timmy got dead. I realize I might be telling Angie too much, but I've got to find out what she knows.

Angie tells me, "I already knew about them pictures. When Timmy got the envelopes from Thorin, I figured something funny was going on between them."

"Funny?"

"Timmy wouldn't let me near the envelopes, not even to touch, like there was something top secret inside. So who were the pictures of?"

"Who?" I say.

"Yeah," says Angie. "Who? You got a hearing problem? I can speak up if you want."

I tell her, "I think they're of Chip."

"Did you see them?" says Angie.

"Not exactly."

"Then how do you know?"

"Maybe it doesn't matter," I say.

"And maybe it does," she says.

"Well, whoever was in those photos, Timmy got a look at them. The police think Timmy was going to report Thorin as a pornographer and rather than risk the scandal, Thorin killed him."

"Jeez," says Angie. "Do the police really think that?"

"What else can they think?"

"Don't they know it can't be Thorin? He loved Timmy."

"Didn't you tell me that 'pure love' can go berserk?"

Angie is silent.

I say, "But none of this matters because now the cops are saying it was an accident, that Timmy fell and broke his neck."

"Fell?" says Angie. "Timmy wasn't the kind of boy who fell."

"Except from grace maybe."

Angie says, "Something ain't right here."

"No kidding, Angie."

"Timmy dies, okay? And I go to the police and make a big noise, and then—"

"Wait!" I interrupt. "You went to the police?"

"Of course I did," she says, "right after you told me about it the other day."

"You said you didn't want anything to do with police."

"Did I?" says Angie. "Maybe I changed my mind. It's a free country. So I go and talk to this big-shot cop, and the next thing I know, my mother's got me grounded, locked in my room."

"Why?"

"She says it's for my own good, for my safety, since people are getting killed in this neighborhood. But when I ask her who's going to hurt me, she says, 'You can't trust those gay people.' "

"Gay people?"

"Right," says Angie. "And then she mentions you, the redhead."

"Me? Your mother knows about me?"

"Right," says Angie.

"How does your mother know me?"

Angie shrugs. Hers is butch too. "Maybe she saw your picture in the paper."

"My picture wasn't in the paper."

"Then who knows?" says Angie. "All I know is my mother makes it sound like you're part of the trouble. But she won't tell me why, and that's what I want to find out. So the only way I figure it is to talk to you. And for that I have to sneak out of the house and hang around here."

"But what trouble could I cause?"

"You tell me," says Angie. "Maybe 'cause you're gay. My family hated Timmy too. They said he was gay, and I shouldn't hang around with people like that. All the time I tried to tell them Timmy wasn't gay."

Angie's denial is still at work, even postmortem.

"But they kept telling me it didn't matter because he *acted* gay and that was just as bad. They said gay people are silly and a waste of time."

"We're not all the same."

"I know that now," says Angie. "But my family is stupid. That's why I disowned them all."

"And that's why they told you to avoid me? Because I'm silly?"

"No," she says. "That's why I know something's wrong. First they say gay people are silly, and now they're telling me gay people are dangerous. So how do you go from silly to dangerous? I mean, Timmy wasn't dangerous. And you certainly aren't."

"Hey!" I protest. "I'm hard as nails underneath."

"Yeah, sure," she says. "Press-on or bonded? Aw, don't take it personally. But face it, you're a nobody, right? So why is my mother all bent out of shape about my safety? And I'm wondering if someone is trying to cover something up."

"Cover what up?"

"I don't know," says Angie. "But she got weird right after Timmy's death."

"Maybe that wedding was on her mind."

Angie looks at me sharply, like I just caught her off guard. "Yeah," she says. "Maybe it was that wedding. I didn't think of that."

"Or maybe . . . ," I say. "Does your mother know Salena?"

"Salena?"

"Salena Hightower, that realtor. The one you were arguing with here at XuX—" Damn! "How *do* you say the name of this place?"

"How do you think?" says Angie.

"Zoo-zoos?"

"Close enough," she says.

So much for the horse's mouth.

"Anyway," I say, "since the last time I saw you, I found out that Salena is pretty thick with the Gardenia clan."

Angie's big brown eyes become narrow. "The who?" she says.

"The Gardenias. They're these big construction people in Boston."

"I think I heard of them," she says.

"You certainly should have. They had an ax to grind with Timmy."

"An ax?" says Angie.

"You know about the SECA project, right?"

"You mean that recreational center?" she says. "What about it?"

"Some big honcho construction guy named Tony Gardenia got killed at the site last fall."

Angie squints impatiently. "Yeah, so? What are you getting at?"

I explain, "The Gardenias blamed his death on Timmy."

"On my Timmy?" she says.

"Surely you knew, Angie, if you were as close as you say."

"I don't know nothing about that."

"Angie, how can you not? There was a court hearing. You were probably there. I can't believe you don't know about it. What are you hiding?"

"I'm not hiding anything, pal. I'm asking *you*, what are you trying to prove?"

"Okay," I say, "I'll tell you. I think the Gardenias killed Timmy as a payback for the death of their son Tony. Or maybe—and this is what I really think might have happened—maybe Salena did it for them."

"Wow," says Angie. "That's a pretty wild idea."

"Everything I've heard points that way."

Angie says, "Exactly where did you hear all this?"

"Not in any one place," I say. "I've been talking to a lot of people, so I kind of pieced it together."

"You got some imagination, I can tell you that." Then Angie says, "Just for your information, Salena was in here the other morning because she thought her husband and Timmy were having an affair. She said she was going to hire a detective. I thought it was you."

"It's not."

"Obviously," says Angie. "But since I was Timmy's friend, Salena thought I'd know if him and Thorin were having an affair."

"And were they?"

"I don't know," says Angie. "Timmy and I had a big fight just before that." Angie shakes her head sadly. "That was the first time we ever had an argument. We were pretty sore at each other too. Before we had a chance to make up, Timmy died."

"He didn't die, Angie. He was killed."

"You think I don't know that?"

"What did you and Timmy fight about?"

"Nothing," says Angie. "It's . . . I don't want to talk about it now." She looks at her watch. "Oh, hey, I didn't realize what time it is. I gotta get home before my mother. If she knows I snuck out, I'm dead meat. See, she gets my cousin to guard me, but I cut a deal with him. He lets me go out without telling her, and in return I don't tell her how he brings his boyfriend over and they play on my bed."

"You're some little pal, Angie."

"Hey, what are you going to do? He's family."

As she unlocks the back door of XuXuX to let me out, I ask her, "You know Myron's dog, Betty?"

"Sure," says Angie.

"Did you ever cut his hair?"

"Myron is bald," she says.

"I meant the dog."

Angie says, "You asking me if I ever cut a dog's hair?"

"That's right."

"Why?" she says.

"Because there was a strand of Betty's hair on Tim's collar. And Myron told me you had just cut Betty's hair the day before."

"So?" says Angie.

"It's possible that hair on Tim's collar fell off your own clothes."

Angie bristles. "You think I was there when Timmy died?"

"He was *killed*, Angie."

"All right!" she says. "All right. He was killed, okay? I said it. Timmy was killed. Now, does that make you happy?"

I say, "It has nothing to do with me or happiness."

Angie says, "Look, I didn't leave no hair anywhere because one, I wasn't there, and two, I clean up after myself, especially if I trim a dog. You think I walk around with dog hair on me?"

"Sometimes you can't help it. When you cut hair it gets all over you."

"Like you'd know?" she says. "You got some weird ideas, pal."

She nudges me out the back door, then she pulls it closed and locks it. But if Angie is in such a hurry to get home, why is she staying in there? As I walk away I wonder if this impromptu assignation was planned. Well, of course it was. Angie told me herself. She's been waiting for me. So how much did I tell Angie in exchange for what she told me? After the grand tally, the ratio isn't in my favor, kind of like the negative help Branco recently accused me of.

28

Since the breakup with Branco this morning, I know the police station is off-limits to me. Yet I have no choice but to confront him again. After talking with Angie I wonder if that packet of photos really did turn Tim Shaughnessy against Thorin Hightower. The question is, how do I see them without asking Branco?

Is it time to enlist Tina's help again?

But Tina says, "Oh, Stanny, I want to help, but I can't put my job on the line. I have a family to think of."

Once again I am reminded of the Great Divide between straights with families and gays with guest houses.

I apologize to her and promise I won't ask ever again.

There's nothing to do but go to Branco and ask him directly. But that vain effort is dashed even before I try, since he's not at the station. His sergeant offers to take a message, but I decline. No sense giving the boss cop something else to stew about.

I head over to Snips Salon to miserate with Nicole. (You can't commiserate unless both of you are doing it.) Lucky for me my Big Sis is in a good mood. The salon has just been named "Best of New England" for the tenth consecutive year by a major Boston television station. Say what, Angie?

I congratulate Nicole.

"Thank you, darling," she says.

"And may the naysayers continue to fail."

"Naysayers?" she says.

"Certain factions within our noble profession are trying to erode the salon's stellar reputation."

"Envy is an awful thing," says Nicole. "What do they know of the years of patience and hard work?"

"Whose?" I say.

"Darling, don't quibble over words."

"How's this for a word, doll? *Betrayed.* Branco has betrayed me."

"Oh," she says. "I can see it's been one of those days. Have a drink, dear. A double."

"No, Nikki. I want to stay sharp and sober and angry."

"Well, if you don't mind, darling, *I* want to celebrate my award."

She pours us both a good snoutful of cognac and makes a toast. "Here's to the next ten years!"

I raise my styrofoam cup in salute.

Nicole downs hers in one gulp and orders me to do the same. I obey.

"There now," says my loving enabler. "Better?"

"No," I say. "Branco has allied himself with a gang of crooks— the Gardenias."

"He hasn't *allied* himself, darling. He's joined by marriage."

"Marriage! Branco?"

"He can't help it, Stanley. He had nothing to do with it."

"Nikki, are you telling me Branco is married?"

"You should know better," she says as she pours us both another drink. "Besides, I thought you didn't care."

"How do you know about this?"

She hands me the drink. "Bottoms up, darling!"

"Nikki, have you been talking to Branco?"

"I wish you wouldn't call him that."

"All right, the crime lord then."

"As far as I know, Stanley, there is no law that forbids my talking to the lieutenant."

"Who called whom?"

"Does that really matter?"

"Yes, doll."

"Why?"

"Because you care about me and he doesn't. At least I thought you did."

Nicole says, "Vito called me—"

"To tell you he got married."

"Nonsense!" she says. "He did not get married, Stanley! It was a relative, so there's nothing to be jealous of."

"Who's jealous?"

Nicole smiles softly. "You poor thing." She takes a sip of her drink. "Vito called me because he's concerned about you. You continue to go places and do things and say things that are dangerous, and he doesn't know how to stop you."

"He doesn't care about me, Nikki, and there isn't any danger, at least not according to him. Branco claims that Tim Shaughnessy's death was an accident. The only danger now is that I might expose him for covering up the murder. That's what he's worried about, and rightly so, since he's on their side—the gruesome Gardenias."

"Oh, dear," says Nicole with a big sigh.

"The Gardenias are at the bottom of it. They're the ones who killed Timmy and Branco knows it. But now that he's part of the family he won't do anything about it, except cover it up."

"More nonsense!" says Nicole.

"No, doll, it's true. And what does Branco say about it? He says Timmy's death was an accident."

"Maybe it was."

"He's obviously got you on his side now."

"There are no sides, Stanley, and there is no betrayal."

"Then why do I feel betrayed?"

Nicole says, "If you really cared about the man you wouldn't be so ready to accuse him. All this time you've put him up on a pedestal like some kind of superman and now you're ready to accuse him of collusion and conspiracy."

"Big words, doll. Have you been doing crosswords again?"

"You can joke about it, Stanley, but it's your mistrust that's become too big. You're treating Vito like some criminal who must be pulled down and destroyed."

"Feet of clay! He deserves to fall."

"And who put him up there?"

"Not me, doll."

"Didn't you?" she says. "Don't you?"

"Are you telling me what I think?"

"Someone has to," says Nicole.

"All I know is Tim Shaughnessy's death was not an accident. Branco says he died of a broken neck. Well, fine. Then I say who pushed him? Tim was knocked down those stairs on purpose."

"All right then, Stanley. Who did it?"

"Any one of those people I've talked to could have done it. Salena Hightower works out on that ridiculous fitness chair in her office. That's a sight on Tremont Street, let me tell you."

"Being a fitness addict doesn't mean she killed Timmy."

I tell her, "But it means she's strong enough. Thorin is too. And Angie. Even Myron could do it, given the advantage of surprise."

Nicole says, "But these people have no reason."

"They do, Nikki! Thorin was afraid Timmy would turn him in to the police for making porn."

"Someone is making porn in Boston?"

"No, it's not porn, but Thorin is afraid that some people might think it is."

"Stanley, it's not that difficult to tell."

"Ask the Supreme Court about it, doll. Anyway, Timmy saw some pictures Thorin had taken and apparently got the wrong idea. So he accused Thorin of the worst."

"The worst what?" says Nicole.

"Of being a pornographer."

"Did you see the photos?"

"Me? How could I? They're police property now."

"That hasn't stopped you before, Stanley."

"Anyway, Nikki, Thorin felt that his love for Timmy was betrayed so he killed him."

"You are obsessed with betrayal," says Nicole.

"Because it's there," I say. "As for Salena, she wanted to help avenge the Gardenias. Angie wanted to . . . well, aside from Timmy's rejection I'm not sure what her motive is. Maybe she and Salena pushed Timmy together."

"But you said Angie loved Timmy."

"And love can go berserk."

"Yes," says Nicole. "I can see that!"

"For all I know, Branco killed Timmy."

Nicole screeches, *"Vito?"*

"Why not? Family comes first with Italians. Maybe killing Timmy was an initiation rite for Branco to become an official member of the Gardenia dynasty."

Nicole says, "You make them sound like nothing more than a bloodthirsty mob."

"Think of the Borgias, doll."

"While you're accusing the world at large," says Nicole, "is there anyone else? Me, for example?"

"Myron Kratz," I say. "Myron wanted . . ." What did Myron want? Timmy's electric trains? Then I remember. "Myron wanted revenge for when Timmy humiliated him at the Home Show."

"Stanley, you're grasping at straws. It's no wonder the lieutenant is so concerned about you. Just hearing you talk like this, I'm worried too—and I *know* you! At least I thought I did."

"Don't worry about me, doll. I'll take this right to the top if I have to—to the Supreme Court." Oh, dear. Shades of Salena Hightower now. I am becoming all of my suspects. "I'm willing to fight this to the end, even if I'm alone all the way."

"If you keep on like this," says Nicole, "that's exactly how you will end up—alone."

"So you're deserting me too?"

"No," she says. "But I'll stay back here on earth, waiting for you to land. I only hope it's a soft landing. Then maybe you'll come to your senses."

"Do you think I've flipped my lid?"

Nicole says, "You are being awfully stubborn, darling—unreasonably so. It's bordering on irrational."

"But what if I'm right?"

As if to signal time-out, Nicole lights a cigarette. She takes two deep drags. Then she pours us each another finger of cognac, which she insists that we drink. Then she takes a few more drags.

"All right then," she says. "Just for argument's sake, let's say there's a chance that Timmy's death was not an accident."

"See? See? Even you admit to the possibility."

Nicole holds up her hand to shush me. "Just let me say this, Stanley. Now, is it possible that you might be looking too far afield for an answer?"

"What do you mean?"

She says, "Maybe it's not a big construction company that killed young Timmy. Maybe it's not familial retribution against a young contractor who may have made a mistake. Maybe it has nothing to do with Timmy or you or photographs or anything. Maybe it's just the house."

"The house, doll?"

"Yes, darling. Your house, if you can call it that."

"Then why was Timmy killed?"

"Because he was there," she says. "Nothing more."

"You mean, an accidental murder?"

"Perhaps," says Nicole. "Or maybe the killer thought Timmy was you. Didn't the lieutenant say something about that at the beginning?"

"Yes, but no sooner did I change my appearance and adopt protective coloration than he said it was an accident. But if I was the intended victim, that eliminates all my suspects, since they would have seen Timmy, not me."

Nicole says, "Maybe it was dark in the house. Or maybe—who knows?—maybe it wasn't supposed to be you either. Maybe it was a mistake that anyone was killed at all." Nicole sighs. "Then again, maybe Timmy really did fall, and all this other business you've been uncovering is just coincidence."

"No, doll. It makes more sense if it's not an accident."

"More *sense?*" says Nicole. "Or more drama? And even if someone wanted to kill you, what would they stand to gain?"

"The house, I guess. Though my death won't guarantee that someone else gets it."

"Do you know that for sure?" says Nicole. "Did you make a will yet?"

"No."

Nicole arches an eyebrow. "What are you waiting for?"

"Old age, doll, just like you. But what difference would it make? How does anyone know if I have a will or not?"

Nicole's mouth twists to one side. "I suppose you're right. It is illogical. Unless maybe someone knows some legalistic loophole somewhere, some time limit on how long you've owned the property. I don't know much about that place you bought." She enjoys her cigarette for a moment. "All I meant to say before was that you may be trying too hard to find a very simple answer in the wrong place."

Nicole rolls the ash off the end of her cigarette, and her last words linger. I savor their message the way Nicole savors her tobacco. It's almost like a revelation, and I badly need a revelation right now. So why not something as ephemeral as Nicole's cigarette smoke?

A simple answer in the wrong place.

"And all this time," I say, "I thought you weren't paying any attention to me."

"As if you'd allow such a thing!"

"Maybe I've been trying too much logic."

"Typically masculine," says Nicole.

"Hardly me, doll."

"You just needed some feminine intuition."

"Like I don't have enough?"

"Evidently not," she says.

"Well, Nikki, maybe I will take a brief intermission from this byzantine intrigue. Maybe it is time to try for a simple answer instead—a two-word answer—something like *the house*."

"That's better, darling."

"Yes, doll. I think I just felt a psychic shift. It's time to keep everything simple and calm from now on. No more operatic grandeur."

"I hope not."

"I promise, Nikki, honest."

"There," she says. "See how easy it is when you quiet down instead of argue? Now, will you please congratulate me properly on winning that award? I'm going to be on television."

"You are?"

"Since we've won ten years in a row, the TV station decided to do a special feature on us. And guess who's hosting the program?"

"Randy?"

"Yes, darling. And it's nice to hear some enthusiasm in your voice."

Knowing that Boston's favorite stud-muffin anchorman will be interviewing Nicole, I'll surely be present for the event, even though I'm not officially at the salon anymore. One thing I'm certain of, I do not want to see Ramon's puss on the TV screen, grinning wildly, as though Snips Salon's ten-year consecutive win is due to his efforts, when I'm the one who slaved for Nicole ever since she opened the place.

Nicole extinguishes her cigarette. Then, very deliberately, she places her hands just forward of her ears and pulls back slightly, stretching the skin on her face.

"What do you think?" she says. "Is this the year for the pull-nip-tuck-and-lift?"

"There's no time, doll. But there are plenty of tricks you can do with surgical tape. I'm sure the TV's makeup department will know them. Just don't spread your nostrils too far."

I lift my cup and repeat her earlier toast.

"Here's to the next ten years, Nikki!"

She holds her facial skin taut as she nods graciously to me.

"Thank you," she says expansively, as though I'm the stud-muffin anchorman.

Everything is quiet at home, and I wonder if leaving my cat with my niece was such a good idea. People who don't live with cats tend to regard them as nothing more than furry furniture. But cats are really little beacons of energy that radiate peacefully within a household. They may not yip and yap like dogs, or jump around wagging their tails with obvious emotion. Yet however silent cats are, you know they are there, because their energy pervades your entire living space. When the cats are gone, the air is too still, almost dead. Just like the little things they sometimes kill.

Overwhelmed by these cheery thoughts, I dial into Hairnet to see if Benjy can help me find anything about my house, some peculiar fact or aberration that might lead to that "simple answer" hinted at during Nicole's revelatory smoke screen. But first I ask him if he can tell me anything more about the Gardenia clan trying to nail Timmy for their son Tony's death.

"Sorry, Pennykins," he says, "but I already told you everything I could find on that scandal, which I'll admit wasn't very much."

"Are you sure, Benjy?"

"Penny-pal, I've given you the facts, the gossip, and the invention."

"I thought there might be one more tidbit."

"Why don't you ask your cop friend? Now that he's part of the Gardenia dynasty, maybe he's privy to family secrets."

"That's just the trouble, Benjy. He's on their side now. I don't think Branco is ever going to talk to me again."

"Oh, Penny, are you two getting divorced?"

"It's uncontested. Now I've got to think about the house."

"The house?" says Benjy. "Stand firm, Penny. Don't yield to the brute. That house is yours, all yours. Don't even give him the back porch."

"Benjy, I meant there may be something about that house that I don't know."

"Like what?" says Benjy.

"I don't know," I say. "A loophole, some legal hang-up that might have slipped someone's attention. Maybe I got that property when I wasn't supposed to."

"But Penny, I'm the one who told you about it, remember? I told you to see that old guy down at the Citizen's Housing Office."

"I know, Benjy. And everything happened too smoothly."

"Penny? Are you looking for problems?"

"No, Benjy. I'm looking for answers."

"Who have you been talking to?"

"My friend Nicole. She's a real person. We were sitting at a table, having drinks."

"Do people still do that?" says Benjy.

"Sometimes they even argue. I think the one-on-one situation is inherently nonobsolete."

"Oh, Penny, I like that. Nonobsolete. That has a nice techie sound to it. Nonobsolete."

"Tell you what, Benjy. When this case is settled, I'll take you out for drinks, and you can see for yourself."

"But Penny, we're talking now, on the telephone. What more do you get by being in person?"

"A warm responsive body instead of a plastic instrument."

"Warm and responsive?" says Benjy. "Oh, Penny, now I hear you! Is that a promise?"

"Benjy, behave. I told you, we both want husbands."

"I still say you want a wife but you're afraid to admit it."

"Afraid?"

"Penny, your last partner was a macho trophy. So this time around if you land some pixie like me, what are people going to say?"

"I don't care much what people say."

"Then why don't we give it a try?"

"Benjy, I offered to take you out for drinks when the case is closed. We can talk spousal politics then, okay? In person. Somehow a courtship over the telephone lacks a certain romance."

"Whatever you say, Penny-wise."

Already the agreeable wife.

"For now, Benjy, can you just help me?"

"I'm all yours, Pen."

"So what about those loopholes? Can you find anything about my property on the Internet?"

Benjy says, "Historical real estate information isn't on the Net yet. It's one of those things you still have to do in person."

"Another nonobsolete situation."

"You know, Penny, you may be on to the next great trend. But yes, you have to do a title search in person," he says.

"A title search?" I say.

"That's what it's called, Penny."

"Where do I go to participate in this particular nonobsolete situation?"

Benjy says, "That would be the Suffolk County Courthouse, love, to the office of Registry of Deeds."

"Thanks, Benjy."

"Anything for you, my Penny-from-Heaven."

Now admit it: Could you date a guy who talks like that?

29

Next morning, bright and early, I'm at the Suffolk County Courthouse, in the office of the Registry of Deeds. The place is as busy as Snips Salon but without the personalized attention. There's a big counter, but no one is sitting behind it. As I look around for anyone to help me, I realize the rules of the road are going to be pretty basic in this place: Here are public records; you are the public; help yourself.

Finally a door squeaks open behind the counter, and a male clerk appears. He's a big guy with a droopy gray mustache that reminds me of a contented old bull walrus. He looks like he was designed and built to be most comfortable behind a bureaucrat's desk. I tell him I want to do a title search on a piece of property.

"Suffolk County?" he says gruffly.

I nod.

He says, "You're in the right place."

"Where do I start?"

"What year did the property last change hands?"

"This year," I say.

The clerk jerks his thumb toward one of the long walls filled with volumes of ledgers.

"What?" I say.

"Over there," he says. "Everything for this year is over there."

I go to where he points me. There's a long shelf of books with this year's date on them. I find the volume that should contain the actual day on which I acquired my dubious manor house, and I pull it down. It's a big book—really big, like a foot and a half wide and two and a half feet high. Though it's not very old, it's been handled by countless grubby hands, so the pages feel kind of oily, like an overcirculated library book.

Sure enough, on the very date the old house at 101 Waltham Street became mine, there's a handwritten entry with my name. I am part of the official annals of the Boston landed gentry. Along with some other pertinent information is a line that refers to another ledger containing information about the previous title owner, who acquired it in 1935. There's also an odd mark in the margin, as though someone tried to wipe the point of a pen there. Still, this is the kind of clean snooping I can handle, so off I go to find that book.

I locate it, and this volume smells like some hapless artifact exhumed from a dark, damp crypt. I open it to the page number indicated in the previous ledger. The name of the previous owner is one Devon Michael Carney. Looks like Devon did all right too, according to the records. He acquired the building for what looks like the equivalent of singing an Irish love song. There's also another one of those odd inky marks—this one's a bit faded—next to the last line of information, which refers me to yet another volume, dated in 1900.

For that one I have to go to a far corner of the floor. The ledgers there are almost crumbly from overuse, and the odor rising from the pages is redolent of the primordial cellar floor. But when I locate the record for my property, I'm not quite ready for what I see. The original owner of my property, the builder of it in fact, was one Angelo Domenico Gardenia. The name gives me a little chill, like I'm trapped in some melodramatic thriller. And there's another one of those strange, inky marks alongside the information.

I've come to the end of the line. Only two people have owned my property before it came into my hands, via the city of Boston. One named Gardenia and one named Carney. That first one sure rings a bell. But what do those inky marks mean? From what I can see, few other records have them. I go and ask the walruslike clerk about the marks.

He says, "Are you here on your own, or do you work for someone else?"

"What do you mean?" I say.

"Are you a realtor?" he says.

"No," I say. "I'm definitely on my own."

"Then you wouldn't know, but those marks mean there's a lien on the property."

"Oh, I know about the lean."

"It sounds like this one goes a long way back."

"All the way to the alley," I say. "The walls are caving in."

"Not that kind of lean," he snarls. "I'm talking about a *lien*. It's like a debt. And technically the current owner has to make good on it. So if you're interested in that property, I'd make sure that lien was cleared up first."

"But I *am* the owner."

"You?" says the clerk with a grimace. "Then you got some work to do, clearing up that lien. You can't sell it like that."

"I don't want to sell it. I just bought it!"

"Bought it?"

"Yes."

"When?"

"A few weeks ago."

The clerk says, "Then what are you doing here now?"

"I'm trying to find out who owned the property before me."

He says, "You should've done that before." He seems to enjoy discovering problems for other people.

I ask him, "What's the big deal if I do it now?"

He chuckles. "You ever hear about closing the barn door after the horses are out?"

"But I own the place, so what does it matter?"

His smile indicates big trouble for me. "You're in arrears."

"Hey, don't get personal."

"You're responsible for that unpaid debt."

"But I just got the place."

"It doesn't matter," he says. "That lien is attached to the property."

"Who did this?" I say. "Who is responsible?"

He grins contentedly. "The answer to question one is the previous owner or owners. The answer to question two is you."

"They didn't tell me about this at the auction."

He says, "You got this at auction?"

"Kind of."

"No wonder," he says.

"No wonder what?"

"Didn't you know?"

"Know what?" I say. Why am I always the last to know? "Auctioned property is sold as is." He seems very happy about something.

"No kidding," I say. "The place is a dump."

There! I've said it. I've admitted the truth. I am finally free of delusion. I have bought a dump. A dump with a lien.

The clerk says, "When you buy something at auction you get everything, including any prior liens on the property. The city discharges all responsibility for any defects in title or any outstanding liens on auctioned property."

"That's a lovely spiel," I say. "Too bad the guy who helped me with the paperwork didn't recite it."

"Which guy?" he says.

"At the Citizen's Housing Office."

A light goes on for the clerk. "Was it that old fellow, kind of ladylike?"

"He had good manners, if that's what you mean."

"Nesbitt," says the clerk. "Poor old guy probably didn't know about the lien. Like I said, the city isn't required to research the title history of any property it auctions."

"So what exactly did I buy?"

The clerk tells me happily, "Looks like you bought yourself a problem."

Not to mention a murder site. Here I thought I'd acquired my own mini-Manderley, and instead I find myself holding the deed to Bleak House.

I ask, "Can I get my money back?"

"Can you get a turnip to bleed?"

"But this is misrepresentation!"

"Did you read your contract?" says the clerk. "Auction sales are final."

"What happens now?"

"You pay the lien or you forfeit the property."

"To whom?"

"To the holder of the lien," he says.

"Who is that? How much is it for?"

"You'll have to go to City Hall for that." He's still smiling. I guess I made his day. Maybe he tortures cats for fun too.

I head over to City Hall fully prepared for defeat, since everyone knows you can't fight City Hall. On my way I think about how many times the same piece of property can change hands. They call it real estate, but who really owns it? A bank, usually. And even if you pay it off (fat chance!), don't fall behind in your taxes, because your real estate—the very security that you, or maybe even your ancestors, acquired and paid for—can be reclaimed with amazing bureaucratic ease, be it by seizure or foreclosure. And then someone else can "own" it again.

At City Hall I explain my predicament to a female clerk with pencilled eyebrows. She says nothing, but hands me a form to fill out, which I do. She takes the filled-in form and makes a sour face. Maybe she doesn't like my handwriting.

She does a bit of looking up on a computer. Then she says to me, "Are you the owner?"

"Yes," I say. "Why?"

"Someone else was in here with a request on the same property. They said they were buying it. Are you sure you're the owner?"

"Only me," I say.

"You know anyone named Tamantha Shaughnessy?"

I falter. "Uh, no," I say.

So! Myron Kratz has been looking up my property. But why him? Isn't Salena Hightower the local girl with the feudal pretensions? Did Salena maybe get Myron to do her a favor?

I ask the clerk, "What did this Tamantha person look like?"

"I don't recall that."

"Was it a woman?"

The clerk twitches her pencilled eyebrows. "With a name like Tamantha, it's obvious isn't it?"

"Not in my crowd, doll."

She does not appreciate the endearing moniker. Maybe I say it too much, the same way Myron "doll-faces" me.

The clerk says, "Do you have any idea how many people come in here every day? And this was a few weeks ago. I just happened to notice it on my computer, that someone was verifying a lien on the same property."

But there is a light at the end of this particular tunnel. It turns out the original lien was held by a long-defunct citizen-owned credit union that went under in the mid-1930s, but not before foreclosing on Angelo Domenico Gardenia, a hapless victim of the Great Depression. The second lien was held by a savings and loan association that crash-landed in the high-flying 1980s. But first they foreclosed on Devon Michael Carney when he defaulted on his home equity loan, the very loan that put in the new foundation of my property. After ruining Devon, the S&L went bye-bye too.

Out of all this financial debris comes the relatively happy fact that I don't owe anyone anything on the property, except for my mortgage to the bank. The city got paid, and I got what I got. It may be a pile of rubble, but it's my pile for now.

At least the foray into the blemished past of my humble abode has uncovered two interesting facts. First, the Gardenias of local fame would seem to have an interest in my place. And second, so does Myron Kratz or Salena Hightower, or whoever was impersonating Tamantha Shaughnessy.

But am I anywhere closer to that "simple answer" I'm looking for? A simple answer in the wrong place? Maybe the place I'm looking isn't wrong enough.

30

Back in the South End, my first stop is Myron's Domestic Art to find out if he's the one who was doing research on my property. It's got to be Myron. Only a dowager queen like him would dare to use a name like Tamantha while on official business. Some joke.

In his store Myron has set up an elaborate electric train layout. He's playing with them as I go in, and he barely acknowledges me. Betty, however, seems to recognize me, and tries to lick my hand.

"Nice doggy," I say, petting him gingerly. Betty may have saved my life, but he's still got a nice set of sharp pointy teeth around that velvety tongue.

"Quite a setup," I say to Myron.

He answers without looking up. "It's a Lionel Silver Anniversary Commemorative Edition. You don't see these very often."

"If ever," I reply.

The sleek silver toy locomotive chugs its way around the longer loop of a figure-eight section of track. Tiny puffs of steam shoot from the train's smokestack. Myron touches a button on the control box, and the little speedster blows its whistle. Betty's ears perk up and Myron's face beams with adoration for his new prize.

I ask Myron, "Where did you get this setup?"

"It was a gift," he says, still not looking up.

"Quite an extravagance," I say. "An admirer, perhaps?"

Finally Myron looks at me. "It's really none of your business, doll-face."

"Are they Timmy's?" I say. "They look like something an eternal boy like Timmy would have."

Myron says, "Would you mind taking your pop-psychology somewhere else? I was having fun until you came in."

I tell him, "I know Thorin didn't get these trains for you because the police caught him before he got them out of Timmy's place."

Myron stops the little train as it enters a tunnel.

I say, "Did you steal them yourself?"

"No, I did not!" says Myron with a choo-choo-like huff. "And even if I did, who is going to prosecute me? Tamantha?"

"His estate can."

"His estate?" Myron laughs. "You think Tammy's estate is going to come charging into my store and accuse me of stealing his trains? Do you even know who is executing his estate?"

"No."

"Well I do," says Myron. "Which just proves how well you *didn't* know Tammy. I, doll-face, I know where to look for things, and I know how to get them."

"Speaking of looking for things, Myron, you were certainly busy looking up information about my property."

"Oh, doll-face," he says, "now why would I do that?"

I feel my jaw clench.

Myron says, "Oh, sorry. You don't like me to call you that, do you, doll-face?"

"Someone was snooping through the records for my property, Myron, and I think it was you."

"Last I heard," says Myron, "that's all public information."

"Whoever it was used the name Tamantha, and I want to know why."

"Why what?" says Myron. "The real 'why' is why are you accusing me of anything?"

"Because you always called Timmy Tamantha."

"So?" he says. "Is there a copyright on that name? Besides, what would I want with your crummy property? Sorry to say it, doll-face, but your house is a mess."

"Don't call me that!"

Betty growls.

Myron says, "And don't you come into my store accusing me of things!"

Now Betty barks. I'm pretty sure what the next step is, and it has something to do with Betty's teeth.

"Nice doggy," I say quietly.

Myron says, "Why don't you go next door and bother Salena? She's been after that pile of broken bricks for years. But there was some problem, like the whole thing was stuck in cement. Then the next thing we all knew, the place is sold, and here you are holding the deed. Miss Salena was ripping mad, so I'd guess she was the one 'snooping about,' as you say. She even mentioned that you might have bribed a clerk to get the place. But you wouldn't stoop to such naughty things, would you, doll-face?"

Once again I don't want to believe it was that kindly old guy who took a shine to me. "We all need a little security," he'd said with a wink. Maybe he fudged some bureaucratic protocol as a favor to me. Now with Salena nosing around, I may end up losing the property. Well, easy come, easy go. If it does happen, maybe I ought to settle for a nice South End condo—some virtual real estate. Then maybe I can settle into a nice gay marriage too—some virtual reality.

I say, "But why would Salena use Timmy's name? They must know her at City Hall."

Myron says, "Doll-face, I really don't know and I really don't care. Now, if you don't mind, I'd like to get back to work here."

I leave Myron to play Casey Jones on the railroad, and I go next door, to the Gateway to Paradise.

31

Salena Hightower, the reigning mogulette of the South End real estate industry, is hard at work as usual. From the big window on Tremont Street I can see her seated at her spring-loaded crossbow exercise machine. I enter the sanctum sanctorum.

"You again?" she says.

"I was just at the Registry of Deeds."

She closes her eyes and holds a contraction, squeezing her elbows together in front of her chest. Every girl knows what that one's for.

I say, "You know the place, right?"

Salena opens her eyes and tries to talk while holding her breath. "I ought to," she squeaks, "in my business."

I tell her it's a bad idea to hold her breath while exercising—me who flunked Slimnastics 101.

Then I tell her I came across an odd thing afterward, at City Hall, how some person named Tamantha Shaughnessy was checking up on my property.

Salena exhales in a *whoosh!* "And?" she says expectantly.

Pull-two-three-four! Hold it. Feel the burn.

I say, "I think Tamantha Shaughnessy is you."

Salena laughs, and in doing so releases the wrist stirrups, which go flying into the air on their spring-loaded steel rods.

She says, "You are one of the silliest people I've ever met. And in this neighborhood that's saying something."

"Admit you were at the Registry of Deeds and at City Hall recently."

"Of course I was!" says Salena. "Sometimes I go a few times a week. It's part of my work. Some of us do work, you know."

"And the people down there know you, right?"

"They'd better," she says.

"Then why did you use Tim's name?"

"I never did!" says Salena. "You just said it yourself. They know me there. I can't go using someone else's name."

"You could if there was a clerk who wasn't yet acquainted with your regal eminence."

"Look," says Salena, "I don't have time for this nonsense. I've got appointments and phone calls, and I'm trying to squeeze in a workout as well. Now, what are you getting at?"

"I want to know why you're interested in my property."

Salena quickly adopts her sunshine voice, as though she's explaining the machinations of the residential real estate industry to a first-time preschool home-buyer. "My interest in that property is the same as any decent realtor who knows the value of a finite property base. I wanted to sell it."

"But then I got it."

"Yes, you did," she says.

"And you think the sale was rigged."

"Rigged?" says Salena with a laugh.

"Didn't you say that the other day?"

She says, "I said there was an irregularity."

"And you were looking for a loophole to annul the sale to me and get the property for yourself."

"All right!" she says. "If it means getting you out of here, I'll tell you what you want to hear. Yes, I wanted exclusive rights to handle that property. Of course I did. Who wouldn't? It was the last undeveloped corner-lot townhouse in the South End. The last one! Do you know what that means? The last one of anything is worth a lot of money. A lot! And yes, so maybe I did carry on when I found out that someone else got it. Who wouldn't? That house was a big prize. But finally I had to shrug it off. What else could I do? In this business you can't afford to be a sore loser. You can't obsess about what's lost and gone." Salena pauses, as if to impart drama to that last line. "Besides," she continues more blithely, "you never know when a new owner will become disenchanted with his trophy and want to sell it."

I ask, "Did you have a client for the place?"

"Of course I did! Do you think I collect real estate the way some people collect dinner plates?"

"Myron's not so bad," I say. Was that my voice? "I can almost empathize with him," I say, "especially after yesterday, when his dog saved me, and you nearly wiped me out again."

"What?" says Salena.

"You turned onto Tremont Street from Berkeley, when the traffic lights were on a walk cycle. You almost ran me down."

Salena says, "You are obsessed with other people's driving."

"When it endangers lives, yes."

She says, "And your life must be very dull if you have to go around accusing successful people of bad driving."

Salena leans forward in her chair and reaches between her legs, where she pulls out a little shelf from under the seat. Then she brings her knees up to her chest and rotates herself on the chair seat. She lowers her back so it's resting on the seat of the chair, and her head is resting on the little shelf. Her legs? Well, they're up in the air now. Yup, right there on Tremont Street, Salena Hightower is portraying Miss Helium Heels for all the locals to see. She maneuvers her inverted body up into a kind of shoulder stand, and stretches her legs and worms her ankles into the stirrups. Then she lowers herself back onto the chair and begins her leg routine. For some mysterious reason, her skirt never rises above mid-thigh. Maybe there's Velcro on her pantyhose.

"This is quite a versatile machine," I say.

Salena says nothing as she pauses with her legs spread open to a near perfect split.

I watch and wait. Salena brings her legs together overhead.

She performs a few more of these scissorlike exercises, then finally she says, "Was there something else you wanted?"

I ask her, "I'd like to know about the client who was interested in my property."

Salena is silent as she opens her legs again into that yawning split.

"Well?" I say.

Salena laughs. "Do you really expect me to tell you that?"

"Are you afraid I'll try to sell my house to them myself?"

"That would be interesting to see," says Salena.

"Or," I say, "is that special customer you? Maybe you wanted the property for a porn studio for your husband."

"Porn studio?" she says with another laugh. And despite the laugh Salena manages to hold the flat-open split against the twanging tension of the steel bow arms overhead. All those abdominal crunches have paid off. "Are you out of your mind?" she says. "Why would anyone waste a priceless piece of property for something as precarious as a porn studio? You can make porn in a cellar."

Speaking of precarious though, I back away slightly from the exercise chair, for Salena's inner thighs are beginning to quake with fatigue. I don't want to be within slingshot range when those bow-arms and stirrups go flying.

I say, "Or maybe that special client is the Gardenia family."

No answer from Salena.

I say, "Some guy named Gardenia lost that property back in the Depression, and maybe the family wants it back."

"Why do you care who it is?" says Salena. "You got what you wanted, didn't you? You have the house. Do you have to gloat over it too?"

I ask, "Is your client still interested?"

Salena brings her legs together overhead, and safety reigns once again. "Why?" she says.

"Maybe, as you said, I'm becoming disenchanted with my new house. Timmy's death has put a bit of a pall on it."

She says, "Do you realize the value of what you have?"

I shrug. "One pile of bricks is pretty much the same as another."

Salena shudders. How can anyone speak such heresy in her office, so close to heaven? She releases her ankles from the stirrups, then swings around and brings herself back to a full upright and locked position. She's facing me like a normal human being now.

I tell her, "When all this is resolved I'll probably sell the place."

"When all what is resolved?"

"Timmy's death."

"A horrible accident," says Salena. "Poor boy."

"Yes," I say. "And I'm oh-so-upset by the awful events on my property that I'll surely want to sell it."

Salena says, "Are you asking me to handle the sale?"

"Will you tell me who that special client is?"

She says, "I'll tell you whatever you want. But first you have to grant me an exclusive contract."

"Isn't my word enough?"

She laughs.

I offer her free hair-care.

She laughs again. "What is this, a game show? I don't want a prize. I want a commission."

Just as well she doesn't take my offer. Her hair needs a regimen of non-FDA-approved experimental chemicals just to bring it within the normal range for humans.

"So," says Salena, "if you want to know who's interested in your property, you'll have to sign an exclusivity agreement with me."

"And then you'll tell me who wants my house?"

"That's right," she says cunningly. "I'll tell you exactly that."

"Okay," I say. "Where do I sign?"

Salena just happens to have a stack of contracts on her desk. All the terms have been filled out already—"a standard agreement," she chirps—all except my name and where I'm to sign it. She prints my name, misspelling Kraychik no less, then shoves it toward me to sign. I sign it, knowing full well that I am protected by the Consumer Protection Act, which says I can change my mind and renege on any contract within three days. Unconditionally, no questions asked, says the U.S. Supreme Court.

I hand the signed contract back to Salena.

"Now that we're in business," I say, "who wanted my place?"

Salena says the name without a moment's pause. "Tim Shaughnessy."

My mouth hangs open.

"That's right," says Salena. "Didn't you know?" She loves the world from where she's sitting. "Here you've been for the last three days, running around like Henny-Penny, and you didn't even know that?" She laughs, a real belly-crunch cackle.

Meanwhile my brain is going clackety-clack, like an old actuarial machine, something Myron would kill for.

Salena is still laughing as she files our exclusivity agreement in a locked drawer. Then she smiles at me, as if to say, Now what are you going to do about *that?*

So Timmy wanted my house? But why?

"But why?" I ask her. "Why did Timmy want it?"

"I sell property," she says. "I don't try to shrink my clients."

Not like me at the styling chair.

Salena says, "If Timmy was sensible he would have subdivided the building into condos. Then depending on the kind of work he put into the place, he would've cleared a few million at least."

So cute little Tim Shaughnessy was also a calculating property developer.

"Or who knows?" says Salena. "Maybe he wanted it for that little girlfriend of his."

"Girlfriend?" I say.

Salena and I have a face-off. She means Angie, of course.

Timmy wanted the house for Angie?

Is that part of the simple answer I've been looking for? Angie?

But the place is certainly wrong—Salena's office. Or does that make it right?

I ask Salena, "If Tim is dead, what good is that agreement I just signed? You can't sell the house to him now."

"That agreement," says Salena, "hardly limits the buyer of your property to a dead person. I have more sense than that. And if you had any, you would have read the agreement before you signed it."

At least the Supreme Court is on my side this time.

Salena says smugly, "Now that we have a contract, I expect we'll get along better."

Not when you get my formal retraction, doll.

As I head for the door I say, "By the way, how do you really feel about Thorin's hobby?"

"His hobby?" she says.

"His interest in photographica erotica."

"You seem intrigued with my husband," says Salena.

"And he seems intrigued with good-looking young men."

"I don't keep tabs on Thorin," she says. "I'll leave that to people like you. I can assure you of one thing," says Salena. "Thorin isn't gay, not unless he's the best con artist in the world. My husband adores my body. He doesn't just make love, he devours me, every inch of me. A man in the closet isn't likely to do that, not with the kind of gusto Thorin does. There isn't a patch of flesh on my body, inside or out, that he hasn't—"

"I get the picture, Salena."

"I doubt it," she says. "Now I've wasted enough time with you, so would you mind leaving?"

Is that a nice way to talk to a new client?

I leave Gateway to Paradise and try to regain my bearings out on the sidewalk. Though I am on a quest for a simple answer, things are becoming more complicated. Did Tim Shaughnessy really want my house? Is that why he was so friendly toward me? Did he have secret plans that went awry? Was the wrong redhead killed that morning after all?

If Tim did want my house, does that mean the Gardenias didn't? But why not? Why wouldn't Salena sell it to them in the first place? She'd have far more to gain from them than from Tim Shaughnessy. Has clever Salena thrown me off the track of that simple answer I'm seeking, merely by implicating Angie?

My mind returns to Tremont Street, and I notice that Salena's husband, Thorin, has been watching me from the window of his store, Domestic Tech, across the street. After his recent escapades with the police, I wonder if his "pure love" for Timmy is still intact. In fact, given his special relationship with Timmy, Thorin can probably confirm whether Timmy really wanted my house.

Why did the ex-redhead cross the street? To find out who killed the other redhead.

32

The display window for Domestic Tech looks completely different this afternoon. Thorin Hightower has removed every one of the two-dimensional bodybuilder mannequins that formerly graced the area. When I go inside I see that he's done the same thing in there.

"Where are all the boys?" I ask.

Thorin explains, "I reconsidered my marketing strategy and decided that the products I sell deserve to be judged on their own merits of quality and design, and not by my artwork."

In other words, he's no longer using sex to sell household goods.

"But didn't you just put those displays up the other day?"

"Yes," says Thorin. "And it was a mistake."

I look around the store, and I'd have to disagree. Without the muscle-bound mannequins adorning the merchandise and enkindling your own fantasies of a perfect home life, Domestic Tech looks like any other appliance store, but with logarithmic prices.

I ask, "Were they too controversial?"

"No," says Thorin. "They just didn't work."

"Maybe they sent the wrong message to people."

"Look," says Thorin, "all I did was change my mind and take the displays down. You're reading things into it."

"How about those photos you took at my place? Have you changed your mind about them too?"

Thorin says, "I have no regrets about any of my work."

I pick up an imported hair dryer that boasts a digital temperature readout—in benign degrees rather than naked truths like "careful!" or "too hot!" or "fire!"

I say, "That was some close call you had with the police."

"Close call?" says Thorin.

"Weren't they holding you on suspicion of Timmy's death?"

Thorin becomes superbly cool. "I don't know who told you that," he says, "but no one was holding me. By the very nature of homicide investigations, the police are obliged to question citizens. For our part, we have the right to remain silent. Since I have nothing to hide, I cooperated with them."

"But you had a lawyer present, right?"

"Were you there?" says Thorin, turning on me.

"Not quite. I meant that you knew enough to have a lawyer with you."

"Yes," he says.

"Especially after last time."

"Last time?"

"That drug rap."

Thorin lowers the lids on his sparkling eyes. "Look," he says, "I really don't appreciate you coming in here and harrassing me like this. But I'll tolerate it for now because I know you're working for the cops. Sorry to break it to you, man, but your cover stinks. Still, as long as you're out on the street bothering the rest of us, I know the investigation is still active. That means whatever I tell you will make its way back to the cops and maybe something will come of it."

How can you disillusion a guy who believes that? Myron too. Both of them really think I'm a dick.

Thorin says, "See, I know Timmy's death was no accident, and I want to know who did it."

I say, "What if it's Salena?"

He says, "Salena didn't kill Timmy."

"How can you be sure?"

"Because I know her."

"How did she feel about your friendship with Timmy? It was kind of an odd thing, wasn't it, for you to be so close to a young gay man?"

Thorin speaks slowly and distinctly, in case English is not my native language. "Timmy and I were not sexually involved."

"What about Chip Holton then?"

"What about him?"

"Do you like him?" I say.

"Like?" says Thorin.

"I've heard that straight guys sometimes get feeling so close to each other that they wonder about taking their friendship beyond feelings."

Thorin says, "Do you think everything comes down to sex?"

"It's pretty basic," I say.

"Some people can get beyond it," says Thorin.

"You mean celibacy?"

"No," says Thorin. "I mean trust. Salena and I build our life on trust, which is something you obviously don't know much about."

"Who met Timmy first, you or your wife?"

"Why?" says Thorin.

I tell him, "Salena said she wanted my property for Timmy."

"For Timmy?" Thorin's words come too quickly. "She told you that?" he says.

"Yes."

Thorin says, "It's true that Timmy did want that house, but Salena wasn't his agent. I don't see how she could be."

"Why?"

"She wanted that place for herself."

"For herself?" I say. "Or for the Gardenias?"

"I don't know who the client was," says Thorin.

"Or did she want it for your budding porn business?"

"It is not porn!"

"Your art, then."

He says, "I don't need to own a piece of property to do my work."

"Not when you can use someone else's."

Thorin says, "Besides, Salena didn't know about those photos until—well, not until all this happened. And the fact is"—Thorin grins—"my darling Salena would never buy that house for me. She has a client list a mile long."

"Which must have made it difficult for you to get a copy of it to Timmy."

"You have all the answers, don't you?"

"Not quite," I say. "Not the ones that count. Do you know why Tim wanted my house?"

Thorin says, "What does that matter now?"

"It matters if he wanted the property for someone else."

"Like for instance?" says Thorin.

"Like Angie," I say.

"The hairdresser?" he says. "I don't think Tim would buy a house for her. They were friends, not a couple."

"Maybe in their own way Tim and Angie were as close as you and Salena are. And who knows? Maybe that closeness bothered you, and you had to do something about it."

"No," says Thorin. "You're just lashing out now."

"What about Chip then? He wants to start a restaurant. Maybe he was trying to get Tim interested."

"You think Chip approached Timmy?"

"Why not?" I say. "He's very ambitious."

Thorin says, "But they never even met each other."

"Are you sure?" I say.

"Why?" says Thorin. "What are you saying?"

I tell him, "You ask Chip the next time you see him. You ask him about the last time he saw Timmy. You might be surprised at what he tells you."

Thorin says, "Why are you always looking for something dirty?"

"Because the truth is often strewn with people's dirt."

Thorin says, "And you think by lashing out at people you'll hear the truth? Maybe you should learn to be a little more generous." Thorin shakes his head in exasperation. Then he sits down. "Maybe if I tell you what really happened with Salena and that property, then maybe you'll see that you are completely wrong."

Every time someone says they're going to tell me what really happened, things get more complicated. Still, I might as well hear Thorin's version.

"I'm listening," I say.

Thorin begins. "When Salena handled the sale of that property to SECA, part of the deal she made with them—she was trying to be a good neighbor, you know?—conscientious, community-oriented, that kind of thing. Understand?"

"Salena?"

Thorin says, "Like I said, you really ought to give people more credit than you do. Anyway, part of the deal she made was that whichever company got the contract to renovate the place, they would have to hire a certain number of bonded gay workers on the site. It was a community-awareness kind of thing, to hire gay construction workers to work on a gay-owned building. Salena thought she was doing something good. Anyway, it was no surprise when the Gardenias got the bid."

"Okay," I say. "So the Gardenias got the contract."

"Right," says Thorin. "But then they hemmed and hawed about the gay part of the deal. They wanted the people they already knew. They weren't in business to support some kind of gay affirmative action. But Salena put herself on the line for the gays, and she finally convinced the Gardenias that it would be good for public relations, especially in this neighborhood."

"Then the accident happened."

"Yes," says Thorin. "And as far as the Gardenias were concerned, Timmy was guilty."

"Even though the court said—"

"I know what the court said!" snaps Thorin.

"How did Salena handle the incident?"

"What do you mean?"

"Whose side was she on?"

"My darling Salena was all business, as usual. She believed the Gardenias partly blamed her for Tony's death, since she was the one who convinced them to do the goodwill toward gays."

"So she felt she owed them something in return."

"I don't know about that," says Thorin. "But she certainly wanted to stay in their good graces. They're an important ally when you're dealing real estate."

"So she turned against Timmy."

Thorin nods.

"That must have been difficult for you."

"What could I do?" he says. "When it came to choosing between Salena and Timmy, well, I couldn't make a choice. I was on both sides. But Salena took care of that too. By turning against Timmy, she turned against me."

"Has it occurred to you that she might have—well, she might have repaid the Gardenias' loss with Timmy?"

Thorin smiles slightly. "You're trying to talk honey, but the message is bitter, baby. Sure," he says, "at first I thought Salena might have killed Timmy. But then I realized killing him wouldn't get her anything. Besides, Salena just doesn't feel like a killer."

"Feel?" I say. That's my kind of technique.

"I live with Salena," says Thorin. "And I've lived with killers too."

"Maybe there's a side of her you don't know about."

"I sure hope that's true," says Thorin, and he allows a tiny smile. "You need a little mystery to keep a marriage alive."

"But the fact is," I say, "Salena knew where to find Timmy that morning, if she heard that message on his machine. All she had to do was show up, surprise him, and give him a push."

"A push?" says Thorin.

"Push him down the stairs. That's what broke his neck."

"He died of a broken neck?"

"According to the police," I say. "Why?"

Thorin squirms uncomfortably. "I heard it was something else."

"From whom?"

Thorin says, "Maybe I'm just remembering wrong. Now that I think of it, they did say that Timmy fell."

Since when do the police tell a murder suspect anything?

"One thing I do know," he says. "It wasn't my Salena who pushed him."

I ask Thorin why he took that drug rap for Salena.

He says, "There were many reasons. I already had a record, and Salena didn't. And at the time she was making money and I was out of work. But the simple truth is, Beauty will be served."

"Beauty?" I say.

"Just look at her," says Thorin.

"I have. What about love?"

"Love?" he says. "What is love when someone looks like Salena?"

Good question.

I say, "Is that how it was with Timmy too?"

"No!" says Thorin. "That was different. I told you, it wasn't physical with him."

"So *that* was love."

After a moment Thorin says softly, "Yes. For me, Timmy was love."

The front door opens suddenly, and Salena enters the store. "Isn't this sweet?" she says. "Two buddy-boys having a chat." Then she says to Thorin, "I hope he's here to pay you for that shipment. It doesn't matter if the contractor is dead now. That order is a make-or-break deal for you, Thorin. You get the money, or you know what."

"Yes," says Thorin. "I know. But the contract never got signed."

"Where is it?" she says.

Thorin says, "Last I knew, Timmy had it."

Salena says to me, "Do you have the contract?"

"Which one?" I say. "The prenuptials between you and me? That's locked away in your file cabinet."

Salena says to Thorin, "What are you waiting for? Why don't you find that contract and have him sign it? Or are you more interested in trading the dead redhead for a live one?"

I remind her I'm not a redhead today.

When Thorin looks up at her, his eyes are wet.

Salena says to me, "And if you're not buying anything, would you please leave my husband alone."

I say, "I believe this is Thorin's store."

Salena spits out the words. "And I believe you're wrong."

Thorin gives a sigh of resignation and says, "The place belongs to her." His voice is spiritless. "If it's got a door and windows on it, my lovely Salena probably owns it."

"She probably charges you rent too."

Salena says, "What we do to each other is none of your business. Are you leaving now, or do I call the police?"

"Have you got Lieutenant Branco's hot line memorized?"

She goes to the telephone on Thorin's counter.

I tell her, "Cool your rotors, doll. You've got this thing about calling the cops on me. I'm going now, see? I've got an appointment anyway."

Outside Domestic Tech I realize that, except for some minor inventive ornaments, Thorin's story is pretty much a da capo repeat of Salena's aria, but with embellishments. Smart accomplices usually do that, plant little inconsistencies to keep their stories believable, though Thorin did stray a bit from the original theme, almost into another whole key. Like, for example, why did he think Tim's death was not from a broken neck? Did he see the autopsy report? Is it possible that Thorin is undercover?

That simple answer is still evading me. I guess I'm still not looking in the "wrong" place.

I head deep into the deepest part of the South End where I really do have an appointment. Yesterday I arranged that introductory workout with Chip Holton at the South End Kinesiological Society. I am about to enter the hallowed realm of the truly fit, the buffed, and the body-conscious.

33

I arrive at SEKS and head down, down, down to the workout floor where I'm supposed to meet Chip Holton. I tell the guy at the desk why I'm there, and he tells me Chip is just finishing up with a client. Then he tells me where to go change.

"Into what?" I say.

"Don't you have workout gear?"

"Not yet. I don't know how serious I'm going to get about this."

"You can't work out without gear," he says. "Go see Jason in the sport shop. He'll fix you up."

Sure enough, big-bosomed Jason shows me exactly what minimum attire I'll need for kindergarten entry into the exalted academy of bodybuilding. It's basically black sweatpants, black sweatshirt, white socks, and black leather cross-trainers. Meanwhile I wonder if I'll ever look like Jason, who is wearing a slate gray Pec-Pouch to great advantage. As he tallies up the merchandise, his big breasts jump around in their elastic vessel. Then he tells me that my starter kit of workout gear will cost two-hundred-seventy-nine dollars.

"But there's no sales tax," he says with a big grin.

I tell him maybe I'll just walk my way through the introductory workout with what I'm wearing.

Jason tells me street clothes aren't allowed on the workout floor.

I find a pair of plain gray gym shorts marked "reduced final reduction" and priced at thirty-five dollars. No redundancy there.

"You'll need a shirt too," he says with a sneer.

I say, "I'm wearing a clean white T-shirt, clean panties, and clean white socks. Wanna sniff?"

"Suit yourself," he says.

"Doll, at these prices I could."

"What about shoes?" says Jason, unamused.

"What about these?" I say, and show him my white canvas tennies.

He orders me to show him the soles.

I do.

It kills him to admit, "At least they're nonmarring."

I put the shorts on my credit card, half-expecting Jason to tell me there's a ten-thousand-dollar minimum for a charge sale. Instead he tells me that sale merchandise is nonreturnable.

I tell him I'm not so sure that I'll be back either.

I open a door marked "boys," which leads to the men's locker room. The first thing in there is the smell. It's a blend of soap and super-sanitized terry cloth, carried by warm, misty air. Oddly, there is no hint of randy, pungent sweat anywhere, or of any expensive colognes. Maybe these guys scrub down before *and* after they work out. They sure look smooth and clean. And do they shave *everywhere?* I mean, I'm naturally smooth-skinned, but I do know there's a gamut of male body hair ranging from porpoise sleek to ursine furry. Yet these guys all look the same, right down to the identically coiffed tuft around their pubes. Some barber in town has an interesting job.

The locker room is very quiet, the silence broken by an occasional rush of water from a sink, or the sound of showers running somewhere within, or an occasional murmured comment about the grueling sacrifices of diet and a strict workout schedule. One by one, as I seek out an empty locker, the "boys" glance at me, evaluate me within seconds, and see that I offer no threat to their rarified enclave. Then they look away, utterly uninterested. At least they don't laugh out loud the way they did in seventh grade.

When I emerge from the locker room, I see someone vanish into the "girls" room, almost like an apparition. Momentarily infused with the testosterone-laden air of the "boys" room, I forget that SEKS is a mixed gym. Still, I swear the person going into the "girls" room was Angie the hairdresser.

I hear someone call my name, and it's Chip Holton. He comes toward me, and his eyes are glued to my legs. For all my physique-related shortcomings, my legs and feet are good. The legs are typically Slavic—long, full-muscled, and naturally powerful—and my feet are broad and highly arched, with a built-in springiness that allows me to jump soundlessly, like a dancer.

For his part, Chip is sporting a stylish new haircut. It looks good, and I tell him so. Actually, I tell him that *he* looks good. Chip takes the compliment in his stride—what else can a god do?—and he explains how he set up a barter deal with one of his new clients.

Now I'm certain it was Angie who went into the "girls" room.

Chip suggests I start out with machines, rather than free weights. He tells me I'll condition up fast with less risk of injury, and I'll learn good form too.

Fine with me.

We start with leg presses.

He gets into the machine and shows me how it works. As he executes the proper movements he explains it all muscle-by-muscle and bone-by-bone. Meanwhile I glance occasionally toward the "girls" room in case Angie comes out. Next thing I know, Chip is out of the machine, resetting it to baby level. He wipes the cushions with a small towel, which he then jams partway into a pocket in his sweatpants. Sweatpants with pockets? Maybe they're custom-made, courtesy of Jason the garment-monger.

"Did you get all that?" says Chip.

"Sure," I say, though I barely heard a word.

I climb into the machine, my eyes still looking toward the "girls" room. Chip kneels beside me and prepares me with the thoroughness of a NASA shuttle launch. Then finally, after another excruciating explanation of levers, momentum, and quantum physics, he orders me to *push!*

I do as I'm told and I basically send the machine into orbit. The resulting metallic clank resonates throughout the gym, and various priests and priestesses look our way to see what has caused the raucous upset.

"Jesus!" says Chip. "You're strong!"

"It's genetic," I say.

Angie has still not come out of the "girls" room.

We move on to leg curls.

Chip lies facedown on the bench, which displays his fine backside to full advantage. But I'm not ready for what happens when he does the exercise. To begin with, his ass clenches. Okay, I'm old enough to understand that. But then, as he lies there on his belly, explaining which muscles are being activated by the exercise—like I can't see, doll?—his butt gets bigger, like it's growing. And finally, when he gives the extra push to complete the exercise, his muscle-ridden ass rises upward and lurches directly at me, like some kind of 3-D movie effect: *The Bubble Butt from Planet Yum-Yum.* Meanwhile Chip is yammering on about levers and fulcrums, all of them with Latin names—these guys just can't get out of church—while all I want to do is dive in and chew.

"Okay," he says, sliding off the machine. "Your turn."

I cast another glance toward the "girls" room just as someone emerges, but it's not Angie.

"You ready?" says Chip.

"T-minus-ten and counting," I say.

Now this is the truth: I get myself settled on the bench, lying belly-down. Then Chip moves away from my head. The next thing I feel are his firm, heavy thighs straddling my waist, or where my waist would be if I had one. It's like he's going to sit down on my lower back. I look over my shoulder and see that he's facing away from me, with his meaty butt hovering just inches over my back.

"What are you doing?" I say.

He turns his head to face me. "I'm holding you down."

Then he turns away and puts his two hands on the backs of my thighs and presses down. "You want to keep all of this still." Chip's hands are strong, and they are guided by an unerring knowledge of muscles. But there is no warmth coming from them. They feel remote. Not like his thighs. His thighs are saying "hello."

He says, "Okay, ready? *Pull!*"

I pull my calves up toward my bum and try to imagine myself looking as magnificent as he did.

"Hold it there!" he says. Then he actually—this is the truth, honest—he actually pushes down on my ass. "Don't let this come up," he says. His hands are very strong, very convincing.

"Yours was up," I say.

"Then I'd better check my form." His hands release their hold on my bum. "Okay," he says, "let 'em down easy. Breathe. Now one more time. *Pull!*"

Again I pull my calves up, and again his hands are grabbing my ass.

"Keep this down!" he says. He gives my nether cheeks a light slap, then grabs hold of them again. "Down!" he says, squeezing my ass with a strong pulsing rhythm.

I say, "You keep kneading bread back there and something's going to rise on the other side." I bounce my bum up and down a few times, which nudges Chip right between the legs.

"Hey!" he says, pulling his hands away quickly. "None of that."

Okay for you to grope, though.

Meanwhile the priests and priestesses haven't noticed our antics. Or maybe they have and they don't care. Maybe a round of

"Ride 'em, cowboy!" is just business as usual for Chip, the straight personal trainer.

He dismounts quickly from the bench and my body. As he does so, he slaps my butt playfully.

Yes, no, stay, go. Methinks this guy might be a mess.

I lift myself off the bench, relieved that my arousal was only a passing notion and not an actual fact. I glance toward the "girls" room once more, and Chip catches me.

"You looking for someone?" he says.

"I thought I saw someone I know."

"You'll get to see a lot of people here."

"Didn't you tell me people come here so they *won't* be seen?"

"Right," says Chip. "But not by the wrong people."

Huh?

As we head toward the "quad" machine, I ask Chip if he ever met Tim Shaughnessy.

Chip says, "You already asked me that once."

"I did?"

"You sure did," he says. "You mean that kid who had the accident, right?"

"It wasn't an accident," I say.

"I thought that's what the police said."

I tell him, "They change their mind a lot. So, you never met him?"

"No," says Chip. "Why?"

"Well, you know Thorin, and Thorin knew Tim, so I figured maybe your paths crossed sometime."

"No," says Chip. "Say, did I tell you I want to start a restaurant?"

"You mentioned it."

"Have you thought about investing?"

"Investing?"

Chip says, "You told me you had some money, so I wondered if you wanted to be an investor."

"You want money from me?"

"Not a handout," he says. "It's more like business partners."

"But I'm gay."

Chip gives me a big brotherly smile. "I'm not asking you to marry me. I'm talking business."

"Some people say being in business is like being married."

He says, "But instead of love it's money." The smile is still there.

"You're serious," I say.

"You bet," says Chip. "For business? Always. Just don't get the wrong idea."

Not at all, doll. Not with you and those wandering hands.

I ask, "Where are you planning to open this restaurant?"

He says, "I'd like to do it in the South End."

"The neighborhood is not exactly a dining wasteland."

"There's always room for a new hot spot."

I ask, "Do you have a place in mind?"

"Are you offering one?"

"You mean my guest house?"

"Why not?" says Chip. "It's a great location for a restaurant."

"After the recent events I'm not sure people will be too eager to eat there, or even stay there."

"I think it'll work in our favor," says Chip. "I think the accident will help business. People will be attracted to the place because of it."

The guy could be right. You never know what morbid fact or event will create audience appeal.

I ask, "Have you raised any money yourself?"

"I'm going to do some modeling."

"Modeling?"

"Don't say it like that!" he says. "I'm through with Thorin and that kind of thing."

What kind of thing? How does he know what I know?

Chip says, "I work hard on my body, and I'd like to get something in return. I can't do competitions because I don't go for the bulk. I don't like that look. I see myself more like an artist who seeks perfect line and proportion."

You hold on to those aesthetics, Chip.

"The only thing left," he says, "is to do a little photo work. Nothing sexy. I mean that. I just want to give the ladies something nice to look at."

"Like your hands?"

He smiles, but doesn't answer.

By the time we progress to the upper-body area of the gym, it's clear that I'll never be a bodybuilder, not even a novitiate. But I am intrigued that a straight personal trainer would come on to me, first by squeezing my butt a few times, and then by approaching me for money. There's no telling what Chip Holton wouldn't do to get what he wants. I tell him there's no need to continue with the workout.

He tells me not to decide too quickly, but it's up to me if I want to leave now, with the workout half finished. There's something patronizing about his tone, though, like he's trying hard not to say "Quitter!"

So what if yet another straight man deems me a wimp?

Then Chip reminds me not to loiter in the shower room.

I go and put my pants and shirt back on. I almost throw the gym shorts into the trash, but I realize they'll make an excellent polishing cloth.

Before I leave I offer Chip a twenty-dollar tip, but he refuses, maintaining that we had an agreement for a complimentary workout, and that means no money. Period. I still can't figure this guy's business ethics.

Outside SEKS I hang around a while, hoping to see Angie come out, but I'm sure I've missed her exit, probably when Chip was giving my backside the twice over. So I head back home, cutting through the South End business area.

34

On my way through the South End I pass by my property. It sits there solemnly surrounded by yellow police tape proclaiming it a crime scene. Too bad that tape wasn't up there before all this happened. And if Tim Shaughnessy's death was really an accident, why isn't that police tape down? The investigation is closed, right? I'll have to check with Branco about getting that tape removed. It means we'll have to talk again, but as with any breakup there'll probably be many "final" conversations, and they'll all be about stupid things like who left the tape up.

I progress through the South End commercial area and see that the storefronts for Myron's, Thorin's, and Salena's businesses are all closed for the day. Business must be good, since it's only four o'clock in the afternoon. I backtrack a bit to pass by XuXuX. I peer into the salon. There's no night-light on now. It's still odd that I've never seen a single client in that place. Is it a front? But for what?

I'm looking so intently into the salon that I don't realize I have company. It's Betty, Myron's dog. Next thing I know, he's straddling my leg and he's got his muzzle in my crotch. First a straight bodybuilder, now a dog. What is my love life coming to?

Something seems to be bothering Betty. He wags his tail nervously and peers up at me anxiously. Then he friskily gambols a short distance down Shawmut Avenue toward Waltham Street. He turns back abruptly and yelps at me, then runs right at me, now barking loudly. He goes for my pants leg, but then backs off immediately. He's already learned that lesson. So instead, he runs behind me and sticks his muzzle up between my thighs and pushes hard. If Betty were a guy, I'd read that message loud and clear. But I'm not sure what the dog wants, and his random jumping around is making me nervous. Does Betty know where each and every one of his teeth are as he snaps those powerful jaws together, so near my tender flesh? He dashes around in front of me again, and that's when I see Myron running up Shawmut Avenue, huffing and puffing his way toward us, his huge oversized sunglasses flashing in the late afternoon sun.

"Doll-face!" he hollers. "Hold on to him!"

I try to grab Betty's collar, but he's moving about too frantically.

When Myron finally gets to us, he's completely out of breath. Still, he manages to scold Betty.

"Bad dog!" he says. "Bad runaway dog!"

Immediately Betty cringes slightly, but he looks up at me, as though I should protect him from Myron's feigned wrath. Meanwhile, the exertion of running has activated Myron's cologne. It's a decent scent, and I have to give the guy credit for using high-class stuff.

"What happened?" I ask.

"Oh, doll-face, just let me catch my breath. What good luck you were here," he says. "Who knows where Betty might have run off to?"

While Myron takes a moment to recover, I ask him, "Is Angie ever open for business?"

"Eh?" he says.

"I've never seen anyone in this salon."

"Oh," says Myron. "She's usually very busy, but ever since that incident with Tamantha . . ." His voice trails off.

"Incident?" I say.

"Do I have to spell *everything* out, doll-face? I mean his death. Tamantha's death. Do you need help with that concept too?"

Myron has regained his breath along with his inimitable wit. He peers into the shop window. "Dark as a tomb," he says.

"Maybe it's your sunglasses."

"Clever you," says Myron. "Were you hoping to be in his will?"

"Whose will?"

"Tammy's," he says.

"Timmy had a will?"

"Yes, doll-face, and Angie is the executrix. Didn't you know? I thought that's why you were looking for her."

"I guess I still think of Timmy as a struggling young contractor, not someone with a will."

Myron shakes his head dismally. "I guess you don't know as much as I thought you did. That's how I got Tammy's trains."

"*You* were in Timmy's will?"

"Not quite," says Myron. "I made a little trade."

"With whom?"

"Who else?" he says with a smile. "Angie."

"What did you exchange?"

"Information," he says. "That's the one thing people know they can trust me with. I never lie," he says, "not knowingly." Then he removes his oversized sunglasses. His black eye is even more discolored than it was earlier. "So tell me," he says, "do you and Chip have a business deal now?"

"A deal?"

"Chip has his eye on your property, doll-face. He wants to start a restaurant. He's even going to ask you to finance him."

"He already has."

"My," he says, "the boy works fast."

"How do you know about it?"

"We talk, doll-face."

"So you're on speaking terms again?"

"We always were."

"First you blackmail him, then he beats you up, then you have brunch together. Is that how it goes?"

Myron says, "Forgive and forget, that's my motto."

"And what is Chip's motto?"

Myron grins. "Just don't hold out for sex, doll-face. You saw what happened to me."

Yet there's a satisfied gleam in Myron's black eye.

Suddenly Betty is tugging at my pants leg again, pulling me in the general direction of Waltham Street.

"Why is he doing that?" I say.

"I think he's trying to tell you something."

"What?"

Myron says, "When was the last time you looked in on your little fiefdom?"

"My what?"

"Your little realty enterprise."

"Just now. Why?"

"Did you notice anything? Peculiar, I mean."

"No. Why?"

"Well, when Betty and I passed by there, he got very upset, started barking and carrying on. Then he broke away and ran off. That's when he found you here."

"Are you saying it was something at my house that upset him?"

Myron says, "I'm not one to guess, doll-face. I'll leave those games to you. But that police tape doesn't offer much security."

"Is someone in there?"

"How would I know? I just hope it's not a repeat performance of—" He pauses dramatically. "I think you know what I mean."

"Myron, who's in there!"

"Doll-face, calm down. Maybe you should go and see for yourself. But with your temper I'd take a Xanax first."

"I'd better call the police first, is what."

"Oh, now," he says. "Maybe you're overreacting. What if it's just two paramours having a final tryst before yielding the property to its rightful owner?"

"They're still trespassing," I say. Then I ask him, "Will you come with me?"

"Me?" says Myron.

"In case there's any trouble."

"Whatever's there, doll-face, it's all yours."

Then Myron takes hold of Betty's leash and leads him away, leaving me standing in front of XuXuX. Betty glances back once, twice, then breaks away from Myron and comes barking at me. Once again he nips at my pants and tugs me toward Waltham Street. But Myron calls out, "Betty! Home, *now!*" Betty quickly runs to Myron, and they trot off together in the opposite direction.

What else can I do but go and assert my rights as a property owner? I must defend my homestead from uninvited guests.

I wonder if I'll ever see people under that roof I actually want there.

35

Three days ago I approached my property eagerly, albeit in a freak snowstorm. I was meeting Timmy, and the day marked the official beginning of the house's big makeover, when the ugly duckling townhouse would begin its transformation into a swank, elitist swan. I should have known better. April Fool's Day is not a good day to begin any serious enterprise.

This time I'm anxious as I approach the house. If Myron is right, all I'm going to find inside are two humble creatures expressing their inevitable physical attraction to each other. No big deal. Fleas do it all the time. Yet I'm uneasy. It's probably the still-fresh image of Timmy's body, which is what I found the last time I was in the house. They say the only way to conquer fear is to face it head-on. So forward I go.

The front door is still locked and sealed, so the amorous squatters have obviously entered another way. I find the secret portal in back. It's the cellar entrance, whose latch has been ripped from its moldering frame. I pull open the creaky door and go inside.

"Hello!" I call out. "Hello?" No answer. "Hello, hello! Whoever you are, you don't belong here, so please leave."

Too much hospitality, not enough concierge.

I creep my way up the basement stairs to the first floor. I call out again, but there's only silence. Then I hear a thump on the floor above me. I call out again. Again no answer, but another thump. There's nothing to do but go up to the second floor. I take the stairs carefully, and I notice again that tread where Chip Holton's foot went through the other morning. The image of Timmy's body flashes back, and something about that broken step isn't right.

Up on the second floor, in what was once a back bedroom, judging by the rotted remnants of floral wallpaper, I find Angie the hairdresser lying on the floor. She's bound and gagged, and she's quite alive.

I go and pull a wide strip of yellow police tape from her mouth.

"It's Chip," she gasps.

I tell her I know.

"How?" she says.

"Just now, that hole in the stairs. Chip told the police he went up the stairs to check on Timmy. But if that's true, the broken tread would be below where Timmy was found. And the broken step is above that. So Chip must have come down the stairs to check on him."

"After he pushed him, you mean?"

"Right," I say as I'm pulling police tape off her wrists. "Or else on his way up—" I can't quite finish the sentence—to kill him.

Angie says, "Right from the start I thought it was Chip. He was the only one without a good reason."

I suppose her logic is as sound as my own, which is based on random guesswork.

"That's why I hired him," says Angie, "as my personal trainer, to see if I was right."

"So it was you I saw at that gym today."

Angie nods as she pulls the rest of the tape off her ankles.

"Chip and me left there together, right after you went out."

"But if you suspected him, why did you come here alone with him?"

"Because I'm a stupe, okay?" she says. "I knew it was Chip as soon as he said Timmy talked to him, because according to the police reports, Chip never saw Timmy alive."

"You saw the police reports?"

"Sure," says Angie. "Why?"

"How did you manage that? The cops don't exactly share their sacred documents."

"There's nothing to manage," says Angie. "I saw them, I read them."

"Did the cops show them to you?"

Angie's eyes say I'm a fool. "You know," she says, "sometimes if you ask for something, it makes more trouble than if you just do the thing without asking. You catch my drift?"

"I think I understand."

"Took you long enough," she says. "So after I read the reports I told Chip I figured it all out. Not too smart, okay? And he tells me he was just repeating what Thorin told him about Timmy's voice. Then he said there was still something here in the house that would prove I was wrong."

"And that's why you came here."

"Right," says Angie.

"And what was the thing?"

"There was no *thing*," she says. "I told you, I'm a stupe. Looks like you are too."

"Where is Chip now?"

"He went out," she says, "but we'd better hurry. He's got some plans for this place."

We descend the stairway to the first floor. Once there, we move quickly along the hall that leads to the cellar stairs at the back of the house. Just as we approach the doorway, Chip emerges from the cellar stairs. He gives me a big smile.

"Welcome home, fag."

He's carrying two big brown paper bags. They almost look like groceries, but I know they're not. I can hear the heavy sloshing sound of liquid within metal containers.

"You're not leaving, are you?" says Chip. "You must've just got here. Although you had enough time to free up your little playmate." He sets the bags down carefully. "Walking back here," he says, "I was wondering how to get you alone. And now you just show up."

"Alone?" I say.

Chip grins. "Not the kind of date you have in mind. See, I accidentally let it slip to Thorin how that kid really died. Lucky for me he missed it, but I figure with you nosing around, it's only a matter of time before it comes out."

I say, "What did happen?"

Chip smiles.

Outside a dog barks.

Myron's voice calls out, "Betty! Come!"

Chip says, "There goes another nosy one."

Please, please, let Betty have watched enough Lassie reruns to know how to go and summon help.

Chip kneels down and opens the bags he's brought. Within them I see the tops of four large metal cans, the square kind with a flat handle that loops over the top. They're the kind of cans used for highly flammable liquids.

While Chip is still kneeling, Angie and I look at each other. We nod in agreement, then make a quick run for it. But as we dash by Chip he grabs my leg and pulls me down to the floor. Next thing I know, he's got me locked in a bear hold. He calls to Angie.

"You run out, bitch, and the fag is dead."

Angie stops. I tell her to go, get the cops. She looks at me, and she's more scared than I am. Maybe it looks worse than it feels.

Chip yanks me closer to him, tighter, squeezing my neck so it's hard to breathe. I squirm for air, I try to pull his hands away, but it's no contest with his strength.

He says in my ear, "Are you afraid of my heat?"

I manage to twist my head around to answer him. "Doll, I'm afraid of your breath."

Chip pulls me up to my feet, and he's still got me locked in that death-hold, grappling me from behind.

Then I feel something hard poking at my butt.

No wonder Chip overcompensates with his muscles.

"Is that your little snub-nose?" I say.

He laughs. "Yeah," he says. "Snub-nose and deadly."

Suddenly there's loud banging at the front door.

"Police!" they say. "Open up!"

Chip squeezes my neck hard and mutters in my ear. "Did you call them, fag?"

Angie shrieks, "Help! Help!"

Then it happens all at once: The front door is bashed open and Lieutenant Branco rushes in with a whole crew of cops behind him.

"Deus ex machina!" I gasp.

Behind me Angie calls out, "Uncle Vito!"

36

With Angie's exclamation I have the second word of my simple two-word answer. It's Gardenia. The simple answer is Angie Gardenia. And the wrong place is my house.

Branco quickly surveys the situation.

"We got a complaint about some trespassers in here." He looks at me. "I recognized the address and thought there might be trouble."

My guest house is notorious already. And with Chip grappling me from behind, things look even more suspect.

I explain to Branco, "It's not what it looks like, Lieutenant. I mean, we're not—"

"Shut up, fag!" says Chip.

Angie says, "It's him, Uncle Vito. I told you, but you wouldn't believe me."

Branco says to Chip, "You can let Stan go now."

"No," says Chip. "He needs to learn a lesson."

I say, "Is that why your little nub is poking at my bum?"

Suddenly Chip's snub-nosed dick is no longer prodding me from behind. I understand why when I feel the warm metal barrel of a snub-nosed revolver under my jaw—warm because it's been in Chip's front pocket. Yup, sweatpants with pockets.

"Okay," says Chip. "I'm in charge now. I want you all out of here. Now! Everyone! All except you."

I can tell by Branco's eyes that Chip means him.

Chip screeches, "Everyone out!"

My ears ring.

Feeling a little desperate, doll?

"The girl too!" His voice cracks with tension.

Branco starts to say something, and Chip jams the barrel of the gun harder into my throat.

"Out! Now! Or the fag dies."

I give Branco a pleading look.

He orders his men to wait outside. Angie slips by me, gives me a last forlorn gaze, then leaves the house with the rest of the cops. The whole exodus takes less than a minute.

Now it's just Chip, Lieutenant Branco, and yours truly.

I look around my house. What a dump! I remember buying it because I wanted to set my life on a new course. Be careful what you ask for.

Chip says, "You were the only one who listened to me."

"Me?" I say.

"Shut up, fag!"

Branco extends his big hands like he's trying to calm Chip down.

I look into the cop's eyes. I want to appear brave, but it's not easy. I want to appear smart, and that's even harder.

Chip says, "You were the only one who acted like you cared. Everyone else just wants something from me. But all you did was listen."

Branco says, "Let him go, son. You and I can talk without you holding a gun to his neck."

"I like it better like this," says Chip. "I want the fag to know who's in control. They're running the whole neighborhood, and I'm tired of it. They look at me like I'm something to have, like their houses and their cars and their dogs. But I'm not one of them. I like my body, and I like what I do with it, but I'm not a fag."

"That's fine," says Branco. "Just let him go."

"No," says Chip. He squeezes my neck harder and says, "You like my body now, fag? You like how it feels? Is this what you want?

This is what Myron wanted. Too bad I can't show you how hard I squeezed his neck, but I need two hands for that, and one of them is occupied." He slides the snub-nose gun up along my cheek, like a lover's caress. "You like that?" he says. "That's not a muscle."

Branco lets out a heavy sigh.

"Mr. Holton," he says. "Please, son, let him go. You and I can talk this over in private."

"No!" says Chip. "I want him to hear. I want him to know how bad it makes me feel when people think I'm a fag."

Like I don't know, doll?

Branco's face becomes tense, as though the situation might be beyond his control. Now I'm getting worried too.

Branco says, "You okay, Stan?"

I try to nod.

Then he says to Chip, "Son, I'm here to listen to you. You take your time and tell me what's on your mind. I'll even sit down. You want to sit down too?"

"No," says Chip.

"Okay then. Just give Stan a little breathing room, okay? He knows you're in control—right, Stan?"

Damn you, cop! Whose side are you on?

I make a small nod.

Branco sits down on the floor. "Look," he says to Chip, "there's no threat to you in here. I'm sitting down in front of you, all right? My crew is all outside. Everything is going to be all right as long as we stay calm in here. So why don't you put the gun down, son?"

Chip pushes his gun into my jaw.

"How do I know I can trust you?"

Branco says, "You have to trust me. I know you're not a killer. I know you don't want to hurt anybody. You're scared, but that's all right. You understand? No one's going to hurt you. I'm here. I want you to talk to me."

Chip's arm releases the pressure on my neck slightly, then he talks.

"Thorin and I used to come here to do photo shoots. The place was abandoned, so we figured there was no problem. That was it. There was nothing else going on. Thorin wanted to do more pictures, but there was no pressure. Still, it got to be on my mind a lot, and it started bothering me. That's when I decided maybe it would be all right to try it, to do a few sexy photos. Thorin promised me that nothing would show if I didn't want it."

Branco nods.

So far so good. This is what was on the police tapes.

Chip continues.

"But that morning when I got here, I saw the truck. I thought it was Thorin's. He said he got a new truck. But when I came in, Thorin wasn't here yet. I figured I had some time, and I thought I was alone, so I opened my shirt. I was trying to get myself in the right mood. And then I unbuckled my jeans. Didn't open them, just unbuckled them. And that's when that kid showed up, up there on the second floor. He was already in here and he was watching me."

Chip's arm tightens around my neck again.

I look at Branco.

He says, "Go on, son. It's all right. It's going to be all right."

Chip's voice sounds dry now. "I don't do that kind of thing in front of other people. And when that kid caught me—I wasn't doing anything, but it looked like I might be. I felt awful. I felt ashamed. But the kid was acting like I came here just for him, like I was some kind of surprise birthday present. He thought I was a fag, and that's when I flipped out."

Branco says, "Just tell me what happened."

"He came on to me," says Chip. "I mean, the kid really came on to me. And I couldn't take it. I kept telling him I'm not gay. I'm not a fag!"

Chip Holton is beginning to remind me of that famous French painting of a pipe entitled *This Is Not a Pipe.*

"I didn't mean to hurt the kid," he says, "but I got worried what would happen if I said no to him and he went to the police. What if he told them about Thorin and me? What does that make me look like?"

"Just tell me what happened next," says Branco.

"The kid was talking sexy to me, and I couldn't take it anymore. I ran up the stairs. That's when I hurt my foot. It went right through the damn stair. The pain was bad, and that made me feel even worse. I had to do something. It hurt so bad. I had to *do something!* And that kid was going on and on. So I grabbed his throat. I just kept squeezing it until he shut up. It took a while, but then he went limp, like when you kill a squirrel or a kitten."

Branco lowers his eyes. He'd guessed wrong. Timmy didn't fall.

Chip says, "That's when I threw him down the stairs. I didn't mean to kill him. It just happened. I hurt so bad, and he was talking sexy, and I couldn't help it. It was all a blur."

Not a blackout, doll?

He says to Branco, "I know it was wrong, and I'm sorry. But what are you supposed to do when a fag comes on to you, just because you look good and have your shirt open?"

Branco stands up now.

Chip says, "What would you do, sir? Just take it? If you do that, doesn't that make you a fag too?"

Branco's face is flushed. His voice is strained when he speaks. "Mr. Holton, I realize this is all very difficult for you, but what you did is wrong. Perhaps it wasn't premeditated, but you did kill that boy, and I have to arrest you. You'll receive every possible consideration because of the situation and your emotional condition, but the fact remains that you killed Tim Shaughnessy."

Chip says, "I said I was sorry."

"That's not enough."

"I didn't know what I was doing. And he came on to me!"

Branco says, "It's time to put the gun down."

"No," says Chip.

"I'm ordering you, son. Put it down."

Another no.

I'm sweating again. Didn't we do this already?

Branco says, "Don't force me."

"You won't hurt me," says Chip.

Branco draws his own gun.

Chip's snub-nose digs into my neck.

I guess this is it.

I close my eyes, a coward after all.

I feel the barrel of Chip's gun scrape against my jawbone. I know it's the microsecond before it's going to kill me. The gun goes off. My ears are split with the noise. I open my eyes to witness my own death. Instead I see Branco's gun sailing through the air in a high arc above me. The cop crumples like a powerful stallion just as his gun lands heavily at my feet.

Chip's hold on me relaxes and I break free. It all feels like slow motion as I pick up the gun at my feet, then realize it's Branco's gun. *Branco's gun!* I swoon. Maybe I am dead after all.

From somewhere back on earth I hear Chip's voice saying, "Hey, fag, are you getting *hard?*"

I whirl around like a ballerina and shoot the snub-nose out of his hand—Calamity Jane in a tutu.

Suddenly Chip is wailing, "My hand, my hand! You hit my hand!"

I answer bitterly. "I was aiming for your heart."

I go to Branco. On the way I pick up Chip's gun—no response for that one.

But Branco lives! He's hurt, but he's alive, and the earth can turn again.

Meanwhile the other cops have heard the shots and they are coming into the house. Branco calls out that everything is under control. But as the cops rumble in, my supersensitive schnoz tells me things aren't quite right. There's something wrong in the air, something like cleaning fluid. I recall the paper bags and the four big cans that Chip brought in with him. I turn to see Chip furiously splashing fluid from the open cans. His hand is bloody, but the wound doesn't stop him. I realize what Chip is about to do, and I think a moment too long about it. As I get up from Branco to go and stop him, he pulls a lighter from the other pocket of his sweatpants.

"*Don't!*" I yell.

Then I'm knocked backward, almost into Branco's lap, by a wall of hot air coming at me. Just as quickly I'm pulled back up by a suction of pressure going the opposite way. I open my eyes and see that the entire back part of my house is on fire, all at once. The cops have barely come in the front door, and they're facing a fireball. I hook my arm under Branco's good shoulder and try to drag him away from the flames. He's heavy, and his strength is jerky, like a big wounded animal. He tries to help with his own legs, but mostly it's my Slavic limbs that propel us toward the front door.

That's where the other cops get him and carry him out of the house. They try to pull me out too.

But I go back for Chip. He's lying behind a wall of flames. He probably got the wind sucked out of him from the initial flare-up. I crawl through the flames and grab his clothes. I drag him through, but the guy is heavy, all muscle, and it's hard to move him, especially since he's unconscious. I thank my mother's genes for providing my best strength when I'm on all fours. So like a big ol' Slavic pack animal, I haul Chip Holton's refined muscular body from the inferno. His sacred garments have started to burn. My ordinary duds too. Once we're clear of the flames I throw myself on top of him and roll us around to smother the fire on our clothes. There's one advantage to being a few sizes larger than chic.

Then the cops come and throw a fire blanket over the two of us. You can have fun with a sexy guy under a blanket, or you can be me.

Outside the house the fire trucks and ambulances have arrived. Two medics are tending to Branco's wound. Angie is standing close-by. Two other medics get Chip on a gurney. They slap an oxygen mask over his face and take his vital signs.

"He'll be fine," they tell me, like I'm his wife.

I gaze down at Chip lying on the gurney.

I mutter softly, "Now call me a fag."

37

"She's his *niece?*" says Nicole.

"Yes, but not by blood," I say. "I thought you knew, doll, since Branco already told you about the marriage."

"We didn't talk details," says Nicole. "I had no idea that Angie was related to him."

"Not by blood," I say again. "She did know him before hand, but now she can officially call him 'uncle.'"

"And wouldn't you like that?" says Nicole.

She and I are at Snips the next morning. We're having coffee al fresco behind the shop, where I've set up a small café table and two chairs. I'm facing the alley, as though there's some magnificent vista to enjoy while I recount last night's grand finale to her. Nicole is trying to stop smoking again, which she does best with a cigarette in hand.

"When did you find out all this?" says Nicole.

"Last night at the station," I say, "after the arrest." Then I explain the details. Angie Gardenia's widowed mother—that's right, Tony Gardenia was Angie's father—recently married a distant cousin of Lieutenant Branco's. Ergo, the Gardenia and Branco corporate name change. An abbreviated mourning period was sanctioned by the Gardenia dynasty for Angie's mother, since Branco's cousin had worked for the Gardenias all his life. He was almost like part of the family. In fact, that's how Angie already knew Branco, through occasional visits with his cousin. And the cousin was so close to the Gardenias that when he proposed to Tony's widow, no eyebrows were raised, at least not in public.

"Probably no one dared," says Nicole. "But why was Angie hiding all this time?"

"She wasn't hiding. Branco was trying to keep her in protective custody. Angie Gardenia was trying to find out what really happened to Timmy too. Like me, she suspected Branco might be covering up a crime committed by her family against Timmy, and she didn't want to believe that. The only way to disprove it was to find out for herself."

"And who called the police yesterday?"

"Myron," I say reluctantly.

"See?" says Nicole. "There's good in everyone." She inhales deeply on her cigarette. By the satisfied glow on her face, it tastes even better outdoors. She says, "But I can hardly believe Chip Holton's reason for killing Timmy—because he was afraid Timmy might tell the police about him."

"That's about it, doll. Chip Holton is terrified of being perceived as gay."

"And is he?" she says.

"No," I say. "But he sure takes homophobia to harrowing depths. And he isn't shy with his body either. The clincher is, I saved Chip's life, and at the station last night he told me he's going to sue me for scarring his hand."

"No!" says Nicole.

"Branco says he has no case."

Nicole says, "I'm just glad you weren't hurt."

"Considering my house is burned to the ground. At least it was insured."

"*That?*" squawks Nicole. "That was insured?"

"I had to, to get that special 'rehab' mortgage."

I feel someone's presence behind me.

Nicole looks toward the door and says, "Oh, my!"

I turn to look.

Towering above me is Lieutenant Branco. He's sporting a shoulder sling that requires his starched cotton shirt to be open almost to his waist. From where I sit there's a good view of Branco's chest. I find myself gulping hard. Branco does not wear a Pec-Pouch.

He says hello to Nicole. Then he asks me, "Are you coming back to work?"

"Maybe," I say hoarsely.

Branco says, "Mind if I sit down?"

Nicole says, "Take my seat," and she gets up.

"Thanks," says Branco, and he sits.

She says, "I have work to do out front anyway."

"Since when?" I say.

Standing behind Branco, Nicole raises one eyebrow, then throws an odd glance down at the cop, which he doesn't see. Then she goes back inside the shop. Branco quietly tells me to close the door behind her. I do, then sit back down.

He looks at me, then looks down. He looks up again and starts to say something. He looks up at the sky, then he looks back at me. Poor guy is hunting around for words. Finally the cop takes a big breath and says, "These past few days have been pretty rough on me."

"Me too," I say.

"Sometimes people say things and do things they regret later on."

"Me too," I say.

Branco looks into my eyes. The air in the alley becomes still and warm, and the traffic sounds fade momentarily. The sight and scent of Branco's skin make my pulse race. He leans toward me.

"Circumstances can change sometimes," he says. "You think you know who you are, and who the people around you are. And then suddenly, you see things . . . how they really are."

"Me too," I say.

"What I'm trying to say is . . ."

There's a long pause.

"I know," I say.

Finally he speaks, but a car horn blows, and I hear Branco say, "I owe you."

"You what?" I say. "You what me?"

He looks down at the ground. He looks up again. "When I saw how you handled that situation last night . . ." Down go the eyes again. "All I'm saying is that you performed as well as any cop I know." Up come the eyes again. "Maybe better. If you were on the force, I'd cite you for a commendation."

I tell myself not to shrug.

"I just did what I did."

Branco says, "You saved my life."

He stands up.

"Get up," he says.

I do.

He comes toward me and puts his good arm around me. He pulls me into his chest and holds me there until I'm suffocated by the scent of clean cotton and his warm skin. From somewhere in another world I hear him say, "Thanks, Stan."

He lets me go, and I slump down in the chair, dazed.

He's holding something out toward me.

I look up.

It's a black leather holster with a gun in it. The gun is a regulation police pistol. Both it and the holster show signs of wear and loving care.

"It's yours," he says.

"You mean yours," I say.

"Yours now."

I take the thing. It's good that I'm sitting down, because my usual perverse response to guns is worse than ever this time. Better, I mean. To deflect attention from it, I ask Branco, "Why did you lose your temper with Chip?"

He replies, "It was the way he was talking, as though certain people didn't matter. Something touched a nerve, and I had to stop him. Believe me, I'm not proud of what happened. My emotional reaction put us all in danger."

"Maybe you ought to work on that touchy nerve."

Branco makes one of his quiet grunts, and I know we're back on safe ground.

From inside the shop comes an absurd knock on the back door.

"Come in," I say.

It's Nicole. I sense someone is with her, and then I hear Angie Gardenia's voice.

"Uncle Vito," she says, "I'm double-parked out there, and they're gonna tag me next time around the block."

Branco says to me, "I'd better go."

I say, "You don't even fix traffic tickets."

"No," he says. When he looks at me now there's no smile, but I know that all our recent accusations of each other have evaporated.

Meanwhile Angie has heard my voice. She sticks her head out the door and sees me. "What are you doing here?"

Branco tells her I work at the salon.

"You do hair?" she says.

I nod.

Nicole pipes in, "Used to."

Angie says, "So you guys are all friends?"

"In a way," says Nicole.

Angie says to me, "If I'da known you worked here, I woulda kept my big yap shut about this place."

I say, "We're even, Angie. I wasn't exactly impartial toward your family either."

"Hey, listen," she says, "for a while there even I was thinking they killed Timmy. And let me tell you, I didn't want to believe that, like my own family was from some opera. But now it's all okay. Even my mother getting married, that's okay now."

She smiles toward Branco. He nods back like a concerned relative.

One last question I have for Angie, and then the case is really closed. I ask her if Timmy really wanted my property.

She says, "Where'd you hear that?"

"Salena Hightower."

"Salena!" says Angie. "She wanted it herself! Salena had some stupid idea that my family blamed her for what happened to my father, and she thought the house might make them feel better." She shakes her head. "And I think I'm a stupe?"

Nicole eyes me.

Okay, so maybe the whole revenge angle wasn't just Salena's need to salve her guilty conscience. Maybe it was partly my need for operatic drama.

Angie says, "But no one in my family did anything connected to your property. Ever."

I say, "What about Angelo Domenico Gardenia?"

Angie's eyes flash. "You know about him?"

"I researched my property too, Tamantha."

Angie shrugs. "Turns out old Angelo was no relation. And using Tamantha for my name was Timmy's idea. I couldn't use my real name down at City Hall because they'd know who I was. In this town, everyone knows the Gardenia name."

"So it was *you* who wanted my property!"

"Why not?" says Angie. "I had this idea to fix the old place up, make it into one of those resort salons. Timmy was going to do all the work. I was even going to have some rooms for people to stay over, kind of like a fancy guest house. But then you got the house, and it didn't happen. I'm kinda glad now. It was a stupid idea."

Nicole smirks at me.

I tell her to shut up.

Angie offers to go bring the car around through the alley, but Branco says, "It's my arm, Angie, not my legs."

The four of us go back through the shop. Branco and Angie

leave together as Nicole and I watch them from the window. Outside they get into Branco's double-parked Alfa Romeo. That's right. Branco has an Alfa too, just like me, but his is a hardtop, and a classier vintage than mine. Angie's driving. As they pull away Branco gives me a parting glance, and Angie beeps the horn.

Nicole says, "Did you and the lieutenant kiss and make up?"

"Pretty close, doll."

"I sensed he wanted to be alone with you."

I show her the holster and gun.

She says, "And what about all those accusations?"

"His or mine?"

"Both."

"All gone."

Nicole says, "She's a virgin, you know."

"Angie?"

Nicole nods.

"How can you tell, doll?"

"It's obvious, isn't it?"

"Not to me."

"No," says Nicole. "I suppose not."

Later that day I'm back at the shop for Nicole's TV special. She looks great. The shop looks great. The local stud-muffin reporter looks great. And Ramon tries repeatedly to get into the camera's frame with his angular, handsome face grinning insipidly. The reporter keeps him at bay, but Ramon is persistent. Finally, right there in front of millions of viewers, the reporter, Boston's own paragon of Southern Gentility, politely asks Ramon if he would "kindly step aside." In other words, Ramon, get your butt off-camera.

During the following summer I offer to help finance the completion of SECA's recreation center. Hell, if I can't join a gym, maybe I can help build one. Besides, who cares about being statuesque? We frivolesques live longer, happier lives. But the Gardenia clan once again exercises its sovereign power. They insist on honoring their original contract to build SECA's recreation center, but now they want to do it *gratis*, just to prove their goodwill toward gays.

Maybe it's just another case of homophobes salving their guilt, but Nicole advises me to shut up and be grateful.

As I sit in my apartment counting the fire-insurance money from my utterly destroyed house, I think maybe I'll build a modest little cottage on the lot, just big enough for me, a small pet, and an occasional overnight fling. No more guest house dreams. If anything, I'll consider a more practical kind of business, something like a first-class cat kennel in my backyard. I can call it The Lap of Luxury.

It's during one of these pipe dreams that I get an urgent Hairnet update from Benjy.

"Penny!" he squeals. "Are you sitting down? You know that hot Italian cop of yours? Wait'll you hear this!"